"A solid, professional tale . . . a good procddural-cum-whodunit."

Publishers Weekly

"Now there is a group of lady sleuths, intelligent, bright, witty. One of the best: Sgt. Norah Mulcahaney . . . a well-plotted, well-written book."

Hartford Courant

O'Donnell fans will be pleased by the fast, high-pitched storytelling."

The Kirkus Reviews

Another Fawcett Book
by Lillian O'Donnell

AFTERSHOCK

Cop Without a Shield

Lillian O'Donnell

FAWCETT CREST • NEW YORK

A Fawcett Crest Book
Published by Ballantine Books
Copyright © 1983 by Lillian O'Donnell

Library of Congress Catalog Card Number: 83-11114

ISBN 0-449-20534-7

This edition published by arrangement with G.P. Putnam's Sons

Manufactured in the United States of America

First Ballantine Books Edition: January 1985

Prologue

IT COST a great deal of money, so only one could go. It had to be the strongest and the smartest. Benita Cruz was chosen. She was young, with a lifetime ahead of her. She was beautiful, a beauty that would at best be wasted in the village of Palmas al Lago, at worst become the cause of her destruction. Her skin was pale like that of the *norteamericanos* and she spoke their language, so she could be easily assimilated. Every member of the family, extending to aunts, uncles, and cousins, contributed to make up the price of her escape. Finally, the pesos were accumulated, and on a moonless night in mid-January Benita Cruz met the "coyote" who was to be her guide, and crossed over. She was led to a safe house where she joined a group of twenty-five women, two men, and a boy from Baja California. She thought the worst was over, from then on the journey would be easy, out in the open. She was wrong.

A second coyote picked them up and moved them through the Marine Corps base at Camp Pendleton, paying off a corporal and a base resident to get them through. In this way, they evaded the immigration checkpoint at San Clemente. Once out, runners met them and took them to a private residence in Los Angeles. That night they were loaded into the false bottom of a trailer truck, pushed in, forced to crawl on their bellies and lie in rows while above them the ostensible cargo of flour was stacked in fifty-pound sacks, one by one, over their heads. So began the long cross-country trek to the cold northeast where jobs were waiting along with the coveted and promised green cards.

In the village, the mother wept. Tears of joy, she assured her husband. Their daughter, their youngest of eleven, six of whom had died before the age of four, was in a land where there was work and opportunity. There was a sense of loss, of course, but deeper also an anxiety to which Pilar Cruz would not admit, even to herself. It was based on rumors, ugly rumors but unfounded. Only one man from Palmas al Lago had made the trip, and he had not been heard of since. That was three years ago. He had not written. He had not sent money to his family, nor made any attempt to have them join him. He had simply disappeared. Julio Cantania had been a good man; it seemed inconceivable that he would leave a young wife and baby girl behind. Inquiries had been made on behalf of the abandoned wife, of course. The men who had acted as Cantania's guides swore he had reached the States; beyond that, their responsibilities ended. Cantania's father-in-law ranted and raged, but he was powerless; without appealing to the authorities—and appealing to the authorities was unthinkable—the inquiries could go no further. The village wrote off Julio Cantania as a man who had been seduced by the affluence he had gone seeking and the wanton pleasure it had brought him. Only the young wife with the baby girl did not believe it, and she waited. And Pilar Cruz, Benita's mother, wondered.

Whatever happened to Cantania would not happen to her child. Precautions had been taken, Señora Cruz assured herself. Extra money had been raised above the fee; Benita carried it in a boodle bag sewn into her girdle. If anything went wrong, if the job she had been promised was not to her liking, she would not be without resources.

Chapter I

SISTER THERESE bustled along Second Avenue, bending into the wind that gusted off the East River. It stung her withered cheeks and brought tears to her rheumy eyes. They gleamed nevertheless with pleasurable anticipation. The sister shivered in her thin navy raincoat, but there was a smile on her dry, cracked lips. With the feast of the Three Kings, the Christmas season was drawing to a close. This might be, undoubtedly would be, her last holiday at Our Lady of Perpetual Help, and she intended to enjoy it to the fullest. She turned the corner at Sixty-first Street, and sheltered from the wind by the understructure of the Queensboro Bridge, was able to walk upright again. But she was tired. As nobody was watching, she gave in to her physical weakness and slowed down.

Sister Therese had been putting on an act for at least ten years—pretending a vitality and resilience that was ebbing fast. For ten years she'd been fighting retirement. At best, retirement was exile. According to church policy, the retired religious were set up in pairs in a location of their own choosing. It sounded good. In a small apartment or cottage a couple of priests or nuns were supposed to spend their last years in comfortable leisure. Actually, they had more difficulty in adjusting than their lay counterparts. They found themselves part of a new and strange community and were given no useful function. Old and often sick, they became withdrawn. They seldom had outside interests or hobbies; there had been little time to develop them. If one of the pair died, the other was abandoned to the charity of neighbors who hardly knew him.

So far Sister Therese had postponed this fate. For thirty-two years she had been teaching in the parochial school, extending her care for her pupils out into the teeming streets, but age was catching up to her; she had to admit it. She could no longer command her strength. When she called upon herself physically, her body did not respond. Her hands trembled; her speech was unreliable—she groped to form words that were crystal clear in her mind. It brought tears of frustration. For she knew her mind was as sharp as ever. In fact it raced, outrunning her ability to express her thoughts. She would start a sentence, mentally complete it and go on to the next, leaving the end of the first unspoken. The children laughed at her and mimicked her, but they understood her meaning and the laughter arose not out of contempt but love. She was secure in that knowledge, for she loved them. The presents in the shopping bag which she clutched along with her purse were for them. Sister gave gifts on the occasion of the arrival of the three kings at the manger, a custom she perpetuated from her childhood in France out of nostalgia and in special honor for the Blessed Infant. As she neared the church and convent, Sister Therese smiled and was ready with the loud cheeriness she used to cover her failings. She feared it would no longer fool Father Boylan. At least not after he read the doctor's report.

Tomorrow she was summoned to an interview with the pastor. She knew what Father Boylan would tell her and she knew that she could no longer offer valid arguments against it. Still, Sister Therese wasn't giving up. If she could not convince Father that she was physically tip-top, she would plead that she was needed.

It was why she'd lasted this long. There were fewer nuns, and funds for lay teachers were scarce. Maybe she could last till the end of the spring term. Passing the residence, Sister Therese continued on to the church and the steps down to the basement entrance of the Shrine of the Blessed Infant of Prague. She felt the need to rest in His presence for a quiet prayer, to renew her request not to be sent away— not yet. Drawing near, she saw the doors of the upper church swing open and a muffled figure hurtling down straight at her. He was lanky, about six feet tall, wearing jeans and a down vest over a dingy gray sweatshirt. His hair was completely covered by a wool cap pulled down to his eyebrows; a wool scarf was wound around his neck and pulled high over his mouth to the tip of his nose—but not against the cold. Sister Therese stood transfixed, wondering at his haste. Not until he reached a raw-knuckled hand out for her pocketbook did she understand.

"No!" she cried out indignantly, and instinctively pulled back.

The mugger grabbed with one hand for the purse and with the other struck Sister Therese across the face and sent her sprawling to the concrete landing. She gasped more in surprise than pain. She let go the shopping bag, but held on to the purse.

As her attacker reached down to wrest it from her, the scarf fell away from the lower half of his face.

"Frank! Frank Salgo!" Sister Therese cried out, and it was her death warrant. She knew it as soon as she saw the knife, before he raised it and plunged it into her breast.

"Frankie . . ." Her soft gray eyes were wide with pity.

Kneeling astride her, he plunged the knife down hard. Blood spurted into his face.

Sister Therese sighed.

He pulled the knife out. It was only a penknife and its tip was broken, so he had to stab her again and again and again. The blood ran over his hand and soaked into the bottom of his scarf. He didn't know how many times he had to stab her to make sure she was dead. After a long while, the bloody knife in his hand, he struggled to his feet and ran.

He got no money. Sister Therese still clutched the plastic purse.

Sergeant Norah Mulcahaney stopped typing. She raised her arms high over her head, slid down on the end of her spine, and stretched her entire five-foot-nine frame. Then, sitting up again, she closed her dark blue eyes and rotated her head to ease the kinks in her slender neck. When she was through, she opened her eyes and stared at the squadroom clock: three-forty-five. She didn't need to see the time to know the shifts were about to change: there was that familiar restlessness as detectives about to go off duty rattled typewriters in the rush to complete reports and slammed drawers as they filed them away, at least temporarily, while those coming on loitered just a little longer in the halls and at the coffee machine. Norah Mulcahaney was not usually a clock-watcher; she had become so only recently. She'd finally learned how to compartmentalize her life. Just in time. Joe had been trying to teach her long enough, but it wasn't something easily taught. In all honesty, Norah had considered her husband's ability to detach himself at the end of the tour as insensitive and lacking in compassion. She knew better now.

What cop didn't start out an idealist? Norah wondered. As the years passed, the ranks were divided by the daily exposure to squalor, violence, the triumph of the criminal over the law, and the subsequent frustration. Some cops turned bitter and became venal themselves. Others cracked in other ways—drinking, womanizing. Some just gave up and quit. Still others learned to put it all in perspective, to live two separate lives. These cops, who appeared hardened, were the ones who kept their sanity, efficiency, and integrity, and so their value in the fight.

It was six years since Norah Mulcahaney, a detective on New York's prestigious but now defunct Homicide North, met and married Sergeant Joseph Capretto of the same unit. Prior to marrying Joe, she had lived with her widowed father. She had two brothers, but when she was fifteen both Pat Jr. and Michael went away to college, then to Vietnam. After they came back, it wasn't long before each married and moved out West, so that in essence she had been an only child. In contrast, Joe Capretto came from a large Italian family. He had seven sisters, all of them married and most with children. Where Norah was shy and introverted, Joe was outgoing, exuberant. Where she was idealistic, he was pragmatic. They fitted. Each gave and also received. They were happy. Their work was an adhesive. There was a time when things had started to go wrong. They grew apart, subtly at first. Maybe it was because they couldn't have children and both wanted them. They tried to adopt—and had to give the child up. That left a deep scar. Norah withdrew into herself. She cut off communication. She would not let her husband reach her. She used the work as a refuge and an excuse to hold him off, though she certainly was not conscious of doing it. And Joe, who cared so deeply for her, could do nothing but wait it out.

Oh, there was no hostility; neither blamed the other. They remained friends, good friends. That was the trouble. They never quarreled. To quarrel might have broken the barrier. They shared the same bed, but they scarcely touched. Norah became desperately shy.

And the change in the city was a part of it. It had become a battle zone with the troops, the police, badly outnumbered. Violence had become ordinary. A knife flashed in an argument over a parking space; a man was killed because his dog barked at night; a boy shot a schoolmate because he didn't like the way he smiled. Muggers attacked at will with no fear of being apprehended, or, if apprehended, with no fear of punishment. Criminals were arrogant and contemptuous of the justice system. Plea bargaining was routine in the most appalling and shocking of assaults. Drugs were hawked openly in Central Park, on Madison Avenue, on Wall Street around the corner from the Stock Exchange. People were shoved off subway platforms into the path of an oncoming train just for kicks. The percentage of homicide cases actually solved dropped alarmingly. Where neither motive nor clues were readily apparent, detectives didn't have the time for the kind of thorough, routine legwork that might turn them up. A case was either quickly solved and the perpetrator apprehended within days, or it was filed away. Norah herself had failed to clear three of her last five homicides. She hadn't given up—she'd been ordered off, and it had shaken her badly. She began to question her own usefulness.

Then her father died. It was cancer of the prostate. And with the current callous honesty of doctors, he had been told that he had six months, or less, to live. All Patrick Mulcahaney wanted was to go home. The doctors wanted him to stay in the hospital for treatments—chemotherapy and radiation. He saw no point.

Though debilitated, he was still mentally and spiritually tough. One night, after lights out, he got out of bed, collected his clothes from the closet, and got dressed. Pat Mulcahaney simply walked out of the hospital. He went through the emergency room, reasoning that one more patient, no matter how pale and shaky, wouldn't be noticed. He was right. It was early February and bitter cold with a fine, sleety rain falling. No cabs anywhere. He walked the long crosstown blocks from the river to Lexington Avenue and the nearest subway. He waited on a drafty platform. When he reached his station, he had to walk again from Broadway to Riverside Drive and arrived at his own front door, teeth chattering and chilled through, to stumble into the arms of his second wife, Eileen.

Though she got him into bed and warmed him with hot tea and whiskey, it was too late. He contracted pneumonia and was dead within five days.

Norah was completely distraught. She railed against the hospital for not letting him go home; she railed against the hospital for not keeping a stricter watch on him. She was equally at odds with herself. She felt no guilt for not having spent more time with him; that was a natural progression of a healthy relationship between father and daughter, not a lessening of affection. However, she did blame herself for not having been more firm with him and convincing him that he should stay in the hospital and take the treatment; she blamed herself for not being more sympathetic and taking him out of there and seeing him safely home to Eileen. She was on the edge of hysteria.

Joe pulled her out of it. He offered the calm security of his love. He insisted she continue the daily routine of life and of the job, knowing that it would restore her. And gradually, Norah and Joe drew close once again. Norah did not link it directly to her father's passing, though she certainly realized that with him gone she had no one left but Joe, that she must cling to him, and to do that she must express what she felt. At the same time, Joe was determined not to let her sink into despondency. He started to make plans for every evening, specific, obligatory, so that she was forced to quit on time and get home. They reactivated old friendships and made new ones. They went to theaters, the opera, the Garden for hockey or tennis or whatever was on. She started to laugh. It was like courting all over again.

Their sensuality was revitalized. It was a surprise to both how easily it came and how much joy it brought. They lived in a perpetual glow. Wherever they were, their eyes sought each other and held with the light of caring. It was noticed, and some, close enough to have the privilege, commented on the new closeness. Both acknowledged it with open delight. That past Christmas was the happiest they had ever shared; New Year's the most festive.

As she closed her typewriter, Norah's eyes were their deepest blue, close to violet, sparkling in anticipation of the coming evening with Joe. Her skin glowed clear, the early lines, discernible when she was troubled or tired, hardly noticeable. Her dark brown hair tied back with a bright red silk scarf was thick and lustrous, her wide brow serene. Norah's only feature fault—a square blunt jaw, usually dominant—was softened by a pensive smile. Sergeant Norah Mulcahaney Capretto was thirty-seven. As she thought of her husband and the coming evening, she looked twenty-seven and felt seventeen.

She clipped the final sheet to the rest of the report and put the whole away in the top drawer. The phone on her desk rang. She picked it up and the dreamy smile disappeared.

The third violent assault on a nun in as many weeks, Norah thought, and the first fatality! The mugging, beating, robbing of priests, ministers, rabbis was no longer considered out of the ordinary. Already the public was taking it in stride, but the violence against nuns still caused indignation, a stirring of the blood. A spokesman for the cardinal's of-

fice expressed concern but stated that churches and
rectories could not become citadels. All caution
would be exercised, but there would not, could not,
be separation of the religious from the people. What
would the reaction be now that a nun had been
killed?

As she pondered, Norah took notes. "Okay, I've
got it," she told Communications, and hung up. She
glanced at her watch. Her replacement was due in
minutes. Undoubtedly Roy Brennan was out in the
hall right now. Detectives were encouraged to "pass
along" unfinished jobs of research, even incomplete
interrogations. This case hadn't even begun. All she
had to do was hand over the address of the rectory to
Roy Brennan with the meager details and he would
get to the scene just as fast as she could and do the
same job. Yet Norah hesitated. Of the three homicide investigations she'd recently been forced to
walk away from, two had involved priests. One human being was the same as another; nevertheless,
she felt that success in apprehending this particular
murderer would somehow make up for the other fail-
ures. Norah dialed Joe's office.

"Captain Capretto, please. Sergeant Mulcahaney
calling."

"Oh, Norah, he's not at his desk," the civilian secretary replied. "Shall I have him call you back?"

"Never mind, Gert. Tell him I'm out on a call and I
won't be home till late. Tell him I'll get back as soon
as I can."

She hung up feeling uneasy. She'd lied—she
hadn't actually gone out. She was letting herself get
emotionally involved. She knew it, but she couldn't
help it. She assured herself that the circumstances
warranted it: Joe would understand. They had
planned dinner out alone, so it wasn't as if they were
inconveniencing anyone else.

Norah scowled. The only one she was letting down
was Joe! That should matter most of all. Just this

once, just this last time, and she'd never do it again, she promised herself as she hurriedly reached for the fur-lined storm coat hanging on a wall hook back of her desk. She was afraid that if she didn't get out fast the assignment might somehow be taken away from her . . . or that Joe might call back and catch her in the lie.

In fact, Joe Capretto didn't get his wife's message till twenty minutes later. He didn't bother to try to reach her. He wasn't even disturbed. After all, police business couldn't be confined into rigid hours. It was inevitable that she would get trapped into working late occasionally. He also expected that from time to time Norah would once again become involved, passionately involved in a case. He had no desire to change her character; it was what made him love her. All he wanted was to temper the intensity of her involvement in her work and increase it in her commitment to their marriage. On the latter, he considered that he was doing extremely well.

He smiled. Joseph Antony Capretto had the classic Italian good looks—dark complexion, straight Roman nose, high brow from which black hair swept back thick and straight, and a smile revealing a row of perfect teeth. Joe had been nearly forty-three when he and Norah married. He'd had a string of carefree and not-so-carefree affairs. Though his widowed mother, Signora Emilia, had constantly urged him, he had not really expected ever to marry. As his mother's only son and with seven sisters to fawn over and wait on him, why should he? Even when he met Norah, he didn't change his mind right away. She wasn't his type, not glamorous enough. Mulcahaney was too tall, too serious. The set of her jaw suggested stubbornness, independence at the very least. He wasn't interested in the rookie policewoman. He wanted no involvement with a feminist.

He found out later that Norah was not a feminist, not in the active sense. All Norah Mulcahaney wanted was to do a good job and leave somebody else to the proselytizing. Joe also discovered beneath her self-sufficient exterior a tenderness and need for affection. He was only too glad to help her fulfill that side of her nature. In the process, he fell in love. She was the woman he wanted. He would never want another.

At that time, Joe Capretto had reached the rank of sergeant and was content. He was satisfied with the limited authority, and also the limited responsibility. Having decided at last to get married, however, he set himself to advance so that he could provide for his wife and the family he expected. He studied, took the exam, and made lieutenant, then captain. Now he was working out of Chief of Detectives Louis Deland's office at headquarters, serving directly under his old friend Deputy Inspector James Felix. Joe's work seldom took him on the street anymore. His hours were regular as any business executive's. Nevertheless, there were times when he had to work late too, though recently he worked through lunch rather than be late getting home in order to set an example for Norah. So actually her message was welcome. It gave him the opportunity to clear up several matters. He knew it would be late when she got through, so he sent out for a roast-beef sandwich and coffee and set himself to his own labors.

He called home at eight o'clock. No answer. She should be through soon, he thought, and decided that he certainly was. He recorded instructions for Gert for the next morning, put on his topcoat, and left his office.

The lights glowed softly in Police Plaza. Number One was a grim, intimidating building, but the setting was pleasant: the plaza itself paved in red brick tiles interspersed with young trees, the nearby bridge garlanded with lights, and the intermittent soft slap of water against bulkheading. All these, along with the surrounding open space beyond which the classic monoliths of the court buildings loomed awesomely, combined into a special kind of urban beauty. People were starting to come down here to live, but so far the converted office buildings and lofts were few, and, as workers in government and finance had long since left, the area was nearly deserted. Some might have likened the abandoned streets and silent buildings to a ghost town, but to Joe it represented order—the cycle of work and rest. He relished the contrast from the day's chaotic activity, savored the silence the echo of his solitary footsteps emphasized. He walked up a short flight of steps to street level, then crossed over to the parking lot where he kept his new dark green Buick Skylark. The lot was enclosed by a high chain-link fence and he had the key to the gate in his hand when he saw that it was already unlocked. It only meant that someone was inside getting his car, but Joe Capretto stopped anyway and listened.

There was no sound.

There should have been the sound of a car starting. At least of a door being opened and shut. But there was nothing. A shiver passed through him. He placed his hand inside his jacket to touch the gun in the shoulder holster.

A woman screamed.

The scream came from inside the lot at the back. Joe pulled the gun and pushed the gate open.

"Police officer!" he announced as he peered into the darkness. "Police officer!" he shouted.

"Help me! For God's sake . . ."

The woman's scream was cut off in the middle. Headlights flashed on, aimed directly at Capretto. As he put one arm up to shield his eyes, the motor started. He raised his gun, intending to shoot out the lights, but the man in the car fired first. Joe didn't move. He stood gasping as though the breath had been knocked out of him, but he knew he had been hit. After the shock, pain would follow soon enough.

Meantime, he still held on to the gun. He tried to return fire, but couldn't pull the trigger. He concentrated all his will, directed all his strength to that one finger of his right hand. Now. He had to do it *now,* before the hand grew too weak to hold the gun, before his knees buckled under. Now, before the car ran him down. It was coming straight at him. The driver wanted to get away, and he was blocking the exit. All he had to do was step to one side, Joe told himself, but his limbs refused to obey. There was no room for the car to go around. Joe braced for the impact. He was hit just below the knees and thrown backward, his head hitting the pavement. Pain struck instantly, cutting a jagged, lightning course through his entire nervous system. Somehow he managed to roll over on his stomach and cover his head with his hands, waiting for the car to pass over him.

"Sh-ee-eet!" Clarence Orton muttered as the car shuddered at impact. Hunched over the wheel, he braced himself for the next obstacle, which was the half-open heavy mesh gate. They hit it, flinging it wide with a scraping sound of metal against metal, but there was little resistance and Orton and his buddy, Willie Abanto, were through. They didn't know and they wouldn't have cared that in passing over the fallen man the right front tire had crushed his spine. They didn't know that he was hooked by his coat to their undercarriage.

Clarence Orton felt the drag but didn't understand the cause. He didn't know that as he and Willie careened through the empty streets, twisting and turning and doubling back in the unfamiliar maze, their victim was coupled to them, that the body was being bloodied and battered beyond recognition. They were only alerted to the fact that something was very wrong when they found themselves in Chinatown and pedestrians stopped along the sidewalk to stare, to point, and finally to yell. No longer able to ignore the impediment, and with the realization of what it had to be, Orton stopped the car in the middle of Mott Street, cut the motor, and flung his door open. Abanto did the same on his side. Not even bothering to slam the doors shut, the two ran.

Nobody chased them.

Chapter 2

BY THE time Norah Mulcahaney reached the Church of Our Lady of Perpetual Help, the streetlights had come on and dusk was blending into night. Overhead, traffic flowed up the ramp and crossed the Queensboro Bridge in a steady stream; it was the height of the rush hour. Below, the debris-strewn block was desolate. Apparently news of the homicide had not yet spread through the neighborhood. Two patrol cars had arrived, not enough to arouse curiosity. Or just enough to keep anyone from showing it? Norah wondered. She noted an upper and a lower church. It was on the steps between that Sister Therese had died.

The aged nun lay head down, legs up, her decent white cotton drawers and thick black stockings exposed. Instinctively Norah bent down and straightened the habit. Not till then did she turn her attention to the wounds. The entire chest area was soaked with blood. Blood had seeped through the navy-blue cardigan and the navy-blue poplin raincoat. It seemed she had been stabbed repeatedly; how many times couldn't even be guessed—the blood from one wound had flowed into another like bubbling springs feeding into a pool. Norah examined the various items that had spilled out of the nun's plastic shopping bag: wool scarves and toques, warm socks, pot holders—all gaily colored and serviceable. Not worth stealing. Or left behind because of an interruption?

Going down the last few steps to the basement landing, Norah knelt to examine the black simulated-leather purse. She could not wrest it free; Sister Therese's grip remained tight in death as it had in life. Norah didn't try to force it. There was no urgency. After the photographers had recorded the scene, the technicians would handle it to make sure that any prints, hopefully the perpetrator's, were not disturbed; then she could look inside. For now, Norah Mulcahaney got back on her feet to find a tall, thin man wearing a Roman collar standing above her.

The priest's face was as gaunt as his frame. Sharp features converged on a large hawk nose. One could stop there and retain the impression of shrewdness, determination, unflinching discipline, or look beyond to the clear brow, gentle brown eyes, and curly hair and see compassion. The priest had been waiting outside beside the dead nun till a call from his bishop had caused him to leave her unattended. He had come hurrying back out just in time to see Norah get out of her car and note her consideration for the dignity of the sister.

"Are you a police officer?" he asked, shivering because he hadn't thought of putting on a coat either time.

"Yes, Father. Are you the pastor?"

He nodded. "Albert Boylan."

"Sergeant Mulcahaney, Father." They shook hands. "I understand one of your lay workers found Sister."

"Yes."

"And that you sent her home?"

"Yes. Shirley Arkin. She was hysterical. She

works on the switchboard and had made arrangements to leave early to do some Christmas shopping.
Every night before leaving she stops in at the lower
church for meditation—she's devoted to the Infant of
Prague. This afternoon was no different, except that
as soon as she started down, she saw Sister Therese
lying on the landing. She had the will to turn
around, walk back up and then to the rectory, ring
the bell, wait for the door to be opened and get inside.
Then she started screaming and weeping.

"It took a while to find out what it was all about,"
Father Boylan continued. "Mrs. Nutten, who was on
the switchboard in Shirley's place, called 911 and
then informed me. Meantime, Shirley had stopped
screaming, but she was just about incoherent. All
she could do was keep repeating Sister Therese's
name over and over. She would have been of no use
to you in that condition."

Norah nodded. "Is there anything you can tell me,
Father Boylan? About Sister Therese?"

He sighed. "Sister was a teacher in this parish for
thirty-two years. Her pupils loved her and so did
their parents."

So they'd be willing, even eager to talk, Norah
thought. The question was: would their comments be
limited to heaping praise on the dead nun?

"Perhaps you could give me a list of the pupils in
her classes, Father?" It was a place to start, she
thought, though certainly the perpetrator didn't
have to be a pupil or a juvenile, or even live in the
neighborhood. Probably he was some punk wandering aimlessly who had seen the frail woman and
marked her for an easy kill. Nevertheless, routine
had to be followed, an association and a motive
sought. Questioning the children and their parents
would be a big job. Norah hoped enough personnel
would be assigned to do it right. Meanwhile, it was
up to her to make sure no evidence at the scene was
overlooked.

While she had been talking to Father Boylan, officers from a special squad called out routinely on homicides began to arrive, among them the assistant chief medical examiner, Phillip Worgan. Worgan was a smallish man, five-foot-eight, with thick brown hair and small sharp eyes behind steel-rimmed glasses. He came from Syracuse, where he had been chief medical officer. He was far more than competent, but even his exceptional skill didn't make up for his abrasiveness. The detectives groaned when they saw Worgan's car pull up, and there was no small talk, no humor—black or otherwise—in their exchanges with him. The only one who felt easy dealing with him was Norah. On arrival, he had gone directly to the examination without a word to anyone. Now Norah joined him.

It was a while before he acknowledged her.

"I can't tell you much more than you've observed for yourself," he muttered in his usual grudging manner. "She died of multiple stab wounds. The knife, from present indications, was small and it required repeated thrusts to do any damage."

Norah sighed; she wished death had come more easily for Sister Therese. "Is it possible that some of the blood belongs to the perpetrator? If there was a struggle, she might have turned the knife against him and cut him." She indicated the spatters on the folds of the nun's headdress and the cuffs of her dark blue coat.

"We'll certainly test for it."

"And for hairs, fibers . . ."

"Yes, Sergeant, yes. We'll check for foreign substances. We're not going to overlook any possibility. But thank you for the reminders."

"I just had to make sure. Wouldn't you, if you were me?"

Was that a smile? Norah wondered as Worgan bent back to his work.

She looked at her watch. Eight! She should call Joe

and tell him she was finishing up. She went the short distance to the rectory, rang the bell, and entered the vestibule.

"Mrs. Nutten? I'm Sergeant Mulcahaney. Is there a telephone I could use?"

As her reward for remembering the name, she was ushered into the office and given a chair at one of the vacant desks while the lay worker dialed the number for her at the switchboard. It rang and rang, but no answer. Joe could have gone down for a paper or cigarettes, Norah thought. Suddenly she was very tired and just wanted to get home. She hung up and asked Mrs. Nutten to get her the precinct. She'd give Brennan a quick rundown and do the reports in the morning.

Roy picked up on the first ring. "Norah!" He didn't even give her a chance to begin. "Where are you calling from?"

"The Rectory on Sixty-first."

"Stay there. Inspector Felix needs to talk to you. He's on his way over."

Jim Felix was coming himself? Norah-wasn't that surprised; she knew Felix was deeply concerned over these crimes against the religious. Still, for a deputy inspector to be coming to the scene suggested the concern reached even higher—to Chief Deland, maybe even to the P.C. She hoped so. She hoped they were getting ready to throw manpower at the problem. Numbers would certainly help. Meantime, if Jim Felix was coming to take over personally, she wouldn't mind, not in the least. At that moment she felt overcome by helplessness, by a sense of the odds being just too great. She had never taken on a case without believing that ultimately through hard work and patience, not to say doggedness, she would find the solution. Norah believed justice required vindication for the victim. Only recently had she been forced to turn her back on this part of what she considered her obligation as a police officer. Brooding, she returned to the lounge to pace nervously in the path worn by the anxiety of her precursors.

She returned to the window several times to look for Inspector Felix's car. Noting that the morgue orderlies were about to remove the body, she ran outside.

"Wait. Inspector Felix is on his way."

Worgan, just on the point of driving off himself, scowled. "Nobody advised me."

"I'm advising you."

His eyes narrowed; then he shrugged. "Whatever you say, Sergeant." He signaled his people to leave things as they were.

Then Norah realized that everyone else had gone: the technical crew, Detective Jonas Farber from the D.A.'s special squad, the radio cars. In fact, the entire area under the bridge clogged with police vehicles a short time before was now clear except for the morgue van, Doc's beautifully maintained Peugeot, and her own modest gray Honda. Shouldn't they have been advised the inspector was on his way? He was, after all, head of the special homicide task force and would be expecting to hear reports. Somebody had goofed. Communications? Once again Norah felt the hot flush of anxiety course through her body. She burned with a sense of impending disaster.

The nerves at the back of her neck knotted and pain pulsed in her shoulders and down her spine. Nor did it ease at the sight of the Olds turning the corner; it got worse. Felix got out of the car and approached the body. He spoke to Worgan, then bent down and studied Sister Therese. Briefly. It was almost a cursory look.

Deputy Inspector James Felix, chief of homicide detectives, was in his early fifties. In the last two years his waist had thickened and his whole figure had lost its litheness, but he was not fat. "Solid" would best describe him. From its rakish mixture of red and brown, his wavy hair had gone completely white, but it was still thick and those green eyes were as clear and alert as ever. He was just back from a week's vacation in the Caribbean, so Norah expected to see him deeply tanned, the worry lines eased, with a general look of well-being. As he approached the rectory, she saw that he was slouching, and as he mounted the stairs, the light over the door shone full on him. Instead of tan, he was a sickish yellow. His face was haggard and in it she read why he had come.

Norah had intended to go and meet Felix, but she let him come to her. She knew now why he had come alone, why the others hadn't waited. She turned ice cold. She couldn't believe it! She let Felix nudge her back into the parish parlor, as though putting off the question might somehow change the answer. Finally, it had to be asked.

"Joe . . . ?" she whispered. "Is it Joe?"

"Yes. He was run over. He's in surgery. I'll take you to him."

Norah was already running for the door, running and crying at the same time.

She got there too late. Joe Capretto was dead. He died on the operating table.

Norah stopped crying. Her eyes were red but dry. "I want to see him," she told the surgeon.

Dr. Charles Monell looked to Inspector Felix and shook his head almost imperceptibly.

Norah caught it. "I want to see him. I want to see him no matter what his condition," she insisted, her voice steady and determined.

"Mrs. Capretto, your husband suffered grievous injuries. The car not only passed over him but dragged him a considerable distance."

Norah flinched. The spasm passed through her whole body; for several seconds every part of it, every nerve and muscle, pulsed and twitched. Her eyes lost focus; they gazed beyond the two men—whether into the past or toward a future that now would never be, they could not tell, but both reached out to give her support.

"I want to see him. It's my right." Her jaw was thrust forward.

Felix knew she would not be dissuaded. He indicated to Monell that the request should be granted.

"Where is he?" Norah demanded.

Lips tight with disapproval, Monell nodded toward the swinging door at the end of the hall. Felix stepped to Norah's side, intending to accompany her, but she shook her head.

"I want to see him alone."

Monell barred her way. "Arrangements have to be made."

"I'm a police officer. I'll make my own arrangements."

Monell met Norah's look, fought it, and gave in. "But," he added one last protest as he stepped aside, "you're making a mistake. It's a mistake," he repeated to Jim Felix as Norah passed through the swinging doors. "It will haunt her the rest of her life."

Felix sighed. "That's why she wanted to see him," he replied.

Charles Monell sagged. Now that the widow was gone, he could give in to his own depression—he had, after all, lost a patient on the table, never an easy thing no matter what the circumstances. He told himself that even if he had been able to save Captain Capretto, the man would have remained a permanent invalid, sentenced to a wheelchair for the rest of his life. He would also have had to undergo extensive facial surgery and would have got back a face bearing little resemblance to the one he'd had before. None of it helped. He started to walk away, then remembered.

"You'll want a complete autopsy, of course, Inspector, but I can tell you now that Captain Capretto was shot. In all likelihood, it happened before he was run down."

Norah wasn't gone long, but to Jim Felix it seemed like an hour. He started after her several times, once actually getting to the swinging doors, but he didn't pass through. A call from Chief Deland cut into the waiting.

"How is he?" the chief asked.

"They couldn't save him."

"God . . ." Deland groaned. Joe Capretto had been his executive officer for only one year, but it hadn't taken a month for Deland to appreciate his value. There was a long pause; then Deland got back to business. "I just got a report. The car that ran him down was stolen. I'm putting fifty men along the route he was dragged to turn up witnesses. Tell Norah."

Felix paced. He had quit smoking nearly four years ago, but now he wanted nothing so much as a drag. Finally he walked down to the nurses' station and bummed one. He'd barely inhaled a couple of times when Norah appeared. He ground out the cigarette in the nearest ashtray and rushed to her. She was calmer than he. Too calm. Shock, of course. It was far from Felix's first experience offering consolation to the bereaved widow or the desolated parents of one of his men, yet he had no set way to handle it, never would have. Each person reacted differently; each suffered in his own individual way. This was the first time Jim Felix had had to deal with a widow who was a cop herself. It should have been easier. It wasn't. While he sorted through the various expressions of sympathy, Norah spoke.

"How did it happen?"

"All we know so far is that he was caught by the car's undercarriage and dragged several blocks. There hasn't been time to reconstruct, but Chief Deland says to tell you he's putting fifty men on the street. And as many more as it takes," he added on his own account.

Norah waited silently, knowing there had to be more, compelling Felix to tell her.

"Dr. Monell found a bullet."

Her eyes flickered. "He was shot? That suggests he was interrupting a crime in progress."

Damn! Felix thought. Now she'd want to go over to the scene herself. He couldn't allow it. "How about Joe's mother? Would you like me to tell her?" he offered, as much to distract her as to be helpful.

A corner of the veil of apathy hanging over Norah had been lifted and dropped again. "Thank you. I should be the one."

"Would you like me to come with you?"

"No."

"Is there anything at all that Sally and I can do for you?"

"Just make sure there's no announcement till the whole family can be notified. Give me till morning. You know how many of them there are."

It was a sad attempt at normalcy, but as an attempt it encouraged Felix. She'd be okay, he thought; Norah would handle it.

Mrs. Emilia Capretto still lived, as she had for sixty-five years, in the Flatbush section of Brooklyn. The squat five- and six-story red-brick buildings were dingier, the treelined streets no longer pridefully clean. There were more people and more stores, but the essential lower-middle-class character of the neighborhood hadn't changed any more than Emilia Capretto herself had changed. She had moved in as a seventeen-year-old bride direct from Bolzano, Italy. She had borne her children, married off the girls, became a grandmother, then a widow, and finally seen her only son married too, all the while adhering to the same set of traditional values. She had never totally approved of her daughter-in-law. Though

Signora Emilia accepted and rejoiced in the liberation—her word—of women, she had hoped that Joe's wife would not be a liberated woman. If Norah had borne a child, Signora Emilia might have accepted her dedication to her job somewhat more graciously. However, realizing the depth of both her daughter-in-law's and her son's disappointment at being childless, Signora Emilia had relented toward Norah, though she couldn't help feeling that the blame was hers.

Signora Emilia seldom went to bed before one or two A.M. She watched reruns of old movies on television. Tonight it was *Dark Victory,* and that was one she could cry over forever. She didn't expect to have her downstairs bell ring at that hour. It brought a tremor of anxiety which, indomitable though she was, she could not repress. It might be a neighbor locked out, she told herself, and went into the large foyer to pick up the intercom.

"Yes?"

"Mamma, it's Norah. May I come up?"

"Norah . . . Yes, of course." She buzzed back, anxiety swelling up and becoming premonition. She hadn't asked if Joe was with Norah. She knew he wasn't. Norah wouldn't be coming at this hour and announcing herself if Joe was with her. Signora Emilia's breathing became labored. There was no need to put on a robe or remove a hair net; Signora Emilia always remained fully dressed in the ankle-length, long-sleeved black dress, black stockings, and shoes that had become her uniform from the day after her marriage, as it did for all the women of her village. All Emilia Capretto had to do was slip off the chain on her front door, open it, and wait for what she now knew was coming.

One look between the women was enough. They embraced. Signora Emilia cried quietly. Norah did not cry. She wanted to, God knew that she wanted to. She had cried earlier when she hadn't known the extent of Joe's injuries, while hope remained; his death confirmed had deprived her of hope and the relief of tears. She held Joe's mother close, gray head nestled against her bosom, dismayed that the woman she had always considered so strong was actually shrunken and frail.

After a while Emilia Capretto pulled away and looked Norah full in the face. She could hardly miss noticing that Norah's eyes were dry.

"What happened?"

"He was shot."

"Dio mio . . ." Joe's mother crossed herself. "You will take me to him."

"It's better not, Mamma."

The old lady's inflamed eyes narrowed, probing Norah's clear ones like a laser. "You saw him?"

"Yes."

"Ah . . . *Figlia mia!*" She sighed and opened her arms. Now she was the one who clasped the younger, taller, sturdier woman and consoled her. It was an emotional transfusion, and when it was done the two women who before had merely gone through the motions of affection were as close as though of the same blood. By common accord, they went into the bedroom together to kneel before the small shrine of Our Lady of Fatima, Signora Emilia's special devotion. After the prayers, they took up the ritual imposed by death upon the living. Signora Capretto busied herself in the kitchen preparing coffee, food, while Norah called the girls one by one: Maria, Rosa, Isabella, Bianca. As soon as the news was comprehended and the call completed, each spouse and family was roused, clothes thrown on, cars backed out of garages. Where there were children too young to be left at home alone, they were dressed and, sleepy-eyed, brought along: Signora Emilia had plenty of spare bedrooms. Celeste and Ron lived in Boston; they would not arrive till midmorning. Lena and her husband, Jake, lived around the corner. They were the ones Norah contacted first, and they came in minutes.

Lena kissed Norah, then, tears streaming, went to help her mother. Jake offered to take over the telephoning, but at Norah's demurral he didn't insist; he recognized that she needed something to occupy her, just as the women in the kitchen did, though the repeating over and over the fact of Joe's death couldn't be easing the trauma. He didn't know what to suggest in its place.

The building tenants, mostly old people who had lived there as long as the Capretto family, were roused. They remembered Joe as a baby, and when they learned what had happened, they too dressed and came to pay their respects and join in the mourning, bringing whatever food they had in the refrigerator. The family and friends closed around the matriarch. It was Jake who, about six in the morning as light was breaking, remembered Norah. He went through the seven rooms looking for her.

"Where's Norah?" he asked when he came back into the parlor. Nobody heard. "Norah!" he raised his voice. "Has anyone seen Norah?"

The talk subsided. Everybody looked around and then at each other.

Norah was gone.

After six years of marriage, she was still a stranger in this family, Norah thought. She missed her father; oh, God, how she missed him! Though she had little regular contact with her brothers, she yearned for their presence now. She felt totally alone. The sociability of the wake intended to ease the pain of the bereaved had intensified Norah's despair. What she wanted, what she needed, was to go home. Nobody would notice, she thought, and so she got her coat and quietly slipped away.

She drove fast, as though time mattered. She raced across the Manhattan Bridge, then up the nearly empty East River Drive, anxious to get home, to the place she and Joe had shared. There his spirit lingered. There she would find solace.

But as soon as she turned the key in the lock and opened the door, she knew it was not to be. Before she even put on the light, she sensed the emptiness. Their home had meant a lot to both of them, and they had shopped, considered, agonized over each purchase and, at the beginning, paid for it out of scant funds. Every object in that apartment, every piece of furniture and ornament, even the rugs and drapes, should have evoked memories and associations. They represented a progression both economic and emotional. Instead, they were now without meaning. Without Joe, they were merely things.

Slowly Norah walked into the bedroom. She sat on the end of the bed, not having bothered to turn on the lights this time.

The phone rang. She didn't answer. Soon it stopped ringing. She was still sitting there in the dark when it started again. She realized that it must be the family and that if she didn't answer, someone would come over. She couldn't bear that. She edged over to the night table and picked it up.

"Yes?"

"Norah! Thank God!" It was Lena, Antonia's mother and Norah's favorite of Joe's sisters. "We were worried about you."

"I'm okay."

"Why did you leave?"

"I wasn't enjoying the party."

"Oh, Norah . . ."

"I shouldn't have said that. I'm sorry."

"We're the ones who should apologize. Norah, listen, you want me to come over?"

"No. No, thanks."

"You shouldn't be alone."

"I prefer it. For tonight anyway."

"Tonight of all nights—" Lena started to argue.

"Please!" Norah cut her off. "I've had just about all I can take."

She hung up. Her hand was shaking; her body was drenched with sweat. She was thinking of the past months, their fulfillment after the long arid period of alienation. The contrast intensified Norah's pain. She turned and threw herself facedown on the coverlet.

Now she and Joe could never make up what they'd lost, Norah thought. Still the tears would not come.

Chapter 3

IT WAS ten-thirty by the bedroom clock when Norah awoke, feeling dazed, as though she'd taken tranquilizers. Automatically she sat up in bed and reached out a hand for the thermos on the night table. It wasn't there. The familiar smell of freshly brewed coffee that usually pervaded the apartment was missing. She looked; the pillow beside her was uncrushed. He was gone. The full impact of what had happened overwhelmed her. Every morning since the first day of their married life, Joe had got up ahead of her and put on the coffee and when it was ready placed a thermos of it beside the bed so that she could have her "eye-opener" while he shaved. It was one of the many small, tender attentions he had lavished on her and which she had come to take for granted. A simple thing, it epitomized Joe's constant love and care for her. The pain welled up inside; what was she going to do without him?

She dragged herself out of bed and headed for the bathroom. It should have been steamy from his shower, the mirror foggy, damp towels draped over the hamper, his scent in the air. It was all neat and arid. Oh, God! How was she going to live without him?

Norah didn't make breakfast that morning. She couldn't bring herself to go into the kitchen. She dressed quickly, picking up the first thing at hand —a navy pantsuit—and fled. But she only got as far as the corridor before she stopped. Where was she running? She had intended to go to work, of course, but all at once she realized that she couldn't walk into that squad room, couldn't stand there and accept the condolences of their friends, hers and Joe's, who would gather around her as soon as she appeared. Maybe she should go over to Our Lady of Perpetual Help and start the interrogations? No, that would be a complete waste; she wouldn't know what she was doing. Norah, who had led such a structured existence, was at a loss. She faced a day without purpose.

Inside her apartment the phone was ringing. Her first instinct was to ignore it; then she thought she might as well answer. She unlocked the door.

It was Jim Felix. "I've got some news for you." He was purposely brisk. "The first thing is that the governor is issuing a proclamation demanding that random, mindless violence against police officers stop. He's backing it with the offer of a twenty-five-thousand-dollar reward for information leading to the apprehension of Joe's killers."

Norah said nothing.

"We've been able to reconstruct the events," Felix continued matter of factly, though inwardly he was distressed at Norah's lack of reaction. "Apparently, as you suggested, Joe interrupted a crime in progress. We traced the tire tracks back to the parking lot where we all keep our cars." He didn't mention that the tracks were made in blood, Joe's blood. Nor did he intend to make that public, though it would certainly have aroused the public's sympathy. To hell with public sympathy! What he was concerned about was the effect it would have on the victim's family, on Norah in particular. "Joe worked late last night—"

"Late! I didn't know that." Suddenly she was paying attention.

"Yes. Gert brought him a snack at about five-thirty, and he was seen by the receptionist crossing the downstairs lobby on his way out just a few minutes after eight. From the plaza he would logically go straight across the street to the parking lot. What we think is that he surprised two youths getting ready to move a car. We've located witnesses who saw two young men in jeans and leather jackets jump out of the car at Mott and Pell, which is where . . . he was found." All at once the routine terminology seemed unnecessarily callous. "We think that Joe challenged the two in the lot. They fired. When he didn't get out of the way, they ran him down."

Car theft! Norah thought. Joe gave his life for a stolen car? A couple of young thugs shot him and then ran over him, dragging him along the streets, mutilating him, only to abandon him and the stolen vehicle? It didn't make sense. Felix had mentioned witnesses—people, citizens, who had stood by and watched?

"We haven't got a description yet, but now that we can offer a sizable reward, undoubtedly someone will come forward."

"Undoubtedly."

"We'll get them, Norah. I promise you."

"Yes." She sighed.

He expected, of course, that she would want to take part in the investigation, at least that she would have more questions. But she said nothing more. It both relieved and troubled Felix.

"Now, Norah, about the funeral . . . Do you want us to make the arrangements?"

"All right."

"Friday at noon?"

"All right."

"St. Vincent Ferrer is your parish church, isn't it?"

"Yes."

"Then the wake can be at Campbell's."

"Yes, all right," she agreed, wanting only to end the conversation. It didn't matter where the wake would be held, since she had no intention of attending. She wasn't going to stand in front of a closed casket making polite rejoinders as well-meaning people who couldn't even imagine what was inside filed by. Let Signora Emilia stand there and accept . . .

"No." She broke into whatever Felix was saying. "No, it should be in Brooklyn. In Flatbush. That would be better for Joe's mother."

"I'll take care of it." Jim Felix paused. Even making allowances for shock, Norah was not reacting like herself. "I'm worried about you. You shouldn't be alone."

"I'm all right."

"Sally wants you to come and stay with us."

"Thank Sally for me," Norah replied. "But I'd rather be home."

"Then at least get someone to stay with you."

"Yes, all right. Yes, I will," Norah promised, and hung up before Jim Felix could pin her down to either who or when.

So Joe had been working late last night, Norah thought. That was because she'd called and put off their dinner. If she hadn't, he would have left at five as usual. At that hour the parking lot would have been crowded. The punks wouldn't have been there; he wouldn't have surprised them in the commission of a crime. *He'd be alive now.*

It needn't have happened, any of it. If she had turned the squeal over to Roy Brennan as procedure required and good sense dictated, Joe would be alive! Why had she been so determined to take on that case herself? Pride. Norah's square jaw quivered, then set as she continued her ruthless self-examination. Having failed to clear three of her last cases, she had viewed the murder of the nun as an opportunity to vindicate herself, to reassert her capabilities. What in the hell had she thought she was doing? Collecting scalps? Notching kills? Her father had always inveighed against the dehumanizing effect of police work, and Norah had made light of his concern. But Patrick Mulcahaney had known what he was talking about: she was as vulnerable as anybody else. Her so-called dedication was no more than ugly pride. It had cost her her husband, the only man she had ever loved or ever would love.

Norah picked up the phone, dialed her precinct, and asked for her own extension.

"Homicide. Detective Brennan."

Roy was another of the original group from Homicide North. In all the years that Norah had known him, he'd held the rank of detective first grade. He could have gone higher; he had the intelligence and the self-discipline; he was simply one of the few who had found his slot and was content. He came from a blue-collar background, married late. So at forty-six he had a young wife and a three-year-old son. He was obsessed with his family. It had to be something heavy to get him to work overtime, Norah thought. What was he doing there when he wasn't due till four?

"It's me, Norah."

"Oh, good. I was just going to call you. I was waiting till . . ."

"It's okay. I wanted to know about Sister Therese. Anything new?"

"There is one thing," Brennan replied. "The poor box was broken into."

"Oh?"

"It wasn't discovered till this morning. A lay worker opened up to get the altar ready for the first mass and found the box pried open and some coins

scattered on the floor. The church was locked overnight, so it could be connected to the murder."

"Anything else?"

"Not yet. That church and rectory are in a desolate
pocket. There are no residential buildings nearby, no
stores, very little traffic. There's not much hope that
anybody saw anything, but we're asking just in
case."

"How about her students?"

"They're all kids under thirteen, and small."
Children under thirteen had been known to kill
—sometimes in panic, sometimes out of sheer
amorality, but it would have taken a robust thir-
teen-year-old to overcome the struggles of the determined nun. "From what the pastor says, they were
all crazy about Sister Therese," Brennan went on.
"The perpetrator doesn't have to be a juvenile or
even live in the neighborhood."

Already they were laying the groundwork for failure, Norah thought—forgetting that earlier she herself had acknowledged those same possibilities. They
were just going through the motions before passing
on to the next case.

"Don't worry about it, Norah; I'm staying right on
top of it. You take it easy. Get some rest. The lieut
said to tell you to take as much time as you want."

Just like that! They didn't even miss her. Overnight, her duties had been reassigned. Nobody had
even bothered to call and consult her on this case or
any of the others she was carrying. Without another
word, she hung up.

Joe's mother had the whole family to nestle
around her and support and comfort her. Oh, they
would have done the same for Norah—the sisters and
their husbands, the children, the cousins and the
aunts—but they had shown their instinctive feelings
that night at Signora Emilia's, and so she didn't
want them. Her own brothers would be there for the

funeral. Eileen, her father's second wife, would be up from Boca Raton; meanwhile, Norah remained alone at home. Though she no longer expected consolation from the inanimate objects that had belonged to them both, the place and those things were her last contact with Joe and she clung to them. But as the time for the funeral drew near, she had to admit that they could not materialize his ghost.

It was a fine winter's day with not a hint of the cruel weather that had just passed and was surely still to come. It was a blessed hiatus. The sun, though not warm, was bright and the azure sky cloudless when the platoons of officers in blue began to line up on the sidewalk of Lexington Avenue in front of the church. Brass buttons gleamed and white gloves flashed in salute as the widow and the mother of the slain officer were escorted up the steps and inside. The rite was set, only the participants changed, Norah thought as she and Signora Emilia were flanked down the center aisle by the mayor and the police commissioner. In contrast to the brilliance outside, the church seemed dark and gloomy, but only at first. After the eyes adjusted, it was seen to be mellow with sunlight filtered through the stained glass to highlight the gilded wood of the immense Christ on the Cross suspended in the nave, to spread a carpet of soft blues and greens on the polished floor, and to illumine the dark box at the foot of the altar steps as precisely as a spotlight.

Joe was lying inside that box, Norah thought, but it had no reality for her.

She took her place with Signora Emilia in the front pew. The family filled four pews behind them. On the opposite side were the dignitaries—commissioners and deputy commissioners, department chiefs—and behind them, Joe's friends and colleagues. Norah had chosen not to wear her uniform. She was here as his widow. She found the pomp and panoply almost impossible to bear, though she had, for the first time in her life, taken a tranquilizer.

Glancing at Joe's mother, Norah noted that the old lady was so wrapped in grief that she hardly knew what was going on. It was cruel, she thought. She had attended such events in the past and had wondered then how the family could bear it. It was a performance put on for the benefit of the rank and file, to show that the department cared. It was a spectacle calculated to impress the citizens, to make them appreciate that an officer had given his life to protect them. *For a car heist!* Norah thought, and wanted to shout it out loud to the somber assembly. They would pity her grief, but they wouldn't hear what she was saying.

She must remember Joe's life, not his death, Norah told herself. Joe had been a fine cop, the best: competent, dedicated. Despite his insistence that a pro didn't get emotionally involved in a case, Joe Capretto had cared as much as any cop she'd ever known, and he had worked many hours of his own time to solve a case. On the street, he had been wary and quick and strong. Promoted to a position of command, he hadn't forgotten the stresses and dangers the ordinary cop faced out there. The only possible justification for this ceremony was to honor a man's life, to honor the man, Captain Joseph Antony Capretto, Norah thought. That was why this family and all the other families endured it. That was why she now sat here in God's church accepting the pain that throbbed through her whole body, which even the tranquilizer could not dull.

"Praised be God, the Father of our Lord Jesus Christ, the Father of mercies, and the God of all consolation! He comforts us in all our afflictions and thus enables us to comfort those who are in trouble, with the same consolation we have received from him."

The people answered: *"Blessed be God, the Father of our Lord Jesus Christ."*

The mass for the dead had begun.

Deputy Inspector James Felix delivered the eulogy. The rest of the mass then went on to its formal conclusion. The pallbearers, eight men who had been Joe's close friends—Officers Schmidt, Brennan, Alvarez, and Inspector Felix with four of the brothers-in-law—lifted the coffin and carried it out into the sunshine. It was quickly placed inside the hearse and those mourners who would make the trip to the gravesite found their assigned transport. The cortege, headlights on, wound its way austerely and ostentatiously down the avenue to the bridge and across it to the immense Mount Calvary Cemetery on Queens Boulevard. The coffin was lowered into the prepared grave, one in a row among other rows stretching along the highway, a vast, seemingly unlimited field of the dead. After the first spadeful of earth was thrown, Norah took her mother-in-law by the elbow and gently guided her back to the limousine. As Signora Emilia bent to get inside, Norah looked over her shoulder to the grave—once, just once.

The next morning, Norah got up at the usual time. She entered the door of the Thirteenth Precinct at seven-forty-five A.M. She went upstairs into the squad room but passed her own desk without even speaking to Matts Wolland, the man she should be relieving. He started to speak to her, but closed his mouth when he saw her face. Norah went straight on to Inspector Felix's office and after the briefest of pauses while his secretary murmured into the intercom, she was waved inside.

Felix was already up and coming around his desk to take both her hands in his.

"Norah, really you shouldn't have come in today. You should take some time off. A few weeks, a couple of months, whatever you need. Go away somewhere. Believe me, it will—"

"I intend to."

"Oh? Well, that's good. I'm glad to hear it."

He looked her over carefully. Yesterday at the funeral she had been all in black; today she wore one of her regular work outfits—gray pants with lighter gray shirt and sweater—yet the effect of mourning remained. Her face was drawn, deep shadows under her eyes, lips bloodless. "Where are you planning to go?" he asked, forcing cheeriness.

"I have no plans. I just want to get away from . . ." A perceptible pause and a look around, then she finished, "from here."

Felix began to feel uneasy. "I think you should. Go south. Go somewhere warm."

Norah didn't answer right away. She took a deep breath and opened her handbag. She brought out a long flat envelope and placed it on the desk in front of James Felix.

"That's my resignation."

Then she pulled out her ID wallet and was about to lay it down beside the letter when Felix reached out and held her hand to stop her. They stood like that for several moments.

"Why?" Felix asked.

"I don't have to give a reason."

"Officially, no. To me, yes."

"I just don't want to be a cop anymore."

"Is it because we haven't found Joe's killers yet? We will. It's early. We'll get them. I promise you."

"You can't promise."

He swallowed. His green eyes filled with sorrow. "I can promise that we'll do everything humanly possible."

"That's not the same thing."

He sighed. "What's come over you, Norah?"

"Joe was killed because he happened to be in the wrong place at the wrong time. He was killed by strangers. They didn't know him; he didn't know them. Two faceless people out of eight million. Your witnesses couldn't or wouldn't describe them. Despite the governor's reward, no one's come forward willing to describe them. How often do we solve this type of crime? What's our clearance ratio?"

Felix didn't answer. To answer would have meant admitting she was right.

"It's got to the point where we don't even try."

He couldn't even deny that. "We're going to do a hell of a lot more than try on this one."

"There isn't a single clue."

"Why are you being so defeatist?"

"For the first time since I became a cop, I'm facing up to reality. You've already dropped the investigation into Sister Therese's death," she accused.

"Who told you that? It's not true. We're still interrogating the pupils and their families."

"Going through the motions."

"All right, Norah, that's enough!" Felix said angrily. "I'll make allowances for your emotional state, but you have no right to impugn the motive and performance of any other police officer. You have no right to assume that others are less dedicated than you."

Norah bit her lip and looked down. "I'm sorry."

He waved the apology aside. Then he picked up her letter. "I want you to take this back."

"No."

"Norah, I swear to you that we will get Joe's killers. It may take time, probably a long time, but we won't give up."

"You mean you'll wait until they commit another crime. But suppose you don't get them on the next one, or the one after that?"

"When they run out their string . . . we'll get them."

"And then what? Assuming you're able to connect them to Joe's . . ."—she hestiated, then forced herself to say the word—". . . murder, their legal-aid lawyer will plead death by misadventure. The bullet didn't kill him. It penetrated the right shoulder and temporarily paralyzed his arm, but didn't do any real damage." At Felix's questioning look, Norah explained, "Doc Osterman told me everything. So long as the shot wasn't fatal, the rest could all pass off as an accident. They didn't mean to run him down; they didn't know he was caught by the undercarriage and was being dragged. And probably that's true."

"Now you're the one giving up. It's still death during the commission of a felony."

"We've lost control. Crime is sweeping over this city like a tidal wave. We're drowning. There's nothing we can do. I used to think I could make a contribution. I used to think that as long as I got one punk off the street, got justice for one victim, it was worthwhile. I can't even do that anymore. I want out."

"Norah . . ." Felix bowed his head and rubbed the open palm of his left hand over his eyes. "I can't believe it's you talking."

"I want to get away someplace where people are decent, honest, uncomplicated."

"There's no such place anymore. It's the same everywhere."

"Not in the rural communities," Norah insisted. "There are fewer people and they all know each other and look out for each other. I want to go where people don't live behind a barricade of locks, where they're not afraid to get involved. I want to get away from the noise and the dirt and the overcrowding. I want to be out in open country."

"You want to run away," he accused.

"Yes, I do. That's right. 'Stop the world, I want to get off!' I've had enough, Jim. I've had just as much as I can take."

"Sure you have." Despite his instinct to put his arms around Norah and comfort her, Felix was uncertain about crossing the barrier of their official relationship. Norah had always held herself aloof in his presence. So he kept his distance.

"You've been through hell," he reasoned. "You're emotionally spent. Don't commit yourself to a course you might regret later." Picking up the envelope, he walked around the desk. "Take a leave of absence, take . . . six months. Then if you still feel the same way, I won't argue. Meantime . . ." He opened the desk drawer and dropped the letter inside. "This stays here." He slammed the drawer shut.

"I won't change my mind."

God, she was stubborn! "All right. Go to your rural Shangri-la. You'll be crazy with boredom in a week. What will you do with yourself? How will you live? Have your thought of that? If you resign now, you won't get anything from the department."

"I'll have Joe's pension, and we've saved. I have enough to last me for a while."

"And then what?"

"I'll find something."

"And throw away your training, years of experience? Abandon your ideals?"

"Ideals are useless baggage."

"Joe wouldn't let you think that, much less say it. One of the things that bound you together, made your marriage strong, was that you shared a philosophy of life and that you expressed it through your work."

"That's all over."

"You're a good cop, Norah. Joe would want you to go on."

She shook her head. "I can't."

Felix sighed. "You don't know anything but police work. You're not trained for anything else."

"I can learn. I'm not too old to learn. I'd like to do something that requires physical effort, outdoors, something to do with animals or farming."

"Mindless."

"Exactly."

Felix shook his head in exasperation. "Have you picked out this elysian small town? How are you going to find it? Close your eyes and stick a pin in the map like pin the tail on the donkey?"

She shrugged. "I haven't thought it out. Maybe I'll just get in the car and drive."

"So that nobody will know where you are or be able to reach you?"

"That's the idea."

Inspector Felix's green eyes narrowed suspiciously. Once again he came around to the front of his desk. "I want you to look at me and give me a straight answer. Are you going to investigate Joe's death on your own?"

"No."

Slipping the strap of her handbag off her shoulder, Norah rested the heavy bag on his desk. She unzipped it and removed her service revolver.

"There. You have my shield and my gun. I'll turn in my personal weapon before the end of the day."

"Guns are easy to come by."

"That's not my fault," Norah said, and thrust out her chin. Then she strode out of Inspector Felix's office.

As far as Norah was concerned, she was no longer a police officer. She walked out of the station house into the tawdry street of discount stores, cheap bars, and greasy luncheonettes, past mounds of black plastic garbage bags, their contents spilling over the sidewalk and into the gutter from the tears where rats had gorged during the night. Automatically she noted the loiterers—whether they were bag people, male and female, old and young and getting younger every day, or drunks who had wandered up from the Bowery, or addicts who came from everywhere; whether they were minding their own business or scouting for a victim. She reminded herself it was not her responsibility anymore, but the thought brought little ease. It was too soon; getting used to being a private citizen would take time. Once she got out of the city . . .

Norah had been honest with Jim Felix: she had no plans. Joe's mother, at last treating Norah with the sincerity of affection she would a real daughter, had suggested that Norah move in with her. When Norah declined, Signora Emilia was sensitive enough not to insist. In the same way, her brothers had offered her a home out west, and even Eileen had invited her down to Boca Raton for as long as she cared to stay. Norah was grateful, but she knew that to find herself, to make a new life, she had to be free of everything that tied her to the old.

Her first idea was to sell everything off and give up the apartment. Radical surgery. She shrank from it. If it had to be, then it could be done later. For now, she would simply close it up and go away—not south, not on a cruise; she was no Merry Widow. Reaching the end of the block where she'd parked the Honda, Norah stopped in dismay. She'd actually had the keys in her hand and started to the driver's side to unlock the door before noticing her tires were slashed. She took a slow walk around. Every one, front and rear. She examined the other cars parked on both sides of the street bumper to bumper. They were intact. Only hers had been vandalized. Because of the police card in the windshield, of course. She opened the car door, reached in, and removed it. She tore it up and dropped it into the wire trash basket on the corner.

And suddenly Norah did feel better. What she had said spontaneously to Felix now seemed reasonable. Why not get into the car and just drive, drive from one town to the next, stay a night or a few days to see how she liked it? Why not? She was under no obligation to anyone to be anywhere, to do anything. Not anymore. She went into the luncheonette she'd noted earlier.

The place was empty of customers, yet the breakfast dishes hadn't been cleared or the floor swept. There was a rancid smell. Norah looked around for the phone and saw there was only a single booth and it had a hand-scrawled sign Scotch-taped to the front: "OUT OF ORDER." The counterman had his back to her. He was smoking, though the sign on the wall proclaimed: "NO SMOKING."

"Excuse me . . ."

He turned, cupping the cigarette in his palm. "What'll it be?"

"May I use your phone?"

"Can't you read?"

"I mean that one." Norah pointed to the hand set on the shelf behind him. "I have to call a garage. Somebody just slashed all four of my tires."

"Yeah? Damn shame." He didn't put much feeling into it; in that neighborhood it was no big deal. Listlessly he waved her around.

"You ought to call the cops," he told her, and opening his palm, raised the cigarette to his lips and took a deep, deep drag.

Norah was just finishing dinner. She hadn't been hungry, but she knew it was important to observe the routine of living—to get up at the usual time, to keep herself and the place clean, to dress neatly, and to eat properly. So she'd cooked the meal, set the table, and served herself. She'd eaten plenty of meals alone when Joe was working late, but then she'd known that he would be coming home . . . Stop that! Stop it. Somehow she got the food down. She was washing up when the downstairs bell rang. She was surprised because she'd made it clear that she didn't want any visitors.

"Yes?" She spoke into the intercom.

"It's me, Gus Schmidt. I'd like to talk to you."

She wanted to say: *No, not now, please* . . . But he was an old friend.

"I won't take but a few minutes. I promise."

So she buzzed him in.

Detective August Schmidt was a thirty-eight-year veteran of the force. He had been a detective for only the last ten, working first with Norah, then for her. Though he maintained a scrupulously respectful attitude toward the sergeant, he thought of her privately as a daughter. Now he stood at her door, gray hair close-cropped, gray face anxious, shoulders squared. Gus wore his good English tweed suit and held the alpine hat with the feather in the headband which he always carried, but had never been seen to wear, on formal occasions.

"I'm very sorry to intrude, Norah."

He rarely addressed her by her first name.

"It's all right, Gus. Come on in. I was just finishing dinner. Want some coffee?"

"No, thanks. I won't stay long." He twirled the hat nervously. "Well, yes, some coffee would be good." He went directly to the sofa and sat down on the edge. When Norah brought the coffee, he took it and sipped, apparently not intending to say another word till it was finished.

Norah had other ideas. "What can I do for you, Gus?"

Reluctantly he put the cup down. "I heard that you were taking a leave of absence."

She nodded. She didn't ask how he'd heard.

Gus licked his lips. "Do you know where you're going yet?"

"No."

"Well . . ." He took another breath, then the words spewed out fast. "I have a place in Pennsylvania, near York. It belonged to Greta's people and they left it to her when they died and now it's mine. It's not much, just a small house on fifteen acres. My neighbors farm the land for me, but the house is unoccupied. I go down in the summer on my vacation and on holidays whenever I can. There's a swimming hole about a half-mile away. It's nice in the summer," he said wistfully. "It's not much in winter. There's not much to do. There's nothing to do. Probably you wouldn't like it."

"Why, Gus . . ."

"There are horses. There used to be horses to ride. I don't know if you ride . . ."

"Yes, I did when I was a kid at camp. Are you offering me your house, Gus?"

"If it would be of any use to you, Norah." The veteran's voice quavered.

Chapter 4

THE ILLEGALS lay prone under the false floor of the dilapidated truck side by side, male and female, pressed together in four rows of five each. They couldn't sit, or even shift position, for they had less than a foot's clearance over their heads. Air holes had been punched in the false floor that was their ceiling, but flour sacks piled high blocked some of them. They had lain so for uncounted hours. They sweated in the foul air; some were unable to contain themselves; some had trouble breathing.

They had crawled in docilely enough. They had been warned not to talk or to make any noise whatsoever. The warning had been unnecessary—they were too frightened to talk, even to cry. Once the truck stopped. They heard the voices of their driver and another man, and thinking they were at yet another checkpoint, twenty aliens held their breaths. When the truck started to move again, twenty pairs of lungs started pumping. There were broad smiles which could not be seen in the foul blackness, though they could sense each other's joy. They expected the truck would pull up at the side of the road at any moment and they would be released into the pure air of freedom.

It didn't happen. Slowly anxiety returned, was passed from one to the next. Stimulated by claustrophobia, it accelerated into panic. It started with Manuel. The child, nine years old, began to cry for lack of air. His mother beat on the floor over her head and began to scream. Her screams were taken up by the other seven women and then by the men. The twenty began to scream and yell and beat their fists and kick their feet against the floor-ceiling those scant inches above their heads. But the flour sacks absorbed the frantic appeal. The driver heard no more than a soft thudding. Not that it would have mattered if he'd heard their full, desperate hysteria; he had his orders and he wasn't new to the game. Meantime, the twenty had so depleted the supply of oxygen with their shouts and exertions that their lungs had to work even harder, compounding the problem. The child lapsed into unconsciousness, and the mother's shrieks took on a keening note.

There was no choice but to endure. It was the one real talent those people shared and they put it to use. Realizing that to lie quiet and still was their only hope, they went into a semicomatose state, even the mother holding her child lying still, suffering the hours and the miles without any conception of where they were or that night had fallen. The cool air did not reach them. They were not even aware finally of the cessation of motion. It was Benita Cruz who first sensed it.

She nudged the man on her right, Carlos Maldonado.

"*Escuche,*" she whispered.

They both listened.

Definitely the truck had stopped. The next sound was the slam of the cab door. Steps approached the rear. They were all alert now, hardly daring to hope. They heard what had to be the rear hatch fall on its chains; then the floor above them began to rumble and heave as sacks were unloaded. At last, with the whine of well-oiled machinery, the floor began to rise, and then, and only then, the night air rushed in so fresh and cool that it made those sweat-drenched bodies shiver. The floor rose no more than an added two feet, but it was enough. One by one, squirming on their bellies, the aliens wriggled out, stood on their legs upright. Except the boy. Manuel Amara didn't move.

"Madre de Dios!" the mother shrieked.

"Shut up, you," the driver snarled with a quick look around.

There wasn't supposed to be anybody for miles, but you never knew, Randy Shaw thought. He was a big brawny blond who at twenty-three already had a beer belly and high blood pressure. "Shut up," he muttered, and reaching in, grabbed the child's legs and pulled. The body fell limp over the side.

"Oh, hell," Randy groaned. "Oh, shit." He shook his head. "Jeez, lady, I'm sorry about this."

The mother threw herself upon the body of her son, sobbing uncontrollably.

Feeling the familiar hot flush and the shortness of breath that signaled one of his attacks, Randy Shaw turned toward the house behind which he'd parked and shouted. "Aggie!"

A redhead, buttocks encased in tight jeans and bosom hanging loose under a Lurex-threaded sweater that glittered in the starlight, sauntered toward them. "You don't need to yell." She stopped short when she saw the inert form and the weeping woman.

"What's the matter with the kid?"

"He's dead."

"Oh, Christ. You shouldn't take kids," she scolded.

"It's not up to me."

"I know. I know. So what are we going to do with him?"

"Get rid of him."

"How?"

Randy Shaw shrugged. "Bury him."

"Not here."

They argued over the boy without regard for his mother, even as she knelt and wept over him.

Benitz Cruz stepped forward. "He must be properly buried with a priest's blessing."

It was on the tip of Aggie Hunniwell's tongue to tell the babe to butt out, but the fact that she spoke English, and pretty good at that, caused her to tone it down.

"We can't do that. You got to understand; we can't do that."

And Benita Cruz did understand, as the rest of the aliens standing there in awe and sorrow and in fear understood. To give the child burial in holy ground and his mother the consolation of it would be to reveal their illegal presence and to risk—no, not to risk, but to invite—being picked up by the immigration authorities.

Benita knelt down and began to whisper urgently to the bereaved mother.

The next morning the group split: five men were to stay and do farmwork. They had toiled on their own arid acres at home and this was work they understood and were looking for. The remaining fifteen were provided with a good breakfast and more appropriate clothing; then they were driven to the Amtrak station and put on a train for Chicago, where factory jobs were waiting. In Chicago they were to be met by another runner who would take the men to their place of employment. All would receive, as paid for, the indispensable Resident Alien Certificate, the much-sought-after "green card," along with a Social Security card. Both forged. The tragedy of Manuel Amara was not forgotten but put aside in the excitement of a new beginning.

Benita Cruz, along with the seven women, was to

go on to New York. She was to work neither in the fields nor factories, but had been promised an office job. She was intelligent enough to realize she had no office skills, but she'd heard the large companies had training programs and they were willing to take inexperienced workers and instruct them and even pay them while they were learning. Benita would have been glad to forgo the pay just to get a chance to learn. To work in a beautiful office with wall-to-wall carpeting and air conditioning, to wear nice clothes and have a steady job and be able to send money home—that was the dream. The basic price to be escorted across the border and into California was five hundred dollars. To Chicago and factory work another hundred. To New York and white-collar work, two hundred more. Benita Cruz, or rather her mama and papa and the uncles and cousins, had paid it. But Benita and the seven women did not even get to Chicago. At Joliet the third runner boarded the train to take everybody off. Benita protested for herself and on behalf of the other women.

This runner had yellow eyes and sallow, dirty skin, greasy hair low on his forehead in a widow's peak that dipped nearly to the bridge of his nose. He said it would cost more. They had already paid, Benita insisted. There was no way to prove or persuade. It was pay now or get on the truck with those bound for the factory.

The money Benita carried in her boodle bag for emergencies was handed over. The others too managed to find enough, whether in cash or treasured trinkets, to satisfy the runner.

Signora Emilia did not approve. She now regarded Norah with that special domineering affection she had evinced only for her son. If her daughter-in-law didn't want to move in with her, that she understood. She was delighted that Norah had resigned from her job, or as good as. A trip, a visit to her brothers out

west, the old lady would have sympathized with
that, even encouraged it, but going to a strange town
in the middle of nowhere, alone . . . well, it wasn't
healthy. Signora Emilia was sincerely worried.
When she saw that Norah would not be dissuaded,
she stopped arguing. Having lost her only son, she
was determined to hold on to her son's wife.

The furniture was covered with sheets; the silver
had been wrapped in nontarnish Pacific cloth and
stored in bureau drawers; the dust catchers—bowls,
ashtrays, vases, framed photographs—were put
away in plastic bags. What life had been left in the
apartment was completely smothered, and so, she
hoped, were her past and her memories. Emotionally
Norah had already shut the door behind her, was
already concentrating her thoughts and hopes forward to tomorrow morning when she would physically leave. The sound of the downstairs bell was a
minor irritation. It was Gus probably, she thought;
he had been fussing, repeating the simple instructions over and over. Or it could be Signora Emilia,
though they'd had dinner to say good-bye the night
before . . .

"Jim Felix, Norah. May I come up?"

She sighed; he'd make another try at keeping her
here. She appreciated that he would bother, was
flattered and touched, but she just wasn't up to the
emotional confrontation. While she formulated an
excuse, Felix was urging:

"It's very important. I think you'll want to hear
what I have to say."

"Of course." She pressed the button that released
the downstairs latch.

Jim Felix stopped just inside her door. He hadn't
seen Norah in nearly two weeks and was totally unprepared for the change. She looked tired, thinner,
with dark circles under her eyes, but that was to be
expected. What shocked Jim Felix was her slug-
gishness; not apathy exactly, but a lack of vitality.

He was taken aback too by the condition of the apartment. The preparations he saw were not for a vacation of a few weeks but for months. *She's given up!* he thought, and dismay was followed by sadness. Never, no matter what the odds against her, had he known Norah Mulcahaney to stop fighting.

Never mind, he told himself, striding forward into the big living room, which had always been so welcoming and was now so strange. What he had to tell Norah would change everything. He was excited and he let it show.

Norah, however, was looking for a place for him to sit. She waved vaguely, reaching to pull off one of the sheets. "I'm sorry."

"No problem, no problem." He was too charged up to sit anyway. "I have news, good news. We've apprehended the two perpetrators who shot Joe and then ran him down. We have them in custody." He grinned broadly.

Norah stood absolutely still. Her face showed nothing, but inside she was in turmoil. Principally, she was surprised; she had not expected that the case would ever be cleared, much less so fast. She was glad because of what it would mean to Joe's mother and the family. She knew that Felix was pleased, and so were Joe's friends. In fact, the whole department would be celebrating the arrest of the cop killers. For herself, it wouldn't bring Joe back.

It was obvious that Jim Felix thought the news would make her change her mind about leaving. On the contrary, it removed the last twinge of anxiety, the last possible deterrent.

Disregarding the sheet, she sat down on the nearest chair. "Who tipped you off?"

"We have a witness. An eyeball witness!" How often did that happen? Felix thought, and gloated, "In fact, she was the intended victim. Apparently she was entering the parking lot to get her car, and when she unlocked the gate, these two followed her in. She got as far as her car, opened the door, and was just about to get in when they jumped her, knocked her to the pavement. The intent was to rape and rob, but Joe interrupted. He saved her. Very possibly he saved her life."

So it wasn't just another car heist, Norah thought. *Oh, God, thank you for that!* She covered her face with her hands, praying silently, and felt the tears well up, waiting for the relief of tears, but none came. After a few moments, she knew that they would not.

"Joe shouted at them, announced he was a police officer. They left her and got into her car. She saw the shorter of the two lean out the passenger window and fire. She saw Joe fall and the other one deliberately drive over him. She picked both men out of the mug books and then out of the lineup. She's prepared to testify in court. There is no way they are going to beat this rap." Felix sat down, folded his arms, and regarded Norah with satisfaction.

"How did she happen to have her car parked in that particular lot?"

He had hoped that she would be too elated to think of that. He should have known better. He stifled a sigh. "She's one of our civilian employees."

"And she waited this long to come forward?"

"She was afraid."

"But now she's not afraid? How come? Because of the reward?"

"Norah, it doesn't matter."

"It matters to me. My husband, a police officer, was killed protecting her, and she didn't come forward. She saw the perpetrators well enough to be able to identify them, but she didn't come forward. She works for the police department, but she didn't come forward. I can understand she was afraid. Oh, yes, I can understand that very well. I don't blame her for it. I blame her for the price of her courage."

* * *

Norah left the city the next morning. Passing under the Hudson River via the Lincoln Tunnel, she picked up Interstate 95 heading south. She veered west on 78 and from then on it was directly west, passing Allentown and Bethlehem, curving slightly east again only to bypass Harrisburg. The panorama consisted of the usual gas stations, cheap food stores, motels, shopping centers; nature was hidden somewhere back of the billboards, she thought, as though the people were ashamed of it. She would have traveled the secondary roads, but after last night she'd wanted only to get where she was going as quickly as possible. There would be plenty of time for breathing free. Swinging away from the state capital, however, Norah found herself away from the tawdry commercialism and in an area of gently rolling semiwooded farmland. Gus had told her that this was some of the richest producing land in the nation. Tobacco, corn, and winter wheat were the main crops. The area around York was known for its apple and peach orchards. It wouldn't be pretty at this time of year, he'd warned, but then, what could be in this part of the country at this time of the year? It was, in fact, the worst time, that bleak period known as the January thaw, though it could come as late as mid-February, when the weather turned deceptively mild, melting snow to slush in the city and to mud everywhere else.

What Norah saw in the thin, watery sunlight was open, featureless fields on either side of the road. Occasionally there was a section of plowed furrows, but mostly the land looked sodden and abandoned. It suited Norah's mood. To have gone to the hot sun, bright water, lush growth of the tropics would have been to set aside mourning. That was not her purpose. At the intersection of U.S. 30, Norah pulled over to study the map Gus had drawn for her. The last of her journey would take her along the famed Lincoln Highway and toward the Susquehanna

River. The turnoff was an unmarked macadam road just short of the town of York Crossing, population 3,421. The first house she would pass on the road would be that of Gus's neighbors Willie and Edda Meyer. Another three miles and she would be at Gus's place.

By the time she pulled up, it was dusk. The half-light was kind to the squat house with its wide, slightly sagging, broad-pillared porch. It was two stories high, without ornamentation, just a good coat of white paint on the wooden shingles and the high-gloss dark green of the shutters. It was as plain and solid as Gus and Greta Schmidt and Greta's people who had built it. The fading violet light tinted the winter sere patch of grass at the front, not formal enough to be called a lawn, upon which several fine old apple trees encroached from the orchard at the back, their gnarled limbs silhouetted against the darkening sky.

Norah mounted the four steps to the porch and put the key into the lock of the front door. It turned easily and she stepped into a small hallway. Her first impression was of warmth and the pleasant lemon scent of furniture polish. She found the light switch, and a lantern-style overhead fixture illuminated the hall. Someone had done much more than just come in and turn on the furnace, Norah thought gratefully. Gus had said that his neighbor Edda Meyer would get the place ready, but knowing that the house had been shut up since his last visit in August, Norah hadn't expected anything so thorough and so welcoming.

Still in the hall, she took note of the plain, yet graceful stairs rising at a slight curve, the random planking of the floor, the neat pattern of the blue-and-white Dutch tiles centered on the north wall. She identified the furniture as Pennsylvania Dutch, good solid pieces, the floor hand-hewn as in the hall, with a scattering of braided rag rugs. She took a deep breath, pulling her shoulders back, as Joe had taught her, held it and then slowly let it out again—releasing with it a myriad of tensions she had not consciously been aware of. She had not really known what to expect, for Gus had been modest about this house. She had been under no obligation to stay if she didn't like it. But this was perfect. She would find herself here, Norah thought; she would come to some resolution.

Upstairs, reluctant to appropriate Gus's master bedroom, Norah chose a small room at the back. Before last light she had put her car in the garage, a separate building that had probably started as a barn, brought her luggage up, and unpacked the most necessary things. Then she went down again to a big old-fashioned kitchen and found, no longer with surprise, that the refrigerator was well-stocked. As she was preparing a light meal, the telephone rang.

"Mrs. Capretto? This is Edda Meyer, your neighbor."

"Oh, Mrs. Meyer, yes. I know that I have you to thank for finding everything in such marvelous order."

"I just called to check that you had safely arrived."

"You're very kind."

"And that the house is comfortable and that you have everything you need, ya?"

"Everything is perfect. You went to too much trouble."

"August is a good friend. Willie and me, we hope you will be our good friend also."

Mrs. Meyer spoke with a slight upward lilt that turned every statement into a question.

"Thank you." Not an Irish lilt, Norah thought; it had a hiss of German, but wasn't that either.

"Tomorrow in the morning we will come. We will show you where everything is. Then also we will take you into the town to show you that, too." She paused. "If you want, ya?"

"Oh, yes, thank you very much."

"Good." There was a pause during which Norah could hear remarks exchanged, asides not for her ears, then Mrs. Meyer spoke directly into the phone again. "Mrs. Capretto? Willie says no need to be fearful alone in the house. We have no crime here."

Norah came as near to smiling as she had in a long time. Gus must have told them that she was recently widowed. He might or might not have mentioned that Joe had been a police officer, but quite obviously he hadn't told them that she was too. Correction: had been. She was just as glad he hadn't.

"I'm not afraid," she assured Edda Meyer.

Of course she wasn't, Norah assured herself as she sat down a while later to eat the ham omelet she'd made for herself. But she surely wasn't used to the silence! She had always thought that the apartment on Sixty-eighth was marvelously quiet at night, but never had she experienced a quiet like this—absolute. Nor such impenetrable darkness. Looking out the window, Norah couldn't see a thing. There were no streetlights, no lights from other houses, no passing headlights. Tonight there was not even a moon or stars. Was it going to rain? Norah found herself tiptoeing as she moved around cleaning up. Ridiculous! She turned on the television in the parlor, loud. After a few minutes, she turned it off; she hadn't come down here to anesthetize herself with television. She was tired. It had been a long day. It was time to go upstairs and go to bed.

Norah awoke to unrelieved darkness. It disoriented her. She remembered where she was, but it still took several moments for her to visualize the room—the position of the bed, the door, the window. What had wakened her? A heavy gust of wind? A passing car? She lay very still listening. Then she heard voices, low voices but unmistakably men's. Out here in the middle of Gus's fifteen empty acres? She found her slippers and got into her robe. She reached for the light on the night table but decided not to turn it on. Then, feeling her way to the bureau, she fumbled for her purse, opened it, and got out the small flashlight she always carried. Automatically her finger spread for the butt of her gun. There was no gun. She no longer carried a gun.

Guided by the beam of her penlight, Norah found her way down the hall and across to the front bedroom and to the nearest of the two small latticed windows, then doused the light. Across the front yard and approximately sixty feet down the road, headlights cut a tunnel of brightness. Through the slats of the shutters she could see an old ramshackle bus, high off the ground, like a school bus except that it was painted gray instead of the usual bright yellow or orange. It was listing off the shoulder of the road on the rear-right wheel. A flat. Two men were bent over examining the damage. After a brief consultation, one of them, short and stocky, looked up toward the house. It was dark and shuttered; she'd been too tired to open the shutters anywhere but in her own room before going to bed. Now, in the grip of sudden and unwarranted anxiety, she was glad. Would they come over and knock anyway? Would they knock and ask to use the telephone? If they did, would she let them in?

They must have decided that the house was unoccupied or else that no mechanic was likely to come at that hour anyway, because they opened the rear compartment and hauled out the spare. While the one in uniform, evidently the driver, got the tools, the stocky blond went around to the passenger door and motioned everybody out. In New York, Norah would have gone back to bed at this point; here, she stayed and watched. She didn't know why. There was something eerie about the scene. The passengers climbed down slowly. In the periphery of the headlights, they appeared as lumpy forms, unusually docile. Probably they'd been sleeping, and suddenly roused, were not yet fully awake. Everybody was oddly silent, she thought. The two men changing the tire talked to each other in low voices. In the city there would have been yelling back and forth, banging and dropping of tools. Passengers would have complained loudly or else made a party out of it.

The blond beckoned to one of the huddled figures. It detached itself from the group and crossed through the headlights. Norah could make out only the general outline, but it was a woman. She was of medium height and wore an outsized shapeless windbreaker over a long, possibly black skirt that dragged at the ankles. Her hair was covered by a kerchief. Suddenly she tripped and fell. Another figure from the group, similarly dressed, ran forward to help. But the man who had beckoned was there first.

As the fallen woman looked up at him, the headlights illuminated her. She was young. She was pretty, with an oval face and full lips. The blond man, his back to Norah, reached out a hand and yanked her to her feet. She shook him off, and as she did so, the scarf fell off to reveal a mass of dark curls. He spoke to her, then led her around to the back of the bus and handed her a lantern to hold so that he and the driver could see to work. An ordinary action, Norah thought, except that the man appeared not to have asked for help but to have ordered.

The girl was not cowed, though she obeyed. Standing by the side of the road, she held the lantern proudly, even defiantly. It was an attitude with which Norah was familiar.

Chapter 5

OLD HABITS are hard to change: though Norah had determined to sleep late the next morning, she woke at the usual time. It was a wintry day, the sun producing the same watery pale light of the day before. Yet she was eager to get up. It was just as well, for the Meyers arrived promptly at eight.

Edda Meyer was a short, rotund, sensible-looking woman. Her full face and her red-gold hair, worn in a braid around her head, made her look on the young side of fifty. But the gold was fading to silver and fine lines scored her rosy cheeks. Her eyes were blue but dispirited; even when she smiled, the strain of the long, hard years as the wife of a small independent farmer showed through. She made an effort to be cheery.

So did Willie. He was his wife's counterpart, or maybe it was the other way around. Squat and chunky, Willie Meyer had the same reddish hair and florid complexion and the same posture of defeat.

Once again they welcomed Norah, looking her over as they did so. Cautiously they offered sympathy for her loss. Obviously they thought her a strange bird and wondered what she was doing here. They took her over the house, explaining the work-

ings of the furnace, the vagaries of the plumbing,
what key went with which lock—things Norah had
already figured out but didn't say she had. That
done, they bustled her out to their van, or was it a
jeep? Norah wasn't sure. They called it the Bronco;
made by Ford, it had four-wheel drive, was brand
new. They were very proud of it.

They were also very proud of the history of their
region and knew it well. York was the first Pennsylvania town founded west of the Susquehanna River,
they informed Norah. In colonial days it was known
as "the breadbasket of America" and it was still an
important agricultural area, though now it also supported a variety of manufacturing. It had been the
site of the Continental Congress from September 30,
1777, to June 1778. York was the county seat and as
it grew and spread it had spawned West York, a rep-
lica of itself, and York Crossing. In actuality, York
Crossing antedated both, going back to Indian days,
when it had been a trading post at the river's bank.
Norah could see that was a source of contention between the inhabitants of the towns. The people in the
region were principally of German descent, but the
tradition was English.

As they entered York Crossing, the first thing Norah noted was the unbroken rows of brick buildings
all under one continuous roof. Nearly every block
was split by an alley. The Meyers explained this by
pointing out that in back of the houses facing the
street were other, smaller houses. They found a
place to park and walked to the central square.

It was immediately apparent that this was the hub
of the business and social life of the town. In addition
to the town hall, courthouse, and post office, all of
brick, there was a small Gothic-style hotel, a modern
supermarket, luncheonette-newsstand, and the ubiquitous bar and grill. This one had lace curtains
strung across the lower half of the plate-glass window. Norah could see that, like any other bar and

grill anywhere, it was already doing business. Some customers were drinking; most were eating. From the relaxed attitudes, she judged it served as the town's social club.

The Meyers introduced Norah around. At the market she met the manager and his wife, who was also the cashier, and their eldest daughter, who was one of the checkers. These people didn't just know each other, Norah reflected, they knew each other's families; they grew up together. They bowled and went to church socials together. Their kids dated and then married. What choice did they have?

Next, the Meyers took Norah to the post office and she met the postmaster, who was baby-sitting his grandson, dangling the infant on his knee behind the general-delivery window. Paul Hoff issued her a key to Gus's box—there was no rural delivery.

The Meyers presented Norah to everyone as "Mrs. Capretto, Gus Schmidt's friend who's staying at his place for a while." They made no mention that she was, or had been, a police officer. She reminded herself again that very probably they didn't know. She also reminded herself that was the way she wanted it, yet it made her feel odd—as though a part of her personality were being denied, a part of her life wiped out.

All the mouths smiled, but the eyes dismissed her. She was a transient. She wouldn't be around long enough to affect their lives; why bother with her? Accustomed to attracting attention, making an impression, and having been warmly received by the Meyers, Norah was let down. Perhaps it was only a small-town reserve, she thought, not so much a resentment of strangers but a shyness. Norah shrugged it off. She hadn't come looking for new friends. She was ready to go back to the house and about to say so when she spotted a beautiful carriage of fine polished wood, canvas-topped, drawn by a sleek trotter. It was driven by a dour figure—a heavily bearded man dressed in sober black and wearing a round hat.

"Is that a Mennonite?"

"Amish," Willie corrected. "The Mennonites have caught up with the twentieth century. They drive cars. Some of them even shave." It was the first hint of a sense of humor. "We don't see much of any 'plain folk' here. Mostly they keep to themselves and do whatever business they have over to Lancaster."

Edda suggested lunch at their house, but Norah declined, pleading that she was still tired and had unpacking to do. Neither of the Meyers insisted, and she was grateful for their tact. They took her back to Gus's place and parted with warm promises of future meetings. That night when Gus called from New York to find out how she was getting along, Norah could honestly answer, "Fine. The Meyers are being very kind."

The days passed with the same grayness of weather, routine, total absence of emotion. It was what Norah had come for. Her feelings were numbed. She spent most of her time walking. She walked the muddy, dreary country lanes in all directions for miles. Sometimes, as she passed a lonely farmhouse, children ran out to lean on the fence and stare at her. Roosters crowed and chickens cackled. Dogs barked and ran at her heels. Always Norah smiled, waved, and kept on stolidly till they fell behind and she was alone again. On the eighth day, the mild weather broke. The temperature dropped thirty degrees overnight. Snow fell. It continued all day. Norah tried to go out but she was afraid to wander too far from the house, for the snow had wiped out the landmarks she'd used to find her way. The day dragged on, and when she went to bed, it was still snowing.

She awoke to bright sunshine in a cloudless sky. She looked out the window of her back bedroom: the bare limbs of the apple trees were coated with crystal and the snow dazzled her eyes. The radio told her that it was four degrees above zero. She dressed quickly, eager as a child to run out and play in the fresh, glittering powder. She had a quick breakfast, bundled herself up, and pulled the door open. Snow was piled up to the level of the porch and the wind had driven it in drifts against her front door. She was snowed in.

She waited five hours till Willie Meyer arrived with his plow to dig her out. By then she was more than restless, she was impatient, chafing at being forced to rely on someone else. Suddenly Norah realized that she was bored. She needed something to do. Joe had always told her that she didn't know how to relax. Then she smiled. This time he would not disapprove of her fidgeting—it meant she was ready to move on to the next phase of rehabilitation.

"Gus said I might be able to do some riding, horseback riding," she mentioned to Willie after he'd tunneled a path from her door to the road and they were having coffee in the kitchen.

He looked doubtful. "In the summer when the tourists come, sure, but now . . . You could try Karl Droste. He has horses. Maybe he'd let you ride one of them."

"I want to pay."

"You could ask him." Willie shrugged. "His place is about five miles down from the fork. Turn right. It's marked. It's the place with the twin white silos. You can't miss it."

It's also got a big "No Trespassing" sign, Norah thought. "I've seen it," she said.

It took two more days before the snow compacted enough for walking—there was still no possibility of using her Honda. Norah set out eagerly. Reaching the gate with its stern sign, she raised the latch and boldly walked through. It was about a quarter of a mile to the main house, but the road had been cleared and she could stride along vigorously. The house was brick, as were most houses in the region. She had discovered that this was due to an abundance of suitable clay; Gus's place was one of the exceptions. The Droste house was larger than it had looked from the road. Grown with the generations, Norah supposed; a wing, a floor added as needed. Yet it was homogeneous. It was true to itself and compatible with the landscape. Norah rang the doorbell.

She had to wait a long time till someone came, a gaunt gray woman with a hard jaw and suspicious eyes. She wore a housedress of a stiff, loosely woven fabric printed in bright red tulips. It didn't go with her expression.

"Good morning. Mrs. Droste?"

"What do you want?"

"My name is Norah Capretto. I'm staying over at the Schmidt place and . . ." she stopped. "Are you Mrs. Droste?"

"No."

"Who *are* you?"

The challenge surprised the woman, took away her advantage. "Ilse Raisbeck," she answered, and Norah's steady stare forced her to add, "I'm the housekeeper."

"I see. Well, Mrs. Raisbeck, please tell Mrs. Droste that I would like to see her."

"Mrs. Droste does not receive visitors."

Ordinarily Norah would have let it go, but the housekeeper's surliness made her pursue it. "Is she sick?"

The woman licked her thin, unpainted lips. "Yes."

"Oh. I'm sorry. Well, Mr. Droste, then. Would you ask him if I might speak with him?"

"He's at the stables." The housekeeper jerked her head to the right.

"Thank you." Norah offered a smile, but the door was already closing in her face. She shrugged and started in the direction Ilse Raisbeck had indicated.

The stables were at the back, not visible from either the road or the front door of the house. Turning the corner and coming upon them, Norah was impressed. She had not expected anything so extensive. On closer inspection she saw that they consisted of three sections like the house, suggesting add-ons. But they were all uniform in style, recently painted, and well-maintained. There was also a small exercise ring, empty. In fact, there wasn't a soul around. The door of the stable on her left was open. Did that mean it was the only one in use? She looked inside.

"Bert?" a man called from the dark, moist, redolent recesses. "Is that you? It's about time you showed up. I've finished mucking out, so you can . . ." Emerging into the sunlight, he blinked. "You're not Bert!"

"I'm sorry."

He wasn't amused. "Damn! That man is so lazy. I'd fire him if I could get anybody else. But he knows I can't." He sighed. "What can I do for you?"

"Mr. Droste?" He nodded. "My name is Norah Capretto. I'm staying over at . . ."

"I know."

"Oh?"

"Sure. You're new. We don't have much to talk about around here." He looked her over with wary interest.

She was swaddled in an assortment of clothing, whatever she'd had on hand that would keep her warm and dry. She'd started with a complete set of woolen long johns, then dark brown cord pants were tucked into high, shapeless rubber boots. A flannel shirt was topped by a thick Norwegian-style sweater, and that by a navy nylon zippered shell. She wore a bright red wool cap pulled low over her ears, and matching red mittens; they were the only things that did match. She must look awkward and at least twice her size, Norah thought self-consciously, then forgot about it.

She took her time sizing him up. He was in his early forties, tall, about six-two, and rangy. His dark hair was liberally laced with gray and swept back from a high, deeply furrowed brow. His brown eyes were deep-set, his features craggy. A white scar burned across the right eyebrow, its whiteness contrasting with the weathered skin. His large nose had been broken just below the bridge. The wound over the eye was an old wound; the other, who could tell? He wore a plaid shirt, sleeves rolled up to the elbows, jeans—work jeans—and high laced waterproofed boots. He carried a shovel. Though he looked as though he knew how to use it, and had, apparently, been using it, and despite his rough clothes, Karl Droste did not look like a farmer. Not like Willie Meyer, for instance, nor like any of the other farmers Norah had met so far. He was as stolid, as reserved, but here was also an aura of . . . breeding. Having asked her business and submitted to her scrutiny, he now waited for her answer.

"I was told you keep horses."

"That's not exactly correct."

At that moment a horse snorted and then neighed from behind Droste, somewhere at the back of the dark stable. Norah raised her eyebrows, but he chose not to comment.

"I'm interested in doing some riding. I would like to rent a horse."

"I don't rent out horses."

Norah looked directly and steadily at him. He was like the rest of them, taciturn by nature. Norah was not easily put off, but she wasn't in the mood for cajoling, either.

"All right," she said. "I'm disappointed, but maybe you know someone in the area who does?"

"Sorry."

"Well . . ." She held out her hand. "Never mind. I'll look somewhere else."

He didn't take her hand, but he returned her searching look with one of his own.

"Why did you come here?" he asked at last.

It wasn't a challenge. It wasn't belligerent, but rather plaintive, and Norah understood he meant York Crossing, not his farm.

"I wanted a quiet place. A place without distractions."

"You got that, all right." He didn't try to hide the bitterness. "Sorry. I didn't mean to pry, but I was told that you are recently widowed, and it seems to me that a place like New York with all its variety . . ."

"No."

There was an awkward pause.

"I have to admit that I didn't expect it to be this quiet," Norah volunteered.

Tentatively they smiled at each other.

"Well . . ." He cleared his throat. "Just how good a rider are you?"

Her smile broadened. "Not good at all. A beginner. I learned when I was a kid at camp."

"You haven't done any riding since?"

"No."

"Well, I do have a horse that might suit you. The fact is, I buy and sell horses. I go down to the sales in Maryland and Virginia, buy horses and bring them up here and keep them till I find a buyer. Sometimes I'll board a horse for a client if the horse was bought from me or if the buyer isn't ready to take delivery. So the horses back there"—he gestured—"aren't really mine."

"Oh."

"There is one, Dandy. He belongs to my wife, but she's not able to ride; she suffers severely from arthritis. She refuses to sell him. She won't consider it. I haven't the time to give him the exercise he needs, particularly lately with the snow and my hired hand not showing up. . . . Well, if you wanted to come by

every now and then and take him out, give him a
little air and exercise . . ."

"Oh, I'd like that. And of course I'll pay . . ."

"No charge. It'll be mutually advantageous. Come
on."

He led her inside into the shadows, into the pun-
gent aroma of hay and manure. Norah inhaled. It
was great. She could make out a double row of stalls;
only three were occupied, and the horses showed no
interest in her at all. Droste stopped at the very last.

"This is Dandy, short for Yankee Doodle."

Dandy was a fine, glossy chestnut stallion approximately fifteen hands high, well-muscled, lean, certainly not looking as though he lacked for exercise.
He had as little interest in Norah as the others. Despite his name and his good condition, he did look
dispirited though, Norah thought. But as soon as
Droste approached with his bridle, Dandy's ears
twitched with interest. Only when it was put on and
he had been led out of the stall to be saddled did the
horse take a good look at Norah.

"This lady wants to take you out, Dandy."

Dandy snorted and began to paw the floor restlessly.

"He hasn't been out for a couple of weeks, so he
may be a little . . . uh, exuberant at first, but he'll
calm down."

Norah was having second thoughts. "I really
hadn't expected to be going out today. I'm not properly dressed . . ."

"You're okay. Just peel off a couple of those top
layers." Having tightened the girth, Droste led the
big chestnut outside.

Norah followed reluctantly.

"I suppose you'd better have the mounting block."

She would have loved to decline, but knew she
couldn't manage without it. "Thank you."

Now I'm in for it, Norah thought as she watched
Droste put the block in place. She clenched her teeth

and summoned forth her memories and her instincts. She stepped up on the block facing the horse's flank, took the reins from Droste in her left hand and placed them on Dandy's neck just in front of the saddle, then her right hand on the cantle, the back of the saddle. He turned the left stirrup for her and she managed somehow to get her foot into it. She heaved herself up but fell short. Oh, God, she was stiff. She tried again, heaved, and felt a shove at her buttocks that sent her sailing. Just in time she remembered to throw her right leg out over Dandy's broad back and her right hand forward. She landed in the saddle with a thud, somewhat embarrassed but secure.

"Are you sure you know how to ride?"

Too hard, Norah thought; I came down too hard.

She looked down and instantly up again—the ground seemed miles away. All she wanted for today was to walk around the exercise ring with someone leading the animal. Of course, she couldn't ask Droste to do that. So she adjusted the reins in her hands, threading them through her fingers—the snaffle passing between the little and the fourth fingers, the curb between the next two, and then the ends of the reins, the bight, followed the palms to come out between thumb and forefinger—very much aware that Droste was observing her closely. She gripped Dandy's flanks with thighs and calves, angled out the stirrups, and thrust her heels down.

"Yes," she replied, chin thrust forward. She must have done it all right, because he made no comment.

"Do you want a crop?"

"No. No, thanks."

"Okay then." Droste lightly slapped Dandy's hindquarters. "You're off."

Oh, God, they were, instantly! Up to then, Dandy had been extraordinarily quiet and patient, and she wasn't prepared either for the start or for the fast pace. Then she realized it couldn't be all that fast, because Droste had no trouble in overtaking them to open the gate. Norah didn't want to leave the compound. A short ride inside the fenced area would have been more than enough.

"I'm not familiar with the countryside," she called out, hoping she didn't sound desperate.

Droste grinned. "Don't worry. Dandy is." He opened the gate.

As soon as he saw that, Dandy broke into a trot. Once through, he increased speed—tucking his hocks under him, he shifted into a canter and then a gallop. Norah's attempts to pull him up were useless. In trying to shorten up on the reins, she lost them. Then her seat was flung forward. All she could do was throw her arms around his neck, grab his mane, and hang on. They galloped faster and faster down the lane, past the barn and the twin silos. With the bit loose in his mouth, Dandy settled into a long and graceful, powerful stride, the snow apparently no impediment. He was . . . exhilarated, Norah thought. He seemed to have forgotten that he had a rider. All she could do was hope that eventually he would tire or get bored and slow down. Meantime, he was relishing the full power of his energies. They were going up a small hill, but even that didn't cause him any extra effort. Then suddenly Norah saw the irrigation ditch. They were headed straight for it. It stretched across the entire slope; there was no way to go around it.

She tugged at the mane. "Whoa!" she shouted. "Stop!" she yelled. He kept on flying. As they approached the open trench, Norah shut her eyes and cringed in anticipation of the inevitable. She waited for the pain as she tumbled off his back and hit the frozen ground. Instead, she felt herself rise, light as a balloon, and when she opened her eyes, Dandy, his four legs tucked under, soared over the ditch without breaking stride. Now she was as exhilarated as he. Her blood surged; the wind stung her cheeks; the cap fell off her head and her dark hair streamed loose behind her. She laughed out loud.

Then, perversely, with a suddenness that turned her laughter to choking gasps and nearly did send her toppling over his head, Dandy stopped.

Her heart pounding, Norah stared down into a huge crater whose sides were gouged stone. An abandoned quarry. Dandy had stopped at the utmost edge. His forelegs still quivered from the strain, but as he turned his head to look at her, Norah had the feeling that he had known exactly what he was doing.

As she patted his neck, glistening with sweat, their steaming breaths intermingled.

"I'm still here, boy," she told him. Then, settling in the saddle, weight slightly forward, thighs pressed to his flanks, she picked up the reins and carefully arranged them. Heart still beating fast, she flicked his flank lightly with her right heel and tugged, also lightly, with her right hand, the pull stronger at the snaffle. Docilely, Dandy turned—away from the precipice.

Norah grinned. Then she gave him a flick with both heels and they started forward at a pleasant walk. He had accepted her, Norah thought. She had made one friend. After a short distance, she grew braver and gave him the signal for a light trot. He responded perfectly and she had no trouble posting to his gait. It was all coming back. She had no desire to nudge him to a faster pace—he might go into a gallop again, and she'd had enough of that for one day. She brought him back to the stable at the same controlled and, she thought, elegant trot, stopping right in front of Karl Droste, who had been watching since they turned in at the gate.

He scowled. "Look at him! He's covered with sweat! You should have walked for at least the last quarter-mile."

Some of her pleasure was quenched, but not all.

Ignoring an offer of help, Norah rose in her stirrups, disengaged the right foot and swung the right leg over, disengaged the left, and slid down. The soreness started as soon as she touched the ground. By tonight, she wouldn't be able to move, but she wasn't going to let Droste see.

"I'll walk him now," she said. "Where's his blanket?"

Norah didn't look back, but she was very much aware that Droste was watching her as she walked slowly around the ring with the horse. After the second time, he joined her and took the reins from her.

"Are you coming tomorrow?" he asked.

After that, Norah went every day. Though she no longer needed help in mounting or handling Dandy, somehow Droste just happened to be around. Occasionally he accompanied her on her rides, and the occasions became more and more frequent. She learned a lot about riding, but more about Karl.

He was no ordinary backwoods farmer. His father had been a Luftwaffe pilot and his mother the daughter of minor nobility. They were perceptive enough to leave Germany before Hitler's Third Reich. Naturally, they were drawn to that part of Pennsylvania which already had a German community. They bought land, but farming was not the same as in the old country. Here, the owner worked side by side with the hands. They accepted that; their fingers dug deep into the soil. At the same time, they did not forget their heritage. In the evenings, Marie Droste played Beethoven on the pianoforte and Christian Droste read Goethe aloud. They made sure their son had the best education available.

As they prospered, the Drostes bought more land. Karl married the daughter of a neighboring farmer and the two properties joined to become the largest holding in the county.

Karl loved the land; that was transmitted in every

word and look. It was also evident that he was desperately lonely for mental stimulation. Talk spilled out of him on every subject. First, he gave Norah tips about riding, then he questioned her—not about herself; after that initial abrupt reference to Joe's death, he never asked a single personal question. What he wanted to know was what she did in New York—the theaters and concerts she went to; what books she read. He had an extensive library of his own and he lent her books and then eagerly waited till she'd read them so that they could discuss them together.

Norah thought Joe would have liked Karl Droste. They would have talked opera together, listened to Joe's favorite records. It was exactly the kind of relationship she needed.

At the same time, she wondered about his marriage. It was the one subject on which he was curiously reticent. Very early on, Karl Droste had explained that his wife, Kate, was arthritic, a semi-invalid. She did not entertain visitors. Whether that was an apology for not bringing Norah up to the house, or a veiled warning for her to stay clear, Norah wasn't sure. It seemed unnatural that he should not make the slightest reference to Kate again, not even in the most casual manner. Did that mean things weren't right between them? Certainly for a healthy man to be tied to a semi-invalid couldn't be easy, Norah thought. Maybe Karl was silent because he didn't want to seem to be asking for pity. She decided that she must respect his privacy as he did hers.

They were prisoners, Benita Cruz realized, literally prisoners. Not in chains, though terrible rumors of such captivity had reached even her home village, but they might as well have been, for they were housed in a structure away from any other habitation; they worked in another similarly isolated place, and they were transported to and fro by armed men.

They had arrived deep in the night and were herded from the bus in which they'd traveled the wearisome days from Joliet directly into this drafty ill-heated building, to lie down fully clothed on hard army cots. They had thought then, and no one had hinted otherwise, that this was merely one more of the stopping places on their journey to New York, freedom, and work. But the next morning they were not rousted out and hurried through a semblance of sanitation to eat and be on their way again. Exhausted, they'd welcomed the extra rest and slept on, well past dawn. A few hours later, their internal clocks roused them, for this building like all the others in which they had sheltered was completely shuttered and light seeped in only through chinks. One by one, the migrants had begun to stir, to sit up. They had long since stopped examining these overnight resting places, but they did then. No one had come to show them where the toilet facilities were, to offer food, to get them going, so they had taken a good long look.

Benita Cruz remembered that first morning.

They were in a long low wooden shed; an old but solidly built structure, recently partitioned with flimsy wallboard. On Benita's side there were roughly two rows of thirty cots each. The next thing that Benita noticed—and this really troubled her— all of them were occupied. Her group consisted of eight women, including herself. These others, these strangers, did not even stir as the light grew brighter. Each huddled under her single army-surplus blanket—no one had sheets—sleeping in exhaustion. Or as though drugged.

Benita shivered. It was cold. Minimal heat was provided by a kerosene heater at each end of the building and by the breathing of the occupants. Fetid body odor and the stench of inadequate plumbing mixed with cooking smells from meal after meal to form a palpable layer never dispelled. Benita had taken off her dress and slept in her underwear. Reaching for the loose jacket and using it as a bathrobe, she folded her dress over her arm and went to look for a bathroom where she could relieve herself and at least have a sponge bath. She found a man she had not seen before, young, heavily dressed, sitting in a chair tilted back against the outside door, feet braced against the opposite wall, mouth open, snoring. His presence neither surprised nor alarmed her. Wherever they went, there was a guard.

Benita cleared her throat. "Pardon, please. I am looking for the bathroom."

Ben Connick stirred, shifted his position slightly. "Excuse me . . ."

He had a cold and his eyes were gummy and stuck together and he had trouble getting them open. When he did, he glanced at his watch before looking at Benita. Ben Connick was twenty-six and handsome in a loutish way. He had dark blond hair greased back, skimpy sideburns, and a small mustache, too small for his fat face. The son of a local farmer, Connick hated hard work, long hours. Every cent cleared went back into the land. He hated the land. So he fled to the cities. But the cities defeated him; he found himself unable to compete mentally; even physically he was outclassed: the young city punks were tougher and meaner and smarter. So he came back, but still looking for the good life, still wanting it to come easy. Here he'd found it. The work was a snap; the spics, men and women, were docile. Pay was good and a free room in one of the outbuildings was provided for him and the other guard. What he earned, he spent, mostly for expensive clothes and booze. The women came free.

But the best part of the job, the part that gave him satisfaction, was the power he held over these poeple. He felt that now as he stared at Benita, who patiently waited for *his* permission. Small eyes still partly gummed together, but glaring with annoyance nevertheless, Ben Connick got ready to blast the woman standing humbly before him for waking him up—before seven, for God's sake! Instead, he gasped. Jeez! she was a real looker. You'd never take her for a Mex. She could pass for a white woman easy. He let his eyes roam over Benita Cruz from the neck down. Nice, real nice. Breasts, just big enough; he could almost feel their soft weight in his hands. She must be one of the load that came last night or he sure would have noticed her before this.

His nose dripped. He wiped the snot with the back of his wrist. "Bathroom's over there." He pointed and brought his legs down so she could pass.

Blushing, Benita squeezed by, taking care not to brush against him.

There were two bathrooms, one for men and one for women. Benita went in, and as there was no waiting line of women behind her, she took her time. Actually, though it was primitive and the water not much more than a lukewarm trickle, this was her first shower since the escape. It felt wonderful. It encouraged her. When she came out, she found Fernando Rivera, Pablo Gutiérrez, and Dalmacio Nuñes, the last of the men in the original group, standing in the small partitioned alcove and conferring in low whispers.

"Que pasa?" She whispered too.

They didn't know.

The guard had gone back to sleep, feet braced as before so that Benita couldn't pass.

"Sir?" she said timidly. "Excuse me, please."

Connick had only been pretending to sleep. He leered at her. "What do you want, sweetie?"

"Could you tell me, please—when do we travel?"

"Tonight."

"Thank you." Benita glanced toward the men.

They'd heard and now turned back to their section of the shed as she proceeded to hers.

"Vamos a la noche," she whispered to the women of her group who were sitting on the side of their cots anxiously waiting.

The rest of the women slept almost without stirring till noon. Then by some instinct they wakened. They eyed the newcomers but didn't speak to them. After washing and dressing, they went to a separate section to prepare the meal on an old-fashioned coal-fired stove. When it was ready, they gestured for Benita and her friends to join them. Still no one talked.

When it was nearly dark, around five-thirty, a bus pulled up close to the building, and everyone, men and women, those who had been there before and Benita's group, were herded into it by the two guards, the one who had been on duty all day and with whom she had spoken, and another. Benita sighed in relief. She hadn't wanted to acknowledge it even to herself, but she'd been worried about moving on. But after a ride of no more than twenty minutes, the bus stopped and everybody got out, filing from the door of the bus into the door of another squat one-story edifice, this time made of brick.

And here they had stayed for the next twelve hours. This was the place they had traveled so many miles and suffered so much hardship to reach. This badly lit, damp, hastily contrived factory with its rows of sewing machines was the destination. The older hands went immediately to their places; the new were assigned a machine and instructed in its use. When they got the knack of it, they were handed a stack of dark blue pants and shown how to sew a white line down each leg. This was the job they had been promised. This was the on-the-job training.

In the morning at first light, they were transported back to the dormitory, where, like the others, Benita and her companions fell exhausted onto their cots.

Days ran one into the other. Sunday and Monday were the same; Friday and Saturday indistinguishable. They lost track of the weeks. Time didn't matter, for the drudgery never changed. They didn't even go to church. For these devout women, that was the ultimate deprivation. Rosaries were fingered in callused hands and prayers mumbled as they lay in their hard beds and drifted into sleep. Yet no one considered running away. Where would they go? They had no money and no friends. They couldn't go to the authorities, for then they'd be shipped back to Mexico. The security over them was minimal, for they were prisoners of their own fear. Benita Cruz knew, as the weeks passed, that if she waited much longer, she too would accept the peonage as unchangeable.

She had no precise plan, just to get away. Each day at dawn and at dusk the bus pulled up to load and unload, and she had not managed more than a quick look at her surroundings. All she knew was that they were somewhere out in open country and that she must get to a town. It was important to get as much of a head start as she could before her absence was discovered. So she would have to leave after they returned to the dormitory from the night's work, and as soon as everyone was bedded down. Above all, she must do it soon, while she still had courage, strength, and desire. Not while there was snow on the ground, though, for then it would be easy for them to track her.

Three days after Benita Cruz had reached her decision, as if in answer to her needs, the good Lord sent rain to wash away the remnants of the snow.

Her preparations were simple: she took up the few belongings which she kept in a box under her cot, and while no one was looking, arranged them under the blanket to look as much as possible like all the other huddled, sleeping forms. Then she crept to the partition to wait until the guard would wake up and leave his post to relieve himself. The guards worked in shifts, but it didn't matter which one was on duty because each drank enough beer so that he left the door several times during the night.

Benita didn't own a watch. The only indication that dawn had given way to morning would be the brightening between cracks in the shutters. She couldn't wait much after that, for the women would be rising and the guard would finally notice that one figure in one cot didn't move. But the light was still feeble when Connick left his chair. The moment the bathroom door closed, Benita ran around the partition, opened the outside door, and quietly pulled it shut again behind her.

In that first instant, Benita Cruz knew only an enormous exhilaration. She threw her head back, flung out her arms, and breathed deeply of the fresh, cold air. Then she looked around. There was nothing much to see. A couple of lesser structures, quite obviously part of the complex, a few barren trees. Otherwise it was all endless flat fields, bleak and featureless, mud brown. But she was neither discouraged nor depressed; she was free! There was a dirt track running east to west, worn into packed ruts. She knew what they were—the tracks of the bus; and she knew where the bus went—to the factory. She set out across the empty, unmarked terrain, sure of one thing only—she was headed in the opposite direction.

Benita Cruz was only twenty-two. Life had been hard in Palmas al Lago, and to survive, one had to be tough. Benita's mind and body had been fired in the crucible of plain food, hard manual work, clean air, and the searing, purifying sun. She was not accustomed to the cold, nor was she dressed for it— wearing only the thin wool dress she'd been given and the black lace shoes which weren't a comfortable fit. She'd been forced to leave the zippered jacket behind under the blanket of her cot. Also, the inactivity of the past weeks—the waiting to be transported, the long hours in the trucks, then the train and the bus—all these had weakened her. Since arriving she'd hardly used her legs at all; it was just sit over the machine and then fall into bed. Her body trembled as she resolutely set out, but her will was strong.

The sun burned through the morning fog, offering little warmth but a tremendous lift to her spirit. How long was it since she'd seen the sun? The land began to slope gently up and down. As she climbed to the top of each rise, Benita believed that she would find houses and people, but one empty vista gave way to another. Then the sun was high. She had no idea how far she had come, but she knew that by now her *compañeras* back at the dormitory would be rising. They would surely notice that she was missing. They would say nothing; they might even take the stuffing from under the blanket so that the guard wouldn't notice. Would they have the courage to do that? She must believe that they would, and keep on moving.

The shadows were lengthening when Benita finally admitted to herself that she must soon stop somewhere to rest. She had been going since sunup without sleep, food, or water. Her steps were growing slower and almost unbearably painful. She had lost any sense of direction. If they had not already discovered at the dormitory that she was gone, they would very soon, because it was nearly loading time. When they loaded, the guards counted heads, and they would be one short. They would search and know that there had been an escape. Then they would come looking for her. It seemed hopeless. Almost resigned to failure, for she knew that, if not caught, she could not survive a night out in the open, Benita saw the house. She had, out of sheer doggedness, and hardly aware that she was still moving, dragged herself to the crest of one more hill, and from there she saw the whole spread—house, barn, twin silos, stables, but better than that, a man, or a woman, on horseback. She waved. Hope warmed her, relief put new strength into her failing limbs. She walked faster. Then she heard the sound of a motor behind her. Turning, she saw a big shiny brown jeep on oversized wheels careening across the fields toward her.

She tried to run. She couldn't. Her body refused. She didn't need to look back again to know who was in that vehicle—but she did—and was stunned at how close they had come in just that short space of time . . . but wasn't it only seconds that she'd stood there immobilized? *Dios mío! Santa Madre de Dios, ayuda me!* How long was it?

"Help! Please, please, help me!" she blurted out. At least, she thought she did, but she wasn't really sure that the words were being uttered except in her mind.

Ben Commick stopped the Bronco but left the motor running. He and Will Haney jumped out. Between them, they dragged her to the vehicle. She struggled, she kicked, but she was weak. She was defeated.

Chapter 6

SITTING ASTRIDE Dandy, Norah saw it all. She couldn't chase the Bronco; Dandy wasn't fast enough. All she could do was watch helplessly as the girl was shoved into the backseat and driven off. She watched as the vehicle disappeared in the same direction from which it had come. If she'd witnessed the incident on a city street, Norah wouldn't have hesitated to report a kidnapping. But a kidnapping out here in the open fields? She hadn't been close enough to identify the men, nor to get the license number. She'd gotten a good look at the girl, though.

Not since the first day she'd come to do some riding had Norah called at the main house. So now she returned to the stable expecting to find Karl waiting, quite openly, for her. But he wasn't there. She removed the saddle, put Dandy in his stall, and ran across the front yard.

Karl answered the door himself. He seemed surprised, and not particularly pleased, to see her.

"I need to use your phone. I have to call the police," she told him in a rush.

"Police? What about?"

"I just saw a girl being abducted by two men."

Quickly he reached for her arm and pulled her inside. With a quick look around, he led her through a small doorway just off the entry and along a narrow corridor blocked off from the rest of the house to a small room that was part study, part office.

"Now, what's going on?"

"I saw a girl, a young girl, being forced into a car against her will."

He scowled at her for several moments. "What you need is a drink." He opened a cupboard and brought out a decanter and two stemmed glasses.

"I don't need anything," Norah protested. "It's the girl I saw who needs help."

"A glass of sherry will calm you."

"I'm not excited." Norah was annoyed, but she decided that Droste was treating her like this out of long habit dealing with an invalid wife. "I don't need sherry, Karl," she said. "I'm not hysterical or upset. I'm concerned. There was a girl being forced into a van against her will. I'm going to call the police."

"Calm down and sit still for a couple of minutes." He came around to the dark green leather sofa and sat beside her. "What can you tell me about her?"

Norah responded eagerly. "She was about twenty-two or -three, medium height, a hundred and ten pounds, black curly hair and large dark eyes. She was wearing a long black dress."

"No coat? No hat?"

"No."

"She was a runaway," he concluded firmly, as though that ended it.

It didn't for Norah. "I said she was in her mid-twenties. Isn't that a little old to be running away from home?"

"Not around here. You've heard of the Amish and Mennonite sects?"

"Of course."

"Mostly they live up near the Juniata River in what they call the Big Valley, but they're also scattered around us in small communities. They're separated from the outside world partly by natural boundaries and completely by their own choice. They came here two hundred years ago, and for them time has stood still—technological progress is the inspiration of the devil. They don't use electricity; they drive a horse and buggy—"

"I saw one of them in town," Norah interrupted. "He wore dark old-fashioned clothing and a round broad-brimmed hat. He had so much facial hair it almost hid his features."

Droste nodded. "Sounds like one of the Buggy Amish, a sect near the bottom of the ladder as far as acceptance of progress goes. There are others not quite so strict. At the top of the ladder are the Mennonites; they drink alcohol, recognize divorce, and generally behave like Presbyterians."

The joke was lost on Norah. "This is all very interesting but—"

"It is relevant."

He continued his lecture, his purpose not merely to convince her that his conclusion was correct but also to calm her. "The Beachy Amish are somewhere in between. They do drive cars, use electricity, even have telephones, if not in the house, then in the barn." He paused. "Did the two men who came for the girl have long hair and full beards?"

Norah closed her eyes to visualize. "The blond had long sideburns and a mustache. The other had curly hair and a thin, wispy beard."

"The Beachy men trim their hair and beards. You said the girl had no hat; did she have any kind of head covering?"

"Nothing."

"Their women wear something so small it's called a 'cupcake.' From a distance you wouldn't have been likely to notice."

"They were very rough with her."

"That's only the start. She will be severely punished."

Norah shook her head. "I don't buy it. The girl didn't have a coat. She didn't carry a suitcase."

"Maybe she saw a chance to get away, unexpectedly, and she took it."

"You make it sound like these young people are in bondage."

"They are loved and protected, but the insidious comforts and diversions of the twentieth century are seeping through the barriers and contaminating them. They want to pass to the outside. They want refrigerators and dishwashers, cars, radios, television. Indoor plumbing. It takes years to get up the courage to run away. Their parents chase them. In the case of a young female, it would be the brothers along with the father. They consider that they're snatching the sinner back from the devil's grasp and restoring her to the Lord."

He gave her time to think about it. "What else could it have been?"

"That's what I intend to find out."

"How can you? You don't know who the girl was."

"If she's a runaway, there will have been a complaint and the police will have a record of it."

He laughed. "My dear Norah, the last thing these people would do is go to the police. They want no outside interference in their affairs, and the police are equally reluctant to intrude themselves unless specifically requested."

Norah frowned. On this last point, she certainly believed him; as for the rest, she certainly wanted to believe him. The last thing in the world she was looking for was to get involved in a police matter. While she brooded, Karl Droste got up and poured two glasses of sherry, and not bothering to ask whether she wanted it, simply put one of them into her hand.

Taking it, Norah noticed that her hand shook.

They sipped in silence.

After a while, his eyes met hers. "Assuming you

do go to the police, what can they do? On the basis of what you have to tell them, what action can they take?"

There were, of course, very specific things they could do, but she was not inclined to reveal her familiarity with police procedure. Also, she was disposed to accept his interpretation of the scene she had witnessed, and would have, but for one thing—the girl herself. If she was Amish and running away from home, what had she been doing riding in a bus with other men and women three weeks ago? For Norah was convinced that the girl she had seen from the bedroom window on the night of her arrival, the girl who had tripped and fallen to her knees in the full glare of the bus's headlights, was the same one she had observed a short while ago in the lane.

Norah didn't tell Karl Droste. On this score she had no reason to keep silent, but she did.

Pain brought Benita Cruz to consciousness. It radiated from her vagina, pulsing, sharp. All her private parts ached. Her breasts were tender; her back and shoulders raw, as though she'd been dragged by the heels across rough ground. Her face felt stiff. Gingerly she put a hand up to her right cheek. It was swollen. So were her eyes; she had trouble opening them enough to see, but she managed. She was in a small room with bare whitewashed walls, minimally furnished. She was lying on her back staring directly up at the ceiling light; its frosted globe did little to cut the glare. She blinked and remembered. She had been brought here by the two guards, Ben and Will. She knew their names because they'd shouted back and forth at each other, alternately encouraging, deriding, gloating. She had been punched, whipped with the buckle end of their belts, and raped by turns. Throughout the night. She had lost count of how many times. She lay on the bed soaked with her own blood. They had used her and left her. But they would come back; she knew it. What would they do then.

Pulling herself up to a sitting position, Benita Cruz swung her bare legs over the side and stood, only to fall to the floor a victim of weakness and nausea. She raised herself to her knees and crawled to the door. She reached for the doorknob. Of course it wouldn't turn; it was locked. There was a window on the other side of the room, but it was too high for her to climb out. Even if she could manage to break the glass and call for help, would anybody hear? Would anybody come?

As in the false bottom of the truck out of Los Angeles, the abused girl passed in and out of consciousness; minutes of waking pain seemed like hours and hours, unconsciousness mere minutes of relief. Then she heard voices. Their voices. Their footsteps scuffling to the door. She heard the key in the lock. She dragged herself as far away as she could and cowered in the corner. The door opened and they were standing over her. She looked up at them out of blackened and swollen eyes, but she would not scream. Benita Cruz had not screamed during the night; she was certain that she had not. At first that had enraged the two bullies, made them more violent and abusive. After a while they had become so obsessed by their own orgy of violence that her passivity was inconsequential. They gorged on their own lust and depravity. What would they do now? Abuse her some more? Or kill her?

They reached down, each one pulling on an arm, and yanked her to her feet. They turned her around, and holding her up between them, forced her to walk out of the room, down the stairs, and outside into the breaking dawn. Every step sent pain shooting through her abdomen, but it didn't matter. They weren't going to kill her. If that had been their intent, they would have waited until it was dark again. There would have been a car or truck to transport her. She had been brought here in the dark; now she could see that she had been held captive in one of the outbuildings close to the dormitory and was being walked back! Though relief did give her some strength, they still had to half-carry her inside and down the aisle between the empty cots. They knew which one was hers and they dumped her on it like a heap of old rags.

Once again, Benita Cruz fainted.

The wheezing motor, the rattling of the broken springs, were familiar sounds. They invaded her subconscious. They alerted her conscious mind to the creaking of the barn door and the weary, dragging steps of the returning workers. Suddenly, all movement stopped. There was a soft gasp, more a sigh, not in unison, but passing, communicated from one person to the next. Benita's eyes would not open to more than slits, so she was limited to a narrow, blurred field of vision. She didn't need even that, for all at once the women were around her clucking and cooing, laying on gentle hands, murmuring consolation. Someone immersed a cloth in cool water and placed it across her brow. The men were shooed out. Someone began to gently remove what was left of her torn and sodden blood-encrusted dress; she had no underwear or stockings. Then she was sponged clean with warm water.

"No te tocarán mas, chica." Viorica Amara, the mother of the boy who had suffocated, bent down close to the thin pillow and whispered into Benita's ear, *"No te tocarán mas; te lo prometo."*

They will not touch you again; it was a promise that could not be kept, Benita thought, and it set her to shivering uncontrollably. Blankets were piled on her; others would have to do without. Then, despite their exhausted state, the women took turns sitting beside her so that she should for now at least feel safe.

But if the guards came for her again, what could the women do? How could they defend her?

They would not come again, Benita decided. They had done what they intended. They could have killed her and dumped her body into any gully where it might not be found till spring. They hadn't. They had wanted to abuse her and make an example of her. They had wanted her beaten, bruised, degraded and humiliated, and then returned for the others to see. She knew it now and so did the rest. That was why they had the courage to sit beside her.

And so they did through the long day till it was time to get back into the bus and go to work. Then they had to leave her.

The girl had waved to Norah and called to her. Though Norah had not understood the words, the meaning had been clear. She'd been calling for help. And Norah had not responded, not then, not later. She had let Karl Droste talk her out of doing the minimal duty of a civilian—reporting the commission of a crime. How many times, Norah asked herself, had she condemned those who were either too frightened or too uncaring and used spurious arguments as an excuse for "not getting involved"? And here she was doing exactly the same thing. She had not answered Karl Droste when he'd asked what the police could do in the circumstances. It was now up to her to make sure that these things were done. She got in her car and headed for town.

The York Crossing police station was another of the ubiquitous brick buildings and located at the back of the city hall. Inside, the layout was standard: booking on the ground floor, lockup and holding pens in the rear. As far as Norah could tell, they were presently unoccupied. They would be occupied on weekends, she thought, with drunks and disorderlies. Squad room, offices, lockers, would be upstairs. Just like home. Except that all this was spanking new, all confetti-flecked tile on the floor, acoustical ceilings, wallboard heating, and flat, fluorescent lighting. She had never believed that she would prefer the grungy old crumbling station house with the clanking radiators and sagging stairs and moldering plaster, but it had character. This place, this could be a supermarket or a dental clinic. She approached the desk.

"Good evening, Sergeant. I'd like to see the chief, please."

"What about?"

"I want to report a crime, Sergeant Fleischman." She took note of his name plaque.

Max Fleischman was a rangy, youngish man with a long, horsy face and sandy hair that was thinning too soon. He wore steel-rimmed half-glasses and they made him look older also, close to forty, which he was not, and very studious—which he was.

"I'll take your complaint, ma'am," he replied in a casual, almost cheery manner.

Norah hesitated. She should have said the matter was personal, but it was too late. "I think it would be best if I spoke with the chief."

Fleischman peered over the tops of his glasses, markedly less pleasant. "Chief Blegen isn't in. May I have your name, ma'am?"

Norah bit her lip. Further argument would only antagonize him. "Norah Capretto."

"Spell it, please." She did. He took pains to get it right. "Okay, Mrs. Capretto, where do you live?"

"I'm staying at the Schmidt place. That's—"

"What do you mean 'staying'? Don't you live there?"

"No, I'm visiting."

"Where is your permanent residence?"

"I'm from New York. Look—"

"Address?"

It sure was different this side of the desk, Norah thought. Now she could appreciate the frustration of a civilian going through what certainly appeared like irrelevant, time-consuming procedures. She started to protest but knew from experience that this would not change anything. She even managed not to sigh. "I live at 150 East Sixty-eighth Street, New York, 10021."

"What crime do you want to report, Mrs. Capretto?"

Norah took a deep breath. "A kidnapping."

He looked up. No question but that he was startled, even shocked.

"An abduction," Norah continued. "A forcible abduction of a young woman."

Now he regarded her skeptically.

"I saw it, Sergeant. I saw the young woman walking across the fields. Then I saw a vehicle, a Ford Bronco, brown, shiny, new, chasing her. When she saw it, she called out to me and started to run, but it caught up with her. Two men, Caucasian . . ." She broke off, swallowing half the word. She'd been about to reel it off: race, height, weight, coloring, and so on. She licked her lips and started again. "They were in their late twenties, I'd say. One was blond, hair greasy slick, with a mustache and sideburns. He was medium height, overweight but not fat. The other was taller. He had brown curly hair and a curly beard. He was on the heavy side too. They both wore the usual cords tucked into boots, and windbreakers. No hats. They grabbed the girl. She struggled, but they were too strong for her. They pushed her into the back of the Bronco and drove away."

Maximillian Fleischman took it all down carefully. "Where did the incident take place?"

"Just outside the gate to the Droste place. That's half a mile from the crossroads of—"

"I know where it is. Any other witensses?"

"No."

"What time did the alleged abduction take place?"

The adjective annoyed her, but it was entirely correct for him to use it. "Four P.M."

The sergeant looked up from his report and pointedly stared at the wall clock. Seven-fifteen. "Why did you wait so long to come in, Mrs. Capretto? Why didn't you call right away?"

It was entirely a fair question and it shamed her. There was no use telling Sergeant Fleischman that she'd allowed herself to be talked out of reporting the incident. She was the witness; she was the one who had seen what happened, and the responsibility was hers alone. "I thought the girl might be Amish and a runaway."

"What changed your mind?"

Just because he worked on a small-town force didn't mean he had to be dumb, Norah thought. "I realized it wasn't up to me to make that judgment."

Fleischman took another, longer look at her over the tops of his glasses. So she wasn't a kook, he decided, just an overly conscientious citizen. "Can you describe the girl?" he asked, reverting to his earlier friendliness.

"Oh, yes." Norah was eager but remembered to choose her words carefully. "She was very pretty. She had dark curly hair and dark eyes. Medium build. Twenty to twenty-five. She had on a long black dress with long sleeves. No coat or hat."

Fleischman put that down. "You said the vehicle was a Ford Bronco."

"Right. Dark brown. Looked brand new. I didn't get the license number."

He didn't ask her how she could specify the model: people around here were very conscious of such things. "Anything else you can think of, Mrs. Capretto?"

Norah hesitated. "You could call the DMV and get the names of owners of any late-model dark brown Broncos in these parts."

"I'll mention that to the investigating officer. Thank you, Mrs. Capretto."

Norah didn't move. "Aren't you going to check your missing-persons sheet? Couldn't you just take a look and tell me if the girl's been reported missing?"

"If the snatch was made at four this afternoon . . ." He shrugged. "Okay." Shuffling through the papers on his desk, Fleischman found the telex report from central bureau and scanned it. "Nobody from around here, ma'am."

"How about anybody answering the description?"

He sighed, but he looked again. It took longer. "Nobody."

Norah frowned. "Who could she have been? Any idea, Sergeant?"

Chewing on his lower lip, Fleischman considered not the missing woman but the one in front of him. Definitely not a weirdo. She was concerned and responsible and . . . something more. He couldn't put his finger on it. Something special. "I'll put the report on Chief Blegen's desk," he promised. "He'll see it when he comes in first thing."

"Will he?" Norah looked straight at Fleischman.

He met her gaze. "Yes, ma'am. Yes, Mrs. Capretto. I will personally call his attention to it."

He didn't mention that the chief wouldn't be in the next morning, that he would be out of town. It would be for one day only. He didn't think it would matter.

Chapter 7

THE SNOW started shortly after ten Monday night and continued into the next morning. It started lightly, then for a span of over four hours assumed the proportions of a blizzard—to the confusion and embarrassment of the forecasters. It tapered off after two A.M., but by the time it was over, eight inches of glistening powder camouflaged the fields, filling in the hollows and softening the countours of stumps and rock outcroppings. The tracks made by the late-model Bronco in the soft earth outside the Droste farm were, of course, obliterated in the first hour. Not that it mattered, for nobody had been assigned to go out and examine them. Sergeant Fleischman did not call the chief's attention to Norah Mulcahaney's complaint when he returned on Tuesday morning. It never reached the chief's desk. Her complaint, along with those of other domestic disturbances, petty thefts, juvenile mischief, littering, and loitering, was shoved to one side in the excitement. Chief Richard Blegen came in late, had barely settled to his second cup of coffee before tackling the paperwork, when the call was received.

The body was discovered by Roy Zacharias Yodel of Raystown Haven. Roy Z.—the middle initial was never omitted, not by Roy Z. himself or by those referring to him, for it was that initial which distinguished him not just from the innumerable Yodels residing in the elbow between the Susquehanna and Juniata rivers, but from the six *Roy* Yodels—had been on his way into town to buy feed. He had been driving the buggy and it was the horse that was responsible. The mare had stopped suddenly and without apparent reason in the middle of the snow-covered track and refused to move. Neither whipping nor coaxing availed. At young Roy Z.'s insistence the animal's fear turned to terror and she began to whinny and rear up on her hind legs, imperiling driver and vehicle. The youth had no choice but to jump down and try to calm Samantha and head her past whatever might be bothering her. As he passed along her flank, Roy Z. caught sight of a form sprawled facedown in the irrigation ditch. He had no idea then whether it was a man or woman. At first Roy Z. thought whoever it was had merely fallen and been injured. He got down into the ditch, and intending to rouse the victim, turned the body over. He then saw it was a woman. He knew nothing about mouth-to-mouth resuscitation; if he had, he would have been too shy to try it. He did shake the woman, but got no response, and he could feel the deep cold through her thin dress. White-faced with awe, he later explained to Chief Blegen that it was her stiffness that told him the woman was dead. Turning the mare around, Roy Z. got back up in the seat, gathered the reins, and headed for the nearest of his Mennonite neighbors who had a telephone. Roy Z. Yodel was eighteen, a big strong farmboy; he had been present at birthings and dyings, but he had never before spoken on a telephone.

It didn't require further use of the devil's instrument for word to spread through the communities of the "plain people." Silently the elders of the various sects materialized from behind the ridges of the fertile valleys which sheltered them and gathered to view the dead woman. They were there before Blegen, though he arrived quickly enough, accompanied by his deputy, Jess Kimmel. As they stood in a half-circle above the trench dressed in their dark baggy clothes and black hats, they seemed instant mourners at an open grave.

At the approach of the two police officers, they parted. In his attempt to help, Roy Z. had rolled the victim over on her back so that all Blegen had to do was bend down to get a good look at her. Though her face was streaked with the snow into which it had been pressed, the characteristic puffiness and blue color of hypothermia was instantly apparent. She had been walking, he reasoned—*why* didn't matter for now. She had been walking and had lost her way and stumbled into the ditch, sustained an injury which prevented her from getting up. The temperature had been down to zero in the night. She had died of exposure. His tension eased. He looked around at the somber assemblage.

"Does anyone know who she is?"

Each man there gravely shook his head.

If they didn't know her, then she wasn't one of any of their sects. There were no strangers in those communities, Blegen had learned. Not only did they all know each other intimately, but they were all related, all family—or just about. That was one of the reasons the names were repeated over and over to the point where even the middle initial often was not enough identification. For example, Roy Z.'s father was John A. Yodel. But there were eleven John A. Yodels in the various communities, so Roy's father was further identified by *his* father's name, Samuel. He was Samuel's John A. Yodel. Confusing at the start, now that he had got used to it, Blegen considered it logical. Two hundred years of narrow breeding had resulted in a characteristic general appearance—thick limbs, round jaw, upturned nose.

The victim, despite the puffiness of her face, didn't fit the pattern.

Blegen got down into the ditch. A closer look revealed that the swelling under her eyes was different from that of the rest of her face; so was the color. Both eyes were blackened and there was a split in her upper lip.

"You said you found her facedown?" Blegen asked young Roy Z.

The boy looked to his father, Samuel's John A Yodel. "He thought she was alive. He was trying to help."

"Yes, I understand," Blegen replied. "I just want to be sure that all he did was turn her over."

Samuel's John A. nodded for the boy to reply.

"Yes, sir, that's all."

Since the position had already been disturbed, he might as well raise her up and look underneath. He did so, but found no sharp stones that might account for the bruises. He sighed and gently laid her down again. Looking around, he saw no purse. He went through her pockets; they were empty. A mugging out here in the middle of a snowstorm? Hardly credible. Blegen looked up at Jess Kimmel. "No ID. othing."

Blegen was depressed. In his nine years as police chief of York Crossing, four homicides had occurred: one, the result of a drunken bar brawl in front of a dozen witnesses; another, a sordid wife beating in the tenements near the iron works during which neighbors had heard the woman's screams but had not "interfered"; the third and fourth, the culmination of an argument over the right-of-way between two farms to a creek—the two farmers carried shotguns and they had killed each other. Each crime had been due to passion out of control, without premeditation, not born of greed or casual contempt for human life, only human frailty. This one was like the others, Blegen silently assured himself. Once he discovered the victim's identity, then he'd know what she had been doing out here alone, dressed in a rag-bag assortment of clothes—the sleeve of the ill-fitting jacket ripped at the shoulder, wearing shoes with thin soles instead of boots, carrying no purse, no identification, no money. He'd know who had mauled and disfigured her.

The snow around the body had been trampled first by the mare and Roy Z., then by the somber specta-tors who had approached from all directions. He would need a platoon of men to spread out wide enough to pick out which prints were hers, and he just didn't have the numbers at his disposal. Proba-bly, Blegen rationalized, the snow had filled in her tracks anyway. He could check the Weather Bureau and find out when the snow had actually stopped. The amount of snow covering the body might have suggested how long she'd been lying there, which in turn might help to fix the time of death. Except that in turning her over, Roy Z. had disturbed the cover.

He didn't have a regular forensic unit, either. Ble-gen felt a wave of frustration, which subsided quickly. To be honest, there was little need for one. When evidence had to be analyzed or evaluated, he sent it on to Harrisburg and the report came back promptly. Blegen gestured to his deputy, and Kim-mel came on the run.

"Get some shots of the body, various angles. You know what we need."

Kimmel did. He was more than a good amateur photographer. He had taken the FBI criminal-analysis course in Washington, D.C., and was well-qualified. He was qualified to be chief, and Blegen knew it. He knew that Kimmel wanted it.

Richard Blegen was an honest man; that was his problem. A twenty-year veteran of the Philadelphia police, he'd had a hard time sticking it out that long. He'd viewed the open corruption around him and re-ported it. For that he was ostracized both by his own once-upon-a-time buddies at the bottom and by the brass at the top. Time after time he'd been passed over for promotion. Blegen's wife nagged him constantly because he didn't advance; they had three boys, all of whom she was determined must go to college. Finally he made detective and was assigned to Internal Affairs, but the stigma of traitor was more than he could bear. As soon as the pension was secure, Richard Blegen resigned.

The demand for experienced ex-police officers was at its height and Blegen had no trouble getting work as security chief for a large chain of department stores. Unfortunately, all was not well there either. He uncovered a scam in which pirated merchandise was being sold along with the legitimate and certain employees were pocketing the difference in the mark-up. He went to the boss, but what he didn't know was that the boss was part of the scheme. Another man was brought in over Blegen. His pride left him no choice but to resign once again.

What he wanted and needed was a place where he could be in actual charge; a calm place, with little corruption and less violence. He read the ads in official journals and applied to every city council, every board of selectmen or board of trustees of every small town looking for a police chief. York Crossing fulfilled his requirements. The Blegens lived here better than in the city on less. They had a comfortable house. Irma Blegen joined the local American Legion Women's Auxiliary, participated in bake sales, picnics, bingo games to aid hospitals, the handicapped, the needy. She sang in the church choir. Above all, she enjoyed her husband's position. Blegen alone knew that it was less than he'd aspired to and less than he was capable of. But he accepted it as compromise. Nevertheless, disappointment showed in his face.

At fifty, Blegen's hair was gray and too thin to cover a yellowish pate. Six-foot-four, a big man, robust, Blegen had let himself go to fat. Looking in the bathroom mirror every morning, he saw a distorted face but went on eating, for he wanted the face that stared back at him to be unrecognizable. He wanted to forget the face of his youth and the hopes it represented.

Deputy Jess Kimmel was nearly bursting with eagerness. At twenty-two, Kimmel had left his daddy's tobacco farm to join the police. As the force was limited technically, he had developed expertise in related fields. He had learned how to use a camera professionally, to lift fingerprints and to read them; he had studied ballistics. Then he had asked Blegen for a recommendation to the FBI course. He was accepted and had passed high on the list, returning to be appointed deputy chief. He'd had high hopes, but the new job wasn't any different from the old. It brought no real additional responsibility or scope. His new skills were atrophying. In this homicide of a stranger, Jess Kimmel saw his chance to show what he could do.

He was of medium height, medium weight, medium coloring. He had lank brown hair and his hazel eyes protruded slightly. In proportion to the width of his shoulders, his head appeared somewhat small and he carried it forward at an angle so that now as he peered down at the snow-turned-slush around the body, he was like a chicken scratching for worms. Having finished with the camera, he knelt beside the body, and raising it by the shoulders like Blegen, he looked underneath.

"She must have fallen after the storm intensified," he observed.

Blegen raised his eyebrows.

"The snow melted and then froze into ice under her."

The arrival of the coroner's station wagon spared Blegen a comment.

* * *

Norah was getting used to sleeping later, but on this morning she awoke at her usual New York working time. It was dark, but it didn't seem unusually so. The first thing that came to her mind even before looking out to see what kind of day it was—for the weather had become the most important factor, the only variant, in Norah's existence—was the visit that Sunday evening to the police station. She had waited all day Monday to hear from Fleischman, expecting to be told that the scene had been examined and the tire tracks of the Bronco found and photographed at least. The phone didn't ring once. She began to have qualms. Was anyone doing anything? Had her complaint reached Chief Blegen? It wasn't till she got out of bed and padded over to close the window that she realized it was snowing again, and hard. A mound of snow had formed across the windowsill and there was a puddle on the floor beneath. Norah felt a sinking sensation that it was too late, that nothing had been done, and with the tracks long since covered over, there was no way of proving the truth of her story. The complaint would be filed away and forgotten. Nobody would even bother to pick up the phone and contact the DMV to get the names of local owners of late-model Broncos, much less go out to interrogate them. Why should they? Her frustration turned to anger—at herself for not keeping on top of it, for leaving it in someone else's hands, a stranger's.

She slammed the window down hard.

Why couldn't she go after the information herself? True, she had no official standing in the community. She had no official standing anywhere. As a civilian she had no right to meddle; the Department of Motor Vehicles probably wouldn't even tell her what she wanted to know. But if she identified herself as a police officer . . . Even if they took the trouble to check with New York, which they probably wouldn't, she couldn't think of anybody who would bother to mention that she was on indefinite leave. What she didn't want was for it to get back to Jim Felix. He'd regard her inquiry as indication that old habits were reasserting themselves. She didn't want him to get that impression; they weren't. At the same time, she had to do something, take action, get things moving! The girl at the end of the lane had appealed directly to her for help. And how had she responded? She'd turned around and placidly walked Dandy back to his stall. Then she'd strolled over to Karl Droste's house and let him hand her a glass of sherry.

What had come over her?

Being a police officer or not had nothing to do with it. She was a human being with a responsibility to another human being. Those two men with the girl were not Amish and not her brothers. They were bullies! The girl was not an errant daughter returning to her father's justice. She had been seized and physically coerced. Norah was breathing rapidly, her blue eyes blazing, her jaw clenched. So what could she do about it now? Go back to the police station, insist on seeing Chief Blegen and make such a scene that he'd have to see her and . . . What? Norah sighed. She had to find a way to back up her story.

All at once, she knew how. With a hint of a smile, Norah started to get dressed. She didn't waste time, just jumped into the same sturdy outdoor things she wore every day. Then she went down to the kitchen. No fancy breakfast of pancakes and sausages topped with genuine maple syrup this morning. Coffee would do. She put the pot on and while it was perking took out the county phone book and flipped through to the Yellow Pages.

Dr. Bruno Gruenwald sank gratefully into the chair across from Chief Blegen's desk. As coroner, it was Gruenwald's duty to preside over the inquest in cases of death not obviously due to natural causes. He was not a pathologist, neither qualified nor authorized to perform autopsies. That he happened to be a doctor was merely a bonus, and the opinion he now offered to the chief was strictly unofficial.

"She was undernourished and in extremely weak physical condition. If she'd stumbled and fallen into the ditch, I doubt she would have had the strength to get up again."

Blegen nodded. "That's the way I saw it. I'm relieved," he admitted. This was his friend, one of the very few in the town that Richard Blegen really trusted. They played chess together before an open fire in the winter, out on the screened porch in the summer. When they weren't playing chess, they were rooting for the Flyers or the Phillies.

"Don't rejoice too soon," Gruenwald cautioned. "The girl had been physically abused, beaten with fists and some kind of metal-tipped object. There were ragged edges on her hands where she'd held them up to shield herself, and the cuts on her face were infected."

Blegen groaned. He'd known in his gut he wasn't going to get away easy.

"Was she raped?"

"My guess would be . . . yes."

It was enough for Blegen. He reached down to the bottom drawer, unlocked it, and took out a bottle and a couple of paper cups.

Norah parked directly in front of the police station. One of the advantages of country living, she thought, was never having to hunt for a parking place or worry about a ticket. She didn't bother to zip up the front of her light gray ski jacket; she was warm with anticipation. Norah hadn't bought mourning clothes—who did nowadays?—but she wore what she had with such apathy that it seemed specifically chosen for drabness. Till this morning. For the first time since she had stepped through the swinging doors of the hospital corridor to view Joe's body, her emotion had been stirred, her interest aroused. Along with that, her determination. Her eyes were bright as she crossed the sidewalk; her square jaw thrust forward. She was elated over her morning's work and she intended to place the information she'd collected before Chief Blegen and no one else. Also, she intended to make sure he followed up on it.

The moment she stepped inside the station, Norah sensed the excitement. Something big was going down. She walked over to the charge desk, on which a plaque identified Sergeant George Hein as the duty officer. He was squat, dark, nearly bald, with a frown cut deep from the side of his nose and up along the bridge to where the hairline had once been. The frown cleaved his face into two, making it difficult to focus on the whole. Hein wasn't any busier than Fleischman had been, but his hands moved restlessly, arranging and rearranging the papers on his desk while he spoke on the telephone. Whether this was a normal nervousness or whether it related to special events, Norah couldn't know, but she suspected the latter. At last he was able to get rid of the caller with a few clipped words.

At Norah's entrance, Sergeant Hein had looked up eagerly, but immediately lost interest. While she'd stood waiting, an officer had peered around the corner from the rear, taken a quick look, and retreated. What were they waiting for?

As she started to speak, a third policeman came down the stairs. Spotting a stranger, he went up to Hein and whispered. The sergeant's eyebrows rose unevenly, pulled out of line by the scar. She had to wait till the two finished conferring for Hein to acknowledge her presence.

"Yes, ma'am. What can I do for you?"

He didn't even know what she wanted, and he was anxious to get rid of her, Norah thought. She was pleasant anyway. "Good morning, Sergeant. My name is Norah Capretto. I would like to see Chief Blegen."

"The chief is very busy this morning, ma'am. Can I help you?"

"No, thank you, Sergeant. I have to see the chief."

"That's not possible, ma'am."

"I have very important information which I can only give to him."

"I'm sorry."

If Hein had probed, tried to find out what her problem was, she might have been more sympathetic with his position; after all, she'd been on that side of the desk. "You don't even know what it's about," she charged.

"I asked and you refused to tell me."

"All right, I'll tell you now. I have information about the abduction."

"Abduction? What abduction?"

"The abduction I reported on Sunday night." Hein's blank look was all the confirmation Norah needed that her complaint had not been acted on, and was now lying at the bottom of a pile on God only knew whose desk. "Sergeant Fleischman took my complaint. He promised to call Chief Blegen's attention to it."

Hein had his own pile of papers, which he now searched through. The report was there and he scanned it quickly. "According to this, the incident occurred on Sunday at approximately four in the afternoon."

"Approximately, yes."

"You weren't exactly in a hurry to report it, were you?"

She couldn't deny it.

"You have something more to add, ma'am? Something you didn't think of before?"

"I now have information that may lead to the apprehension of the perpetrators."

The scowl divided his face—one side expressing

puzzlement over her language and the other uncertainty as to just how seriously he should take her. "Well, ma'am . . . uh . . ."—he consulted the report—"Mrs. Capretto. If you'll just give me this information, I'll see to it that—"

"That's what Sergeant Fleischman said. This time I want to see the chief personally."

The two sides of his face came together and the irritation was doubled. "I told you he's busy."

"I'll wait." Turning her back, Norah marched over to a row of varicolored plastic chairs against the far wall and sat.

Hein started to try to dissuade her, sighed instead. "Wait as long as you want, ma'am . . . Mrs. Capretto. Wait all day."

He promptly forgot her as the front doors opened and two medics, identified by their shoulder patches, entered the station carrying a collapsed gurney between them. "Third floor," Hein instructed, indicating the elevator. He didn't leave his desk or use the telephone, yet somehow word of their arrival spread through the building and every man on duty found a reason to come down to Booking.

Maybe somebody had had a heart attack, Norah thought, and found herself, like everyone else, waiting for the elevator to come back down. When it did and the doors opened, a patient was lying on the assembled gurney and the medics were maneuvering it out.

Norah gasped. The patient was in a body bag. "Wait!" she called out as they passed her. She caught up. "Who is it?"

The medics were nonplussed. They looked to Hein for help.

"Please stand aside, ma'am."

"I want to know who that is."

Hein came out from behind his desk. "Will you stand aside and let the medics pass, please." The "please" was added to remind himself that he must not physically remove the woman.

"Has the body been released? Are you taking it to the funeral parlor?" Norah asked the medics. "No," she answered her own question aloud. "The funeral parlor would be sending their own people. Where are you taking the body?"

"That's none of your business," Hein told her.

"You don't have a morgue in this building, right?"

"One last time, Mrs. . . . uh . . . Get out of the way."

"I want to view the body."

Hein was trembling with indignation. "Just who do you think you—?"

Norah pulled herself up, head high, chin up, eyes boring into Hein's. "I intend to view the body. I can do it here or I can follow the medics to wherever they're taking her."

Hein hesitated. He could let the woman follow the medics, then whatever she did would be on somebody else's head. She was a crazy and he'd be well rid of her. He started to tell her to go and do whatever she wanted; then he realized that she had said "her." How in hell did she know?

He swallowed. "Look . . . Mrs. Capretto. Viewing a dead body is not nice."

"I know."

"So why do you want to do it?"

"I think I know who she is."

While Hein tried to decide, another voice, heavier, authoritative, came from the stairs.

"Let her look."

It was Blegen. He was accompanied by Gruenwald, who went over to the gurney and opened the flap.

Norah looked down at the once-lovely face. She examined the blackened eyes, the swellings and lacerations with a deep and growing sadness.

"What's the rest of her like?"

"Do you recognize her?" Blegen countered.

"Oh, yes. It's the same girl."

"Who is she?"

"Don't you know?" Norah retorted.

"You said—"

"I said I might know who she is, and I do. She's the same girl I saw forcibly abducted on Sunday afternoon. I reported it. I don't know her name." She took a deep breath. "How did she die?"

"Hypothermia."

Norah stared at the distorted face. She noted a small mole on the right side of her jaw. "Maybe, but she was beaten first, sadistically abused. You *are* ordering an autopsy?"

"I appreciate your concern, Miss . . . ah . . ." As the chief hesitated, Hein put the report into his hands. "Ah . . . Mrs. Capretto. I'm Chief Blegen. I assure you that everything possible will be done to discover the victim's identity and the circumstances—"

"Was she raped?"

Blegen sighed and gave up. "We won't know till the autopsy."

"The position in which she was found should indicate . . . Unless she was moved. Was she?"

"The position was disturbed by the person who found her." Blegen waved the medics off, with a look said goodbye to Gruenwald, and then devoted himself exclusively to Norah. "Shall we go to my office, Mrs. Capretto?"

He escorted her to the elevator. They got out on the second floor and walked down a corridor painted blue on one side and yellow on the other—the new institutional cheeriness, Norah thought. She was surprised once again to be remembering the One-Three and its bile-green decor with affection. Blegen held his office door open for her and waved her to the chair recently occupied by Gruenwald. He took his own seat and set himself to read, very carefully, the report Hein had given him.

When he was finished, he put it down and considered Norah with the same thoroughness. Not a busybody, he thought, but a concerned citizen; solid, the kind who, once she took up a cause, could be a pain in the ass. "According to your own account, Mrs. Capretto, you were a considerable distance away, yet you're prepared to identify the young woman you saw and our Jane Doe downstairs as one and the same?"

Norah didn't attempt to justify herself, to explain that the light had been exceptionally sharp, that having seen the victim once before aided recognition; she offered no more field for challenge. "I am," she stated flatly.

"I take it she had not then sustained the injuries you observed on the victim downstairs?"

"No. But it is the same girl."

"And the two abductors, could you identify them?"

"Not positively."

Blegen sighed. To continue to try to shake her testimony would only result in making her more certain in her own mind. He got up. "It was good of you to take the time to come in. Mrs. Capretto. I wish that all citizens . . ."

Norah didn't move. "When was she found and where?"

Blegen stared at Norah, and she stared back.

Well, what could it hurt? he thought. It would all be in the papers soon enough. "Her body was discovered this morning in a ditch in a field between Shrinestown and Mt. Wolf."

Not so far from where she'd first seen her, Norah thought. "She could have been raped and beaten and then dumped and left to die," she speculated. "Or maybe she managed to get away from her assailants, but her injuries were so severe she couldn't make it to shelter. Either way, those men are responsible. They killed her."

"We'll have to see."

"Isn't it stretching coincidence to suppose that another perpetrator or perpetrators are involved?" Indignation welled up inside Norah. She balled her hands into fists, clenched her teeth, but held it back. Arguing would do no good. The two louts who had committed the assault had to be apprehended. Cause and effect should then be evident even to Chief Blegen.

"What is your interest in this, Mrs. Capretto?"

The question startled her. "I have no personal interest," she replied. "I saw a young woman forced into a car. I reported it Sunday night. This afternoon, approximately forty-eight hours later, I come in with additional information, only to learn that she had been brutally beaten, raped, and murdered."

Blegen sighed.

"At the very least, the beating was a contributory cause of her death."

"Ah . . ."

"I know; 'We'll have to see.' She could also have died on their hands. So then they *had* to get rid of the body. They dumped it in a ditch, where if not for . . ."—she raised inquiring eyebrows—"if not for a chance passerby, she might not have been found till spring."

"One of the first rules of police work, Mrs. Capretto, is not to draw a conclusion till all the facts are in."

"You asked me why I cared."

"Yes, of course." His flabby face sagged. It was barely three o'clock, but he was beat. He needed another drink, but he couldn't unlock the drawer and bring out the bottle till this woman left. He got up and reached a hand out across the desk. "I will personally look into it."

Norah didn't take his hand and she still didn't get

out of the chair. "I came in today because I have some information which should be useful."

"Oh yes?" He frowned, but he did not sit again. He lit a cigarette.

Norah ignored his broad hint. "The vehicle in which the girl was abducted was a Ford Bronco. I know because my neighbors, Willie and Edda Meyer, recently bought one. I had a ride in it and they pointed out all the features to me. It occurred to me that there probably weren't all that many late-model dark brown Ford Broncos around. I looked up the dealers and discovered there was only one this side of Harrisburg. I drove over there and told the salesman I was interested in buying but I wanted to talk to someone in my area who owned a Bronco and get his opinion first before committing myself. He looked up the records and found that he had sold four within the last year." Norah pulled out her notebook and flipped the pages.

"He gave you the names?"

"Why not? Sales aren't so easy these days. Naturally, I couldn't ask him what color each one had bought, but your men can find that out easily enough." She paused expectantly. "Don't you want to take down the names, Chief?"

Blegen sat down heavily. He found a pad and pencil.

"My neighbors, the Meyers, as I told you, bought a Bronco just a couple of months ago. As it happens, it's dark brown. Another neighbor, Karl Droste, owns one, but it's light gray, and I was at his place when I observed the incident anyway. The third owner is a Mrs. Millicent LaBate, whose address—"

"I know Mrs. LaBate's address."

"All right. The last is a Mr. Frederick Elicker. The address I have appears to be his place of business . . ."

"He owns the local drugstore."

"I see." She closed the notebook and put it back in her handbag.

"That was very enterprising, Mrs. Capretto, but these people are personally known to me as responsible, law-abiding citizens. I don't think they're going around abducting young women. You have vouched for the first two. Mrs. LaBate is recently remarried but she's a York Crossing girl born Millicent Lee and married to Albert Youse, also a local. Mr. Elicker, as I said, is our pharmacist. I'll vouch for them."

"I'm not vouching for anybody," Norah countered, "and I'm not accusing anybody. I'm trying to trace a particular vehicle of a specific make and year." She bit her lip. "If we . . . if you locate it, it's possible that the owner didn't have it in his possession at the time in question. He might have lent it out, or it could have been used without his knowledge or permission. In other words, it might have been stolen. Maybe the vehicle has been reported as stolen."

"We'll check it out."

"It would certainly be worthwhile examining each of the vehicles." Norah looked straight at Blegen. Surely he knew that she meant examining by technicians for traces of the victim's presence—for her hair, fibers from her clothing, even her blood.

"Has it occurred to you, Mrs. Capretto, that the vehicle you observed might not be owned by anyone from these parts? That both the victim and the alleged abductors might be foreigners?"

Again Norah decided not to contest the "alleged," but she suspected that the chief was trying to get out from under by dubbing both victim and perpetrators as "foreigners." She couldn't understand what difference it would make to the investigation. "The girl was on foot; how far could she have come? I'm talking about the first time. The second time . . . well, were there tire tracks in the snow?"

"Not by the time we got there."

"So it all hinges on the time of death."

Blegen looked hard at her. "You seem unusually familiar with police procedure, Mrs. Capretto."

"My husband was a police officer."

"Ah . . ." He took a deep drag of what was left of his cigarette, and the accumulated ashes at the tip broke and spilled down the front of his shirt. He didn't notice; he was watching Norah. "Because of the extreme cold, I doubt that the medical examiner will be able to make anything but the most general estimate."

It was almost as though he didn't want to solve the case, she thought. She reminded herself that he regarded her as a civilian and might be holding back on that account; no pro appreciates advice from an amateur. She assumed that Richard Blegen had come to his present job from some big-city law-enforcement agency; that was usually the way. Some men thrived in the more limited milieu, and others went to seed. To which class did the man nervously lighting a fresh smoke belong? She had no right to assume that he was anything but competent and sincere.

"I came down here a little over a month ago," she told him. "January 21, to be precise. During the first night, I was awakened and I went to a window at the front of the house overlooking the road. I saw that a bus had broken down about fifty yards along. It had a flat, so the passengers had to get out to lighten the load. One of the passengers was a young woman; she passed in front of the bus and stumbled and fell within the direct beam of the headlights. I had a very good look at her." Norah took a deep breath and fixed her eyes on Blegen's. "It was the girl I saw being abducted and the one I saw on the table downstairs."

Blegen ground out the barely lit cigarette. "You're sure?"

"The girl held the light for the bus driver and another man while they changed the tire. The bus driver will certainly remember her."

Chapter 8

NORAH CONSIDERED the bus driver the best lead toward tracing the victim's destination. Once they had that, it shouldn't be difficult to find out her identity. Unfortunately, she couldn't give Chief Blegen the name of the bus line. In fact, she didn't recall seeing a name lettered along the side, but it could have been on the front or on the opposite side. Obviously it wasn't a regular run or Blegen would have immediately commented and she would have noticed a regular passing. So it had to be either a tour bus or a charter. Even so, tracing it and the driver would be routine. Norah shied away from making any more suggestions. Actually, she'd said more than she'd intended, but resistance was always a spur. She hoped that in addition to locating the driver and interrogating him, Blegen would also order an expert examination of the suspect vehicles, but she wasn't optimistic. The interview concluded, she was the one who offered her hand. The chief took it without any great enthusiasm.

By the time Norah got back to the house, it was close to five and turning dark. She was restless. It was too early to start dinner. She couldn't settle to her reading. She turned the radio on to the local station. The newscaster mentioned the discovery of the body of an unknown woman by Roy Z. Yodel. It was assumed that she had died of exposure. No speculation as to who she was or where she came from, no description, not even the usual characterization as "attractive," which the young woman certainly deserved. No mention of an assault. Certainly not the way this crime would have been reported in New York, Norah thought, and caught herself up short. How many times had she denigrated big-city reporting, the so-called "freedom" of the press that resulted in pandering to sensationlism? Such reporting frequently impeded the work of the police and the prosecution of the culprit.

She was up again the next morning at seven. It was one of those glorious days that often follow a storm, cold but bright and full of promise. As Norah set out for her daily prebreakfast jog, she noted tips of green along the front of the house and bordering the path where some of the snow had already melted. Crocus? Hyacinth? Maybe early tulips? She would call Gus and ask if it would be all right to do a little gardening, put in some flowers—maybe vegetables. She did not dwell on the fact that she had no plans to stay long enough to see the flowers bloom or harvest the vegetables.

Without conscious intent, she turned east toward the Meyers' place. As she had learned to do, she went directly around to the back.

The husband and wife were seated at the kitchen table eating hot oatmeal with applesauce while a pan of fried eggs sunny-side-up kept warm on top of the big cast-iron stove. The aroma of zucchini bread came from the oven. Edda wore one of the housedresses made out of feed bags: all the women ran them up on their sewing machines. It was actually a pretty fabric of light green with butterflies printed all over it. The feed companies vied with each other in producing fancy designs to attract the farm wives. Willie wore rough work clothes. The daylight hours would be precious in months to come, but for now they need not be thriftily husbanded, so both husband and wife greeted Norah warmly, ready to spend a little time in sociability.

"Sit. Sit, Norah, yet awhile. Will you have some breakfast with us?" Edda offered, the ladle already in her hand and hovering over the pot of oatmeal.

"No thanks. I'd love some of your good coffee though."

Edda poured and Willie indicated the empty chair beside him.

Norah sat and the coffee was placed before her. "Delicious. I don't want to keep you from your work." She looked from one to the other.

There was always work, she knew, even with snow on the ground. The chickens, for instance: by now Edda had already fed them, piebald bantams she raised to sell, the money being for her own personal use—what in the old days was called "pin money." After breakfast, Willie would work in the barn getting the machinery in good order for spring, while Edda would be washing the dishes and doing the housework. Then, of course, there would be more baking and cooking: eating was a major interest among the Dutch. It was a life of hard physical labor and simple values. It appealed to Norah.

"I came by because I wondered whether Chief Blegen had contacted you?" Might as well ask straight out, she thought.

The Meyers exchanged glances. As usual, Willie answered. "What about?"

"The girl who was found in the ditch."

Willie started to shake his head, then remembered. "Ah, sure, sure. We heard on the radio. Mama, you remember, we heard last night."

"Yes, on the radio, we heard."

Willie regarded Norah. "Why would Chief Blegen talk to us?"

"I suppose just to ask you if you'd seen anything."

"What should we have seen?"

"We were to Lancaster right after church," Edda put in. "To a symposium . . ." The word was not familiar to her. "On Small Farm Management, it was. Sponsored by the Agriculture Department."

Farmers were never more than one jump ahead of the next loan payment. Each year after the crops were harvested and sold, the bank was repaid, repairs to house and machinery took up the rest of the profit, and it was back to the bank for next year's loan. The small landholders had a harder time of it because they couldn't use the labor-saving and cost-efficient methods of those with large tracts. So now Norah could appreciate that any kind of discussion or lecture that might help to improve the return on their labors would be well-attended. It would also serve as entertainment, an opportunity to get together. There wasn't much doing in the county after the fair in October and the American Legion show in February. A symposium by the Agriculture Department would have been as exciting for the older people as a dance on Saturday night for the young ones.

"We didn't get home till late Sunday night," Edda stumbled on, despite her husband's glaring signal to be quiet.

Why had she mentioned Sunday? The body had not been found till Tuesday morning. Yesterday. The girl had died either the Monday night or early Tuesday, but Edda was offering an alibi for Sunday. Norah hadn't mentioned what she'd seen on Sunday, nor had there been any reference to the abduction in the newspapers or on the air. She had come simply to get a line on what Blegen was doing, never thinking that her neighbors could be implicated. And, of course, they weren't. Nevertheless, Norah knew she would have to go to Lancaster and check it out.

"I wonder if I could ask you a favor," she asked as she stood up to go.

"Sure," Willie answered promptly. "Anything. Almost," he added, smiling with a rare touch of humor.

"I'd like to borrow the Bronco for the afternoon."

"Nah, I'm sorry, Norah. It's in the garage yet. Brand new, and already the brakes are slipping." He shook his head. "Nothing works nowadays. The big companies—they have no conscience. They take your money, but they don't give value. A week already it is in the garage waiting for a part to come from Philadelphia."

"How did you get to Lancaster on Sunday?"

"We went with our friends Rudi and Hilde Steff," Edda told her.

"How nice." Norah beamed. Now she could admit that she had been worried, just for a second. "How nice," she repeated.

Norah jogged back the two miles to the house. She fixed and ate her regular breakfast, not as elaborate as the one the Meyers had offered, then considered what to do with the rest of the day. She decided to take a ride into town for the papers. As usual, she headed for Abner's, a dark, narrow store resembling a European tobacconist's that carried an infinite variety of magazines and out-of-town papers. As she entered the main square, Norah was surprised to see a line snaking from Abner's door along the sidewalk as far as Schirmer's Bar and Grill. She got on the end to discover of all things that the run was on the York Crossing *Weekly Gazette.* It had scooped the York, Lancaster, and Harrisburg dailies.

DO YOU KNOW THIS WOMAN?

Beneath the headline was an artist's rendering of the dead girl. It was certainly less ghoulish than a postmortem photo. Such photos, Norah thought, were not easily recognizable because they lacked the personality of the living person and they were so deeply distressing that the viewer instinctively looked away. Somewhere between her own memory of the girl herself and the artist's attempt to imbue character, there was the reality.

She'd misjudged Chief Blegen. She had thought his insistence that the victim was a stranger was an attempt somehow to pass responsibility for the investigation to someone else. In fact, he was doing his job, following his own procedure and priority. Norah itched to go over to the station, but she got back into the Honda instead and, paper on the seat beside her, went back home.

She couldn't settle down. Though she wasn't hungry, she fixed herself lunch and didn't have that much trouble eating it. If she went on like this, she warned herself, she'd get as fat as everybody else around York Crossing. So Norah, who had had problems with her weight in the past, resolutely returned the slice of apple pie to the refrigerator. Exercise would work off the extra calories and the excess energy. She'd go over to Droste's and have her ride. Maybe Karl would be around. Solitude was healing, but she was beginning to need someone to talk to.

Usually she walked, but all of a sudden it seemed important to get there, so she took the car. When she arrived, the place appeared deserted. Karl wasn't at the stables; neither was Bert Hadley, the hired hand. By now she knew how to put Dandy's bridle and saddle on by herself, but she didn't like to just take him without someone's okay. So she walked to the house. As on her first visit, Ilse Raisbeck opened the door and barred Norah's way.

"I'd like to see Mr. Droste, please."

"Not home. He went to the town."

Which town? Norah wondered. "When will he be back?"

The housekeeper shrugged and was about to close the door when an airy yet commanding voice called from upstairs, "Ask the lady to come up, Ilse."

Instantly Ilse's dour expression moderated and she stepped aside.

With the exception of her one visit to the house, when Karl had immediately shunted her down the corridor to his office, Norah had seen nothing of it. She had assumed it would be middle-class-comfortable and she was unprepared for the large open foyer and the clean uncluttered sweep of staircase, the formal French window at the landing, the elegant chandelier. It was more Maryland or Virginia antebellum South than Pennsylvania Dutch. She knew that Droste had married the daughter of a neighbor; maybe Mrs. Droste's people came from the South and this had been their house.

"Mrs. Capretto?" The voice floated from the nearest open door just as Norah reached the top of the stairs.

Following it, Norah entered what could accurately be called a bed-sitting room. A large canopied four-poster was swathed in eyelet ruffles and dominated one side; an intricately inlaid rosewood desk piled with papers, the other. Katerin Droste was lying on a chaise at the broad bay window. She was a slight woman with a thin face that looked longer and thinner framed by the abundant mass of dark hair. The sun drew flashes of auburn from it. Her eyes were green, with a slight upturn at the outer corners. Her face was pale, her skin very fine but fretted with tiny lines. Nevertheless, they did not spoil the impression of beauty. She wore an ivory satin peignoir and her legs were covered with a thin pastel wool throw. She smiled warmly and extended a hand.

"I'm Kate Droste."

"I'm Norah Capretto."

"Yes, I know. Karl has told me, and I've watched you." She turned her head to indicate that she had watched from the window. "Your riding has improved a great deal."

Norah grinned. "Dandy's been my teacher. I have to thank you for letting me ride him."

"And I you for giving him the exercise that I can't."

The formalities were simply a device to let each woman size up the other. Gradually, though Karl never spoke of his wife, the impression that there was little rapport between them had grown. She believed the marriage was an obligation, even a burden. A marriage could go wrong in all kinds of ways, Norah thought, as hers nearly had, but this was not a woman who could be ignored. She would demand a response—if not love, then hate . . . or pain.

"You're very pretty," Kate Droste remarked. "Karl didn't tell me how pretty you are."

Norah wasn't often called pretty. Attractive, yes. Joe had thought her beautiful. She bit her lip.

"What did you want to see Karl about?"

She shook off her memories. She opened her big, commodious policewoman's handbag, which felt so light now that she no longer carried a gun, and took from it the *Gazette* with the drawing on the front page. "I wanted to show him this."

Kate Droste reached for it and studied it. "Chief Blegen was here yesterday evening with a copy of this. He asked Karl if he could identify the girl, but of course he couldn't. He said you claimed that you saw her, or someone like her, heading toward this house."

"Heading in this direction," Norah corrected.

"The girl is a complete stranger."

"Mrs. Droste . . ."

"Call me Kate."

"Kate. The girl apparently was on the run. She was seeking shelter and help. This is the only house for miles around. That's all I intended to suggest to Chief Blegen."

"The poor thing." Kate Droste sighed and was all warmth again. "It's a pity we couldn't have done something for her." She tapped the newspaper photo. "You're certain this is the girl you saw?"

"Absolutely."

Kate Droste shrugged. "Well, the police will know soon enough who she is. This is a small community. We all know each other. It won't be long till someone identifies her, then the mystery will be solved."

"Chief Blegen thinks she's a stranger."

"Any stranger in these parts is remarkable, Norah. May I call you Norah? A stranger is noted, speculated upon, discussed. As I'm sure you've been, Norah." The smile was not quite so open; the green eyes were narrowed. "Wouldn't it make more sense to trace the two . . . abductors?"

"I didn't get a good enough look to give more than a general description."

"Perhaps they were the strangers. If so, they're long gone by now." She leaned her head back against the pillows and closed her eyes.

Norah frowned and got up. "I mustn't take any more of your time."

The invalid opened her eyes. "Were you planning to ride this afternoon?"

"Yes, I was."

"Dandy's been a little off his feed. I think he should stay in for a few days."

Norah nodded. "Of course. I'll call before coming again."

"That would be best."

Their eyes met and Norah left.

Norah walked the short distance from the house to the car. She hesitated, then on impulse turned and went over to the stable and opened the door. After the bright sunshine it took several moments for her eyes to get accustomed to the gloom, but she knew her way and by the time she got to Dandy's stall she could see well. He whinnied with pleasure at her approach. She stroked him and looked him over. He seemed fine. She was no expert, but she knew Dandy, and his coat was glossy and his eyes alert. From her pocket she brought out a carrot and he accepted it eagerly.

"Good-bye, Dandy," she said, and turned regretfully away.

Outside, she looked up toward the house and the second-floor bay window. She couldn't see her, but she was sure that Kate Droste was watching.

Norah raised her hand and waved.

Blegen had come to check her story, of course, Norah thought as she drove off. Karl couldn't do more than attest to what she'd told him. Surely Blegen had known that. His coming at all suggested he was taking her seriously. Just how seriously, Norah decided to find out.

She headed into town. The residential section was at the west end and more individualized than anything Norah had seen so far. The houses were not all brick, but some also of stone or wood, and detached, with landscaped suburban-style plots. Number 32 Walnut Street was Victorian, ornate, decorated with cupolas and fretwork. It had a porch wide enough for a small hotel. Norah climbed the well-swept stairs to a door whose fanlight was Tiffany glass or something very similar. She had to ring twice before making herself heard over the whine of a vacuum cleaner inside. Finally the door was opened by a chubby young freckle-faced girl. She wore an oversized feedbag pinafore that just about enveloped the skirt and sweater she had on underneath. A faded red bandanna covered her head, but wisps of carrot-colored hair escaped at her forehead and ears. Instead of examining Norah, she was ruefully inspecting a torn and grimy fingernail. She put it into her mouth and tried to nibble it even.

"Mrs. LaBate?"

"Who wants her?"

"Norah Capretto."

"Norah who?"

"Ah, just say . . . a neighbor."

The teenager shrugged. She left Norah standing just inside the door and climbed halfway up the stairs before shouting, "Miz LaBate! Neighbor woman wants you!" Then she clumped back down and without so much as another look at Norah headed for the rear. The screech of the vacuum announced she had no time to waste.

"Mrs. LaBate?" Norah inquired of the woman who peered over the banister at her.

She was as unexpected and as much of an anomaly in the farming community as Kate Droste. She was a wispy dyed blond. She dressed and carried herself as though she were in her early forties. Her clearly stated image was city-sophisticate. She wore an accordion-pleated, bat-sleeved loose blouse of a filmy material in a chocolate brown, overpainted by hand in blues and yellows. Her pipestem pants were brown satin. Large shell earrings dragged at her small earlobes and stretched them out of shape. Her light blue eyes were bright, the pupils unusually large. On closer examination and taking into account the care with which she descended, Norah decided that Millicent LaBate was a lot older than she tried to appear.

"Hello?" She smiled inquiringly. "Bridie!" she shrilled. "Bridie Deely, turn that thing off!"

In the sudden silence, she went on screeching, "*What can I do for you?* I'm sorry. What can I do for you?" she repeated at a normal level.

If she had come as a police officer, Norah would have shown her ID and the interrogation would have been simple and straightforward. With the Meyers she'd had the leverage of Gus Schmidt's friendship. The interview with Kate Droste had been initiated by her, but here and now, Norah had no excuse and no rights.

"My name is Norah Capretto. I'm visiting at Gus Schmidt's place. Do you know Gus?"

Millicent LaBate shook her head, and her earrings clinked musically.

Norah pursed her lips.

"Ms. Capretto, I don't mean to be rude, but I haven't much time."

"Of course, I'm sorry." Norah fell back on her initial ploy. "I was referred to you by a salesman at Ruxton Motors. I understand you recently bought a Ford Bronco."

"Yes, that's right." She waited, curiosity overcoming impatience.

"I feel a little foolish," Norah apologized. "Frankly, I hadn't expected anyone like you. I mean, you're more the Mercedes type."

Millicent LaBate was pleased. She preened herself. "I do own a Mercedes. I bought the Bronco for my husband, to use at work."

"I see. I should have guessed. Is your husband a farmer?"

"Roger?" Mrs. LaBate was hugely amused. "He's a designer. He did this outfit that I'm wearing now." She turned in place for Norah's inspection.

"Most unusual."

"Yes, isn't it?"

In the back, the vacuum started up again. "Bridie!" Mrs. LaBate yelled.

"I gotta finish! I gotta get home and do homework," the teenager yelled back, and kept the machine going.

"The young don't have any respect for their elders anymore," Millicent LaBate shouted close to Norah's ear. "Do you know how much I pay that girl? She's never on time. She comes late and leaves early." Shaking her head, Mrs. LaBate stopped shouting and waved for Norah to follow down the hall and to the right into an old-fashioned conservatory. It had a leaded-glass roof and glass walls on

three sides. On every table there were shallow
dishes in which white narcissus were being forced,
some already blooming. Forsythia branches stood in
floor vases, their buds swollen. The furniture was
white wicker with blue-and-yellow-flowered chintz
cushions. The late-afternoon sun brought the temperature up an extra ten degrees.

"We haven't got around to redecorating in here,"
Millicent LaBate explained. "We're going to replace
the glass with pierced brick and build in platform
furniture. Roger's redesigning the whole space."

"It's quite lovely as it is."

"My first husband, Albert, liked it. He was very
conservative. I think one should keep up with the
times though, don't you?" She tilted her head coyly.

And with a young husband, Norah thought as the
vacuum was turned off on the order of a deep male
voice. Then footsteps approached and the inspiration
for Millicent LaBate's style and philosophy appeared. This time, Norah was not surprised. Roger
LaBate was typically a rich woman's young stud. He
was six-two, broad-shouldered, narrow-hipped, with
blond wavy hair—Norah could detect no dark roots.
The clothes he wore—faded jeans, plaid shirt, and
zippered jacket—were rough country style, but their
superb fit and quality was strictly city. The jacket
particularly so; it was made of a glove-soft maroon
doeskin—a spot of rain would have ruined it. One
quick, all-encompassing glance of his dark brown
eyes was all Roger LaBate needed to assess and dis-
miss Norah. He passed by her and went straight to
his wife.

"Millicent, darling."

Next to him she seemed diminutive and almost
disappeared within his embrace, which was passion-
ate to the point of embarrassment for a third party.
She emerged from it, however, rosy with pleasure
and pride.

"Roger, this is a newcomer to our town. Mrs . . . uh . . . ?"

"Capretto."

"Hello." He made a point of his disinterest, keeping his eyes on his wife.

She loved it. "Mrs. Capretto came about your Bronco."

"My Bronco? What about it?"

"I'm interested in its performance. I understand you use it in your business. What business is that?"

"We manufacture designer jeans," his wife replied with pride.

"Is that so? Your own design, Mr. LaBate? I understand you created your wife's lovely ensemble."

Glowing, Millicent LaBate again anticipated her husband. "No, we manufacture Calvin Kleins. We sell to some of the biggest department stores in Philadelphia, even in New York. Someday . . ."

Roger LaBate's pat on the hand was his way of telling her to be silent.

"Sort of like a franchise?" Norah asked.

"In a way," LaBate replied.

"I didn't know there was any kind of manufacturing done around here. Except for the iron works, of course."

"Ours is a very small operation. We use only local people."

"I see. Where is your plant?"

"I'm sorry, Mrs. Capretto, we have an engagement and have to be leaving shortly. What is it you specifically wanted to know?"

Norah hesitated; in her role of intrusive neighbor she was limited. "Just how you like the Bronco? I'm considering settling here, buying land, and farming it. I figure I need something in a four-wheel drive to get around and look at properties."

His dark eyes were openly suspicious. "And you came to us."

"Mr. Cummings at Ruxton Motors gave her our

name," Millicent put in anxiously to ward off his displeasure.

For a moment Norah thought he was going to challenge the explanation. Then his thick, fleshy lips lifted in a slight sneer. "It's a good buggy, but it's not that easy to handle. I wouldn't recommend it for a woman. I'm surprised that Cummings is trying to sell it to you."

"Oh, well, thanks. I appreciate your honesty," Norah said.

"That's what you came for, isn't it?"

One of the things she'd come for, Norah thought as she walked down the front path to the street, was a look at LaBate's Bronco, and there it was, parked in the driveway—big, high off the ground, and shiny brown.

Her questions regarding it had not seemed to disturb Roger LaBate, so she concluded Blegen had not paid him a visit. However, Norah wondered as she got into her small Honda, easily maneuverable for a woman, why he had been so reticent about his manufacturing plant. Surely its whereabouts must be common knowledge? All at once she had a keen desire to see the place. She stopped at the first gas station for directions. It was as easy as that.

It was the usual one-story brick, three miles out of town on a secondary road sprawling in the middle of nowhere. There was no lawn, no plantings; that type of "beautification" was for the big industrial parks, Norah thought. This didn't even have a sign over the door. Since it was the only building in sight and since it must be known to all, she supposed there wasn't any need. On the other hand, it looked so desolate and uncared for, without so much as a gleam of light showing through the frosted windows, that if it hadn't been for the rows of cars parked neatly around it, she wouldn't have known the place was in use. It most definitely was. As Norah sat in her car across the road, a side door opened and the employees, mostly women, began to file out. The last one, a man, locked up; then he too got into his car and drove off.

Norah headed for home.

When she got there, she found Chief Blegen sitting on her front porch.

"Good evening, Sergeant Mulcahaney."

Norah didn't reply till they were inside, till she'd hung up her jacket and pulled off her cap, till she'd led the way into the parlor. Dusk had fallen, so she flicked on the lights. Indicating the wing chair for Blegen, she chose the settle that stood at a right angle to the fireplace. They faced each other.

"How did you find out?"

"I asked," he answered. "First I asked Detective Schmidt, your host, then your commanding officer, Inspector Felix."

"Why?"

"You were making a nuisance of yourself."

Norah flushed. "Who complained?"

"Nobody. I observed you. You were meddling in police business."

"You had me tailed!"

"I didn't need to. Everybody knows what goes on in a small town."

It was the second time in two days that she'd been told that, Norah thought. "Gossip," she said, and shrugged.

"The only thing we have to talk about is each other."

"Then how come nobody knows anything about the dead girl?"

"Because she's not from around here," he reiterated wearily.

"She died here. Or doesn't that matter?"

"You have no right to take that attitude."

"I'm sorry." Norah wasn't one to remain apologetic for long, however, nor on the defensive. "As a private citizen I have every right to visit another private citizen and ask any questions I want and that he cares to answer."

"Until it becomes an invasion of privacy."

"How can it?"

"Roger LaBate claims that you entered his home on a flimsy pretext and subjected his wife to interrogation about personal matters."

"So there was a complaint. Believe me, all I asked either of them about was their Ford Bronco. I didn't even ask him if he was using it Sunday night or Tuesday morning, just how he liked it."

"It could be construed as entrapment."

Norah gasped. Her eyes blazed. "No, sir, Chief Blegen. I understand entrapment. Entrapment is causing a suspect to commit an infraction which he would not otherwise have committed. Whatever crime Mr. LaBate may be guilty of had already taken place before I entered his home and 'invaded his privacy.'"

"Why didn't you tell me you're a police officer? Why did you present yourself falsely?"

"I didn't intend that."

"It's professional courtesy for a law officer to make himself known to the local authorities."

"If he intends to operate in their jurisdiction."

"What the hell do you call what you've been doing?"

"What any citizen has the right to do." She glared back. Then she sighed. "I've resigned from the NYPD."

"According to Inspector Felix, you're on leave."

She frowned. She didn't have to explain anything to Chief Blegen, she decided. "I don't want to get involved in this case, and that's the truth, but I feel responsible. I feel I should have done more for the girl when she was seized."

"Like what?"

"Chased the car, followed the tracks, called the police right away."

"Why didn't you? Call right away, I mean?"

"I let myself be talked out of it." She took a deep breath, held it for a couple of seconds, then slowly exhaled. "I apologize, Chief. I have been meddling, but I promise from here on to stay out of it absolutely."

"I came to ask you to give us a hand."

Norah waited for just a second. "You *want* me to help? You're actually asking me to take part in the investigation?"

"That's right. You're a trained and experienced detective. We need all the expertise we can get."

Norah shook her head. "I'm sorry. I really would prefer not to. I came here to get away from the job. I came because . . ." She got up and walked to the window, her back to Blegen.

"I know your situation. I wouldn't intrude on your grief, but we have almost no one trained in homicide work. We have no facilities. . . ."

Norah turned around. "Homicide?"

"Yes." He scowled; his shoulders sagged. "The medical examiner discovered a bullet hole in the back of the victim's head. It was hidden by her hair. The bullet had lodged in the base of the skull and was recovered. It was a twenty-two, fired at close range."

Chapter 9

"*THE BULLET* was the direct cause of death?" Norah asked.

"Not exposure? Not the beating?"

"That's right," Blegen replied.

"Was she raped?"

"Brutally and often."

"So she tried to get away once more," Norah mused aloud. "This time when they caught up with her, they shot her. I suppose the ground was too hard to bury her?"

He nodded.

"Still, just to leave her there . . ."

"In a ditch."

"But without any kind of cover, any camouflage of branches, gravel . . . Of course, it was snowing." She shook her head and stared contemplatively out the window.

Dusk had become night. Norah had learned to listen for and recognize the night sounds—a stray dog foraging for food, an owl hooting, the scampering of rats, but it was too early for that. She could hear nothing, and see only her own image mirrored in the dark glass. Gradually it was superimposed by Joe's face—mutilated. She shuddered and turned back to the chief.

"If I wanted to go back to work, there are plenty of unsolved cases in New York. I wouldn't do you any good anyway. I didn't clear one of my last three assignments."

"According to Inspector Felix, you're one of his top people."

"He knows you're making the offer?"

Blegen nodded.

"You don't need me. There's nothing to be done that can't be handled by your own men. It's all routine. Get your late-model dark brown Broncos examined by experts. If they find anything that can be traced to the victim, you've got it made."

"You mean LaBate's vehicle. We can't touch it without probable cause. You know that."

"And the pharmacist's, Elicker's. Check alibis. If either LaBate or Elicker can't come up with one, then surely you can get a search order."

"Okay, but even if we can prove the girl's presence in a particular vehicle and you testify that you saw her dragged into it against her will, that was on Sunday. She wasn't killed till anywhere from twenty-four to forty-eight hours later."

Norah sighed. "You've got to start somewhere." She walked over to Gus's plain but serviceable desk and picked up the much-handled copy of the York Crossing *Gazette.* "It's hard to believe that nobody around here has ever seen this girl." As she had so many times before, Norah studied the likeness, but this time she looked not at the face as a whole, but feature by feature, separately. "Have you noticed the cheekbones? They're unusually high and prominent. The space between the eyes is wide. The shape of her face is triangular. Could she be an Indian?"

"Her complexion—"

"I wasn't thinking of an American Indian. Maybe from Mexico or South or Central America?"

"There would be a copper tone to her skin."

"Unless the Spanish ancestry was predominant."

"What would anybody from Mexico or Central America be doing up here?"

"Working."

"No. There would be records, a work permit."

"If she was brought into the country illegally—to work as a domestic, say—then of course there wouldn't be a record and the employer wouldn't be eager to step forward."

"The women around here mostly do their own housework."

"Kate Droste has a housekeeper."

"Ilse Raisbeck has been with Kate since Kate was a child. She's more of a practical nurse, anyway. No, if the local women get any help at all, it's for a few hours a day from a local hired girl."

Like Millicent LaBate's Bridie, Norah thought, recalling the sullen, recalcitrant teenager. She also recalled Roger LaBate's defensiveness about his factory and his volunteering that he used all local help. She hadn't asked. His wife hadn't mentioned it.

"Could it be that she was brought here with others as cheap sweatshop labor?"

"Everything's unionized here." Blegen reached under the jacket to his shirt pocket for a crumpled pack of cigarettes. He pulled one out, straightened it more or less, lit it, and sucked deeply.

Meanwhile, Norah was also remembering her first night in the house and the bus that had broken down. She visualized the knot of silent, ghostlike figures huddled together at the side of the road. Illegal aliens. "They'd have to live somewhere, be clothed and fed. If one of them ran away . . ."

"Don't you think that if something like that was going on, people around here would know?"

Norah looked straight at the police chief, whose

flabby face was oiled with sweat. "That's the question."

"This is a God-fearing community, Sergeant Mulcahaney. If you've learned nothing else about us, you should have learned that."

"All right, they don't know. Or maybe they don't want to know. So the personnel records of every manufacturing plant within a radius of ten or fifteen miles have to be examined."

"That means notifying Immigration and Labor. We don't have the authority."

"You're investigating a homicide."

"The farmers are giving up, selling out, moving away. This town, this county, needs the jobs these factories create. If I go in and make trouble, maybe cause them to go bust, nobody's going to thank me."

Now Norah began to understand. "How long have you been here, Chief?"

"Nine years. But I'm still a foreigner. Always will be." Ash from his cigarette spilled down his shirtfront.

"And that's why you want me." She sighed. "You want me to take the blame."

"You'll be leaving in a few weeks. A couple of months at the most, and you'll be gone, back to New York," he pleaded. "I have nowhere to go. Twice before in my life I've been forced to resign; I'm too old to go through that a third time. If any of the plants around here move away because I've harassed them, what kind of reference do you think the town council is going to give me?"

Norah moved quietly among the sewing machines, up one aisle and down the next. The women were curious, but not one moved her foot off the treadle or raised her head until Norah stopped beside her. To each one, Norah showed the drawing of the murder victim and asked: "Do you know this girl? Have you ever seen her?"

She would have been surprised if any one of them had said yes. What she was really doing was looking over LaBate's workers, the workers he had described as local. With the exception of the drivers who were out making deliveries, the sixty women at the machines were, as far as Norah could tell, exactly as he had said—born and bred, checked out by name and address, by physiognomy and speech, each and every one from the town of York Crossing. She was prepared to concede that the drivers were too. Just the same, Norah kept doggedly on until she had spoken with and examined every person there.

From the glass-enclosed office and observation post set on a wooden platform about four feet higher than the rest of the floor, Roger LaBate watched her progress. The shipping clerk was going over invoices; the accountant worked on the books. Whatever it was that LaBate normally did, he wasn't doing it now.

"Well?" he asked when Norah came up.

"Nothing."

"You could have spared yourself the trouble, Sergeant."

She shrugged. "All part of the job."

"Now what?"

What she would have liked would have been to get a look at the books. "How long have you been running this operation, Mr. LaBate?"

"About two years. A little more."

"I understand that Mrs. LaBate was just about ready to declare bankruptcy, but you turned things around."

"Millie is not a businesswoman. She has other talents."

"I didn't think you were a businessman. I thought you were a designer."

He worked his lips in and out thoughtfully. Then he grinned. "I never sold a single design in my life, Sergeant Mulcahaney. I couldn't get a job designing.

I couldn't get a job in an atelier sweeping up the cuttings."

Why the sudden attack of honesty? Norah wondered.

"Before I married Millie I earned my living as a nightclub performer. I had my own act."

She was not really surprised, and only mildly interested. "What kind of an act?".

"A little singing, a little dancing, some fast patter."

"And that's where you and Mrs. LaBate met?"

"Right. Millie came to the place the odd time she was in town on a selling trip. What she had going here, what her first husband, Albert, left her, was a cottage industry. They made Pennsylvania Dutch-style quilts and comforters. They were very good quality and all that and the department stores stocked a few, but it's a limited market. Anyhow, she used to invite me to sit with her between shows; she was very generous with her tips. Then she started to come in on a regular basis, to confide her problems, ask my advice."

Norah could imagine the small-town widow, lonely, reduced to paying for attention, maybe gratification, struggling to handle a business she didn't understand, and the big-city, small-time entertainer getting past his prime and searching for some kind of permanency. Roger LaBate—a stage name probably, not that it mattered—ten pounds lighter and in the flash of the strobe lights, must have been the realization of her fantasies.

"Obviously, she had the physical plant and access to local labor," LaBate continued. "What she needed was a product. Well, I had a few friends in the rag trade. I got her the contract for the Calvin Kleins. We can't turn them out fast enough."

So it was a good deal for both, Norah thought, at least on the financial level. As a marriage, certainly the lady had given every indication of satisfaction. "Thank you for being so forthcoming," Norah said.

"Hey, why not? We all do what we have to do. Life is a series of accommodations, right?"

"Right," she agreed. And he had told her only what she could have found out on her own. "So thanks again, and I'll be going."

"That's it?"

"Unless you have a suggestion?"

"Me? No, Sergeant."

"Then I have one. It's very dark in here. Why don't you clean the paint off the windows and replace the frosted glass with clear? You'll cut down on your electric bill."

"According to our studies, electricity is more efficiently used if the daylight is blocked out. Anyhow, it's the machines that pull the heavy load."

As everyone who ever paid a gas or other utility bill knew, rates had soared and were continuing to rise astronomically. The retired elderly were having trouble keeping their homes lit and warm. Often it was a choice between electricity and food. In spite of that, Norah was appalled as she examined the ledgers placed before her at the electric company's main office. The differences between the bills paid by the Albert Youse Company and the present LaBate's were hard to accept. When she asked for an explanation it was pointed out that the number of units being consumed had tripled. Additional sewing machines had been installed and additional help hired. Norah hadn't thought to ask the length of employment of the women to whom she had spoken. They were mature, most past middle age, and she had simply assumed they'd been there since the time of the previous owner. It would be simple to ask LaBate how many workers he'd added. On a hunch, Norah decided to ask his wife instead.

* * *

"Oh, certainly the business has expanded greatly."

This afternoon Millicent LaBate wore black leather pants and a bulky white knit overblouse. She had festooned herself with heavy gold jewelry that clanked with her every movement. It was all too much for her. She seemed lost and shrunken as a snail inside its shell. She looked bent, as though she were actually carrying a load. In the background the vacuum whined, indicating that Bridie Deely was on the job. Millicent LaBate closed the parlor door to shut it out.

"I can't think of you as a police officer. It seems strange calling you 'Sergeant.'" Her smile was strained.

"Call me Norah."

"Thank you. The business has expanded, but I don't know the percentages, Norah, the cost and profit breakdowns." She shrugged and the gold bangles clanked. "When Albert was alive, I took care of the books. He taught me. I didn't mind. We had no children; it gave me something to do. But Roger doesn't want me to work," she concluded pridefully.

It covered the wistfulness, Norah thought, and almost, not quite, masked the resentment.

"He's hired office staff, of course, and drivers for the trucks. We never even had trucks. Albert used to make the deliveries himself in our station wagon. We didn't have all that many to make."

"I was thinking of the number of women on the machines."

"We employed forty. There were times we didn't need them, but once hired, Albert never laid anybody off."

Norah didn't ask how many there were now; she knew there were sixty. That should have meant an increase of a third in the use of electrical units. But according to the clerk at the utility company, the unit use had tripled. For convenience, taking each machine as a unit, that meant one hundred and twenty. There was only one explanation: Roger La-Bate was running an extra shift.

That was why the windows were blacked out, so no one would know the plant was operating at night. But why was it important that no one should know? Was he pirating copies? Under cover of the legitimate contract to manufacture Calvin Klein jeans, was LaBate making extra copies and pocketing the full profit? If so, he certainly wouldn't be using local workers.

Norah became aware of Millicent LaBate's eyes fixed on hers with unmistakable anxiety.

"I really wish I could be more helpful, Norah." Millicent LaBate got up, definitely indicating that she wanted Norah to go.

The woman had been friendly and helpful; suddenly she was defensive. Whether or not she'd had any suspicion before that all was not right at the plant, she did now. Norah knew only too well the depth of loss and loneliness that engulfed one after the death of a beloved husband. She knew many women who had willingly deluded themselves as to the price of a new young lover. She was afraid that in Millicent LaBate's case the delusions could not be maintained much longer. She was sorry it had to be that way.

As usual, Roger LaBate put the Ford Bronco into his driveway at five-thirty promptly. He opened his front door without a key; nobody in York Crossing locked the door. He called out, "I'm home."

There was no answer.

"Millie!"

He shouted up the stairs, but there was no response. He called and looked into the front parlor. Wherever she was, whatever she was doing, she always ran out to kiss him. So he was a little anxious when he went back to the conservatory and found her among the forced narcissus and the blooming forsythia, sitting on the blue-and-yellow couch looking as though she were in a trance. Her face was streaked with dirt, her coiffed hair disordered and showing patches of pink scalp. Dust and dirt soiled her white knit blouse, and several threads had been caught and pulled, bunching it up over one hip.

"My God, Millie! What's happened?"

She blinked a couple of times; then her eyes focused on him. She pointed to a pile of ledgers on the coffee table in front of her. "I went up to the attic and I got out the old books. I compared them to the current accounts."

"You went into my desk?"

"I have a right to know what's going on. It's my company."

"Thanks for reminding me."

"I didn't mean it like that." She was instantly contrite. "But, Roger, the amount of fabric you're ordering, the thread, the number of boxes, doesn't match the volume you're turning out. It's too low."

"You can't compare jeans to comforters."

"I can compare dollars and cents. I want to see the accounts receivable." She sucked in her breath at her own temerity, but money at this moment took precedence over passion.

"You've got it all in front of you," he retorted stiffly.

"I thought we were doing so well. According to this, we're barely breaking even." She took a deep breath. "Are you pirating copies?"

"Of course not! Though I'll tell you frankly, I've been tempted. But we don't need it." He sat down beside her and took her veined, age-spotted hands into his. "I don't know what's come over you, sweetheart. You're making money, more money than you've ever had before. Why do you want to fuss?"

"If you're doing anything illegal . . ."

"What could be illegal?" He shrugged elaborately,

sensing that she was willing to be placated. "Come on, love, what you need is a drink. You've got yourself all upset over those old books, and they bear no relation to current costs and practices." As though that put an end to it, LaBate gave her tense hands an extra squeeze, then went over to the drinks table to fix the martinis that had become an evening ritual.

But she was still anxious. "Why do you keep the books here instead of at the plant?"

"Because I don't want anybody nosing around." Playfully he tapped the end of her nose with his forefinger. "All right, all right, this is the truth. I've been cutting corners, fixing the books, upping the costs and lowering the sales on account of the IRS. Hell, sweetheart, if I didn't, we'd end up handing the government all our profits. Everybody does it. It's self-preservation." He sighed. "I've got a deal with some of our buyers—you'd be surprised which ones— the biggies, a couple of the chains. Anyhow, I give them a hefty discount and they sign an invoice for less pieces. They pocket a personal profit and we cut down on our taxes. Okay?"

"Do you have to?"

"We're living high. If you want to keep the Mercedes and go on buying expensive clothes and taking winter vacations in the Caribbean . . ."

"Suppose you get caught?"

"We're partners, love. If I get caught, you go down with me. But we won't get caught; I promise." He handed her the martini he'd taught her to like, or to pretend to like. "Drink up."

She did so obediently.

He sat down very close and buried his lips in the curve between her neck and shoulders. She flushed with gratification and excitement and drank some more.

"You'd be surprised the things people do to get past the IRS. And how many do it," he murmured. "It's that or go under, believe me." While he held the martini glass in one hand, he reached down inside the loose cowl collar and felt for her breast with the other. She moaned softly. "Let's get rid of this thing." He set the glass aside and pulled the bulky blouse off over her head.

"Not here, darling."

"Why not? Why not here? We've never done it here before." He unhooked the bra. "I don't know why you wear this thing; you don't need it." With just a hint of roughness, he yanked it off. "You're beautiful," he said. "What we need is another drink."

He left her sitting bare-breasted while he went to get it.

When he came back, he was carrying the pitcher. By the third refill, Millie LaBate had kicked off her shoes. Barefoot and bare-breasted, humming a tune only she recognized, Millie was dancing enticingly before her young husband. Her eyes were dilated, her wispy hair disheveled. Arms outspread, she began to twirl madly to the beat of the cymbals and tambourines inside her head—faster and faster till she was gasping for breath, till the blood rushed to her head and she sank unconscious at Roger's feet.

He looked at her thin, painted face, puckered lips. He examined her raddled arms and legs, her shriveled tits. Dumb woman, he sneered. Dumb, dumb. Then he picked her up in his arms, she wasn't much of a load, and carried her upstairs to her bedroom. He kicked the door open, flicked the light on with his elbow. The bed was neatly made up, so he put her down on one of a pair of pink satin boudoir chairs. While he was stripping off the spread, he heard a thud behind him and jumped. He whirled around. No, she hadn't come to; she'd only slid off the chair, hitting her head on the soft carpet. Folding the spread, he placed it on its special rack and turned back the bedcovers. Then he picked up his wife, limp and unresisting, carried her to the bed, and laid her down between the sheets. She was breathing in rasping gasps, sucking for air. God, what a sight! Her eyes opened; they were red and unfocused, but if she didn't see clearly, she sensed his presence and reached out thin arms. Sighing, he bent down to take off his pants. One more time, he thought, one last time. Then he went down on top of her.

When he left her, she was quiet; the breathing was more normal, though her color was still high. He took a look around the room, considering what else he had to do. Put her things away, then make sure everything was right downstairs. And, of course, get rid of the old ledgers. As for the current books, Millie was right—he could afford to be a little less greedy, charge off fewer costs and show more profit. He set to work with a clear head—after that first martini, Roger LaBate hadn't touched a drop.

Bridie Deely was never precisely on time getting to work. It was a small gesture of independence, an assertion that she worked because she pleased to do so, not because she had to. In fact, despite her surliness, Bridie did please; in her father's house all the children were required by age twelve to earn their keep. If she were not employed as a domestic at Miz LaBate's, she would be out in the fields, or wading in the muck of the pig pens, or ankle-deep in chicken-shit. Also, though she wouldn't admit it, Bridie Deely liked the job. To her the house was the epitome of style and elegance. As she scrubbed, dusted, and polished, she imagined it was hers. She was very much attracted to the master, and when she was alone, she dressed up in the madam's clothes, writhing in front of the pier glass in accompaniment to her daydreams.

Today Bridie was later than usual. It was St. Paddy's day, and for the first time ever there was going to be a parade. A whole bunch of the kids were going. She had asked for the day off, and she hadn't got it.

Papa wouldn't have let her go even if she had, but she was sulking anyhow. So it was three-thirty before Bridie Deely put her key into the lock of the La-Bates's front door.

The house was silent and empty. Miz LaBate wasn't even home to notice her tardiness, Bridie thought with surging resentment. She was so frustrated she even considered turning right around and walking out again, but she knew that sooner or later her employer would be back, and if she wasn't there, she could get fired. There was no hope of getting a similar job, for few of the local ladies took hired girls on a five-times-a-week basis, and to bring home the same money would mean breaking her back in a different house each day of the week. Plus which, she'd get a strapping from Papa. Then there were other considerations. . . . So Bridie hung up her black raincoat, a hand-me-down from her older sister, took off her knit beret and stuffed it into the coat pocket. In the kitchen, she donned the working pinafore over her school costume and tied the faded bandanna over her red hair. Today was Wednesday, the day for the upstairs bathrooms. Gathering the powders and brushes into a plastic bucket, Bridie went up to the second floor.

She made up his room first. Picking up his pajamas, she held them to her cheek, inhaling the mixture of body scent and Aramis cologne before hanging them up in the closet. She changed the sheets slowly, dreamily, smoothing them with what amounted to a lingering caress. A quick flip of the dustcloth took care of the rest, and she passed through the connecting bathroom to the other bedroom. Hers.

The door was closed. That was unusual. Bridie hesitated. She was thirteen, but she had a pretty good idea of what might be going on. She tapped lightly but got no answer. She turned the handle and pushed the door open partway and sneaked a look.

Miz LaBate was in bed, alone. Nervously Bridie licked the beads of sweat off her upper lip. Nobody in York Crossing stayed in bed all day, not unless he was sick.

"Mis LaBate? Ma'am . . . ?"

No answer. No movement.

Bridie opened the door the rest of the way and went in. She looked like she was sleeping, Bridie thought; then she saw that Millicent LaBate's blue eyes were wide open. She started over but stopped halfway and screamed. Still screaming, she ran out of the room, down the stairs, and into the street. She didn't stop screaming till one of the neighbors heard her and came out. Her head nestled against the woman's ample bosom, Bridie Deely's screams turned to sobs.

Chapter 10

WHAT ROSALINDA Miller deduced from the hysterical girl in her arms was that her friend across the street had suffered a stroke. The two women had been close. The friendship had strengthened when Millie Youse lost her first husband. But with her second marriage to a younger, handsomer foreigner, it had turned into a jealous, backbiting rivalry. A stroke! She'd asked for it, Rosalinda thought with a moment of satisfaction so fleeting, so deeply buried that she was not consciously aware of it before responding to the crisis. She called the police, who in turn summoned the medics. Then Rosalinda ran across the street into her old friend's house and up to her bedroom. At the sight of the diet-starved body and the puffed, cyanotic face, all the old differences dissolved into tears. When the police arrived, she stopped crying and demanded the presence of Chief Blegen. Mrs. Miller's husband, Eric, was a member of the town council. Blegen arrived promptly along with Jess Kimmel and a creditable turnout of officers.

It was five o'clock before anyone thought to call the dead woman's husband. He came immediately. Behind him was Norah Mulcahaney, who had spent the latter part of the afternoon staked out in her car across from his plant. When LaBate saw the police cars on the block and the neighbors out on the sidewalk, he charged up the front steps. Norah followed, not too close.

LaBate raced directly to the master bedroom. Norah went up too.

"Millie?" he called. "Millie!" He entered, but Blegen and Kimmel standing together blocked his view of the bed.

"What's going on here? What's this all about? Where's my wife?"

Blegen sighed. "I'm afraid she's gone."

"Gone? Gone where?"

The officers separated and LaBate saw the shrunken figure in the big bed. "Millie . . ." he whispered. He went over to her, but he didn't touch her. "Millie?" He turned around. "She's dead."

"We're very sorry, Mr. LaBate," Blegen murmured.

"What happened?"

"We don't know."

"What do you mean, you don't know?"

"Exactly that."

"She was all right when I left for work this morning," LaBate offered, shifting from anger into bewilderment.

"You're sure?"

"Of course. I wouldn't have gone otherwise."

"What time did you go?"

"The usual time, eight."

"And she was fine?"

"I've said so." LaBate frowned. "Well, I didn't talk to her. She was sleeping. I didn't want to disturb her."

"I see." Blegen strolled about the fussy, feminine room. He opened the two closets and looked inside. "You have separate rooms?"

"That's right."

"Did you sleep here last night?"

LaBate sucked in his breath and appeared ready to blast the chief, then changed his mind. "We had a few drinks downstairs and we both got a little high. We came up here together, but Millie fell asleep on me."

"You mean she passed out?"

"All right. Yes."

"You're sure that's all it was?"

"It wasn't the first time."

"Okay. So you left her to sleep it off and went . . . ?"

"To my own room." He indicated that it was on the other side of the bathroom.

"But you're positive she was all right?"

"She was snoring."

He looked around. Nobody smiled.

"How about this morning? Was she snoring this morning?"

LaBate frowned. "I'm not sure."

"How about her color?"

"What about it?"

"What position was she lying in?"

"I don't remember."

"Like she is now?"

LaBate took one quick look. "I didn't pay any attention. I thought she was asleep, I told you. I called, she didn't answer, and I went away."

Norah listened and kept to the background. Richard Blegen was handling the interrogation extremely well and he was far from finished.

"Did she have a heart condition?"

"I think she took pills for high blood pressure."

"You think?" The chief sighed heavily and LaBate flushed. "She was not a young woman," Blegen remarked, as though musing aloud. "Before she passed out, did you have sex?"

Once again LaBate appeared to be ready to protest, and then thought better of it. "Yes."

"So: sex, alcohol, high blood pressure—that could have done it."

LaBate tried not to look relieved. "Poor Millie."

"If her personal physician confirms that she had high blood pressure . . . Who was her personal physician?"

"God, I don't know. She didn't tell me these things. She was very sensitive about the difference in our ages and she was always trying to minimize its importance. But she must have records, an address book. Downstairs, in what used to be the study . . ."

"We'll find it."

For the past few minutes Norah had been quietly wandering around. Like the chief, she had looked into the dead woman's closets, but where a mere scanning of the garments had sufficed him, Norah examined each one. She'd also searched the bureau drawers. At last she came to stand beside the bed and look at the woman herself.

"Chief . . ." She motioned for him to join her. She spoke quietly. "Notice her face?"

"Cyanotic, sure, but . . ."

"It's been washed."

"Oh?"

"Mr. LaBate claims he and his wife came up here together, went to bed, and started to make love. Then she fell asleep on him."

"Okay, so she got up in the night and washed her face."

"Not likely. Notice that it wasn't a good job; there's makeup all around the hairline." She pointed to the remnants of powder base that had turned an orange color in mixing with sweat. Then she led the chief to the bureau and opened the second drawer. She picked up a set of beige lace panties and matching lace bra. There was no apparent body odor, but stains indicated they had been worn. Next she opened the closet door and held up the hanger on which the black leather pants and white overblouse had been put away. "Look at the dirt down the front of the blouse. No woman, no matter how much of a slob, and Millicent LaBate was anything but that, puts her used underthings back in the drawer or hangs her dirty clothes up with the clean. If her husband undressed her, why didn't he just leave everything on a chair? Wouldn't that be the norm?"

Blegen waited for Norah's conclusion.

"I was here yesterday afternoon and Millicent LaBate was wearing this black-and-white outfit and it was absolutely fresh, not a spot on it."

Blegen summoned LaBate from the corner to which he had retreated. "Is this what your wife was wearing last night?"

"No. Millie was meticulous in her person. As soon as something had even a little spot on it, it went right out to the cleaner's. Here . . ." He strode to the closet, and rummaging through the tightly packed dresses and suits on the rod, pulled out a bright red jersey jumpsuit. "This is what she had on."

"Thank you."

LaBate accepted the dismissal and went back to his corner with lassitude. He kept his eyes on the two officers.

"She could have changed," Blegen suggested.

"Right, but if she got herself so dirty that she had to change her clothes and wash her face, why didn't she put on a whole fresh makeup?"

"What are you saying?"

"That there has to be an autopsy no matter what her physician says."

"Are you suggesting drugs?"

"The autopsy will tell."

"Autopsy!" The word jumped the space like an electric charge between open terminals. "There's not going to be any autopsy!" LaBate jumped to his feet. "I'm not going to have poor Millie hacked up."

"Don't you want to know how she died? Why she died?"

"Frankly, no. She's gone. Nothing's going to change that."

Blegen sighed. He exchanged a glance with Norah. "I'm sorry, but the law requires it."

Norah went downstairs. She looked into the conservatory where she'd last spoken with Mrs. LaBate. There were traces of last night's carousing: empty cocktail glasses, the pitcher with the dregs of cocktails and melted ice. Wandering through the other room, she noted that the fireplace in the front parlor held a heavy residue of ashes—paper ashes, not wood or coal. She picked up the poker and sifted through with care.

Had Millicent LaBate burned papers? Was that how she'd got herself so dirty? Or was it Roger who had lit the blaze? Either way, it had been a thorough job, for Norah could find no remnant large enough to warrant trying to reconstitute.

Roger LaBate made no further effort to attempt to stop the autopsy. In fact, his protest took on an emotional integrity when the results were learned. His wife's death was due to cardiac arrest. She had indeed suffered from high blood pressure, as he had stated. The stimulation of alcohol and sex had been too much for her.

According to the lab analysis, the smudge on the white sweater was dust, not soot. There was also a liquid stain which had been caused by spilling her martini. Norah was more interested in the dust smudge. Where could she have got that dirty? In the basement or attic. Blegen wouldn't let her go back and look through them. The death was now officially "due to natural causes." They had no more rights.

But the uneasy feeling that her visit to Millicent LaBate had somehow stirred things up persisted. Norah couldn't shake it off. The mornings suddenly became too quiet again; there were no afternoon rides on Dandy anymore since Kate Droste had quite openly warned her off. Karl hadn't called, so either he didn't know about his wife's dictum or he had accepted it. There was nothing to occupy Norah while she waited for Roger LaBate's next move. In her will, Millicent LaBate had left everything to her "beloved husband." *Everything* consisted of the house and factory, little cash. He could sell off both properties or he could keep the plant going. In these times, land was going cheap. He could elect to stay in business and put the operation in charge of a manager while he moved back to the city. So far, he was staying. So far, he was conducting himself as usual. The day of the funeral, with quiet dignity he received his neighbors in the house that was now his. The very next day after that, he went back to work driving the Ford van as usual, leaving Millicent's Mercedes in the garage. It was evident that LaBate was going to behave with extreme circumspection. The legal daytime manufacture of designer jeans continued. Nothing happened at night.

At least Norah couldn't discover it. A stake-out was impossible without cover. There weren't any trees or bushes, never mind buildings, in which to hide and observe. She couldn't park her car among the other cars in the rutted parking area because every vehicle was known, and anyhow, at the end of the day everybody went home and hers would be the only one left. She finally worked out a system of driving over at various hours of the night, parking at a distance, then walking to the factory. Always, no matter the hour, she found it shut and silent and dark. Yet she remained convinced that there was, or at least had been, a second, illegal shift. Apparently Roger LaBate had suspended it. Of course, he could have moved it to another location, but that would have meant buying a whole set of new machines, and isolated buildings equipped with sufficient electrical power couldn't be that readily available. Nor did she believe that he would shut down permanently; the money was too good. No, he would wait her out.

For how long? Certainly it was harder on him than on her.

Should she help him? Should she pack her bags, close the house, and pretend to go away? He would wait a few days to make sure she wasn't coming back, then start up again. And she could catch him in full swing. To convince him, she would probably have to actually go back to New York, open up the apartment, make it look genuine.

It was ten o'clock on Friday night, a full week after Millicent LaBate's heart attack. Norah decided that she would go out to the plant just once more.

On this final occasion, Norah parked nearly half a mile back on an unpaved track which she had often followed when riding. These nightly forays had honed Norah's five senses. She had learned to find her way in almost total darkness; the glint of starlight off a stone, the reflection in a puddle was enough to guide her. She could feel the texture of the terrain right through the thick soles of her rubber boots—packed earth, grass stubble, furrowed field. And she could anticipate a shift in grade. She could identify sounds too—from a fall of small stones or gravel, the snap of a branch. She could differentiate between the passage of a wild creature and a human. Like all good cops, Norah Mulcahaney had always been able to sense a presence. Back home on a stakeout in an empty house or outside on an apparently deserted street, a tingling along the spine, a heating of the blood had been enough to warn her of danger. Here in the open and on this night, her sixth sense alerted her. Though no light showed in the LaBate factory and it appeared as deserted as usual, Norah was prepared to back her instinct that someone would show even if she had to wait all night.

Then she heard it—the low hum and rattle of a motor. Almost immediately after, the headlights appeared and a van, or bus, materialized out of the darkness. There was no time to hide and no place to go, so Norah threw herself down on the ground, lying flat below the shoulder of the road, absolutely still, her head turned sideways so she could watch. The bus pulled up by the building's side door. Its lights went out. It took only a few seconds for Norah's vision to adjust once again, plenty of time to observe the passengers as they got off one by one, shuffling the few feet from one door to the other, silent as ghosts and almost as insubstantial. It was a repetition of the scene she'd witnessed from the front bedroom of Gus's house on her first night. The transfer completed, there was a flash of light from inside LaBate's before the door was pulled shut. Careless, Norah thought, but how could they know anyone was watching? Already the bus was backing out and turning. It was gone without even having stopped long enough to shut off the motor. Everything was as before. It had happened so fast that Norah could almost believe she hadn't seen it.

But she had. In a regular stakeout she would have had a partner and a backup and they would all have been in radio communication with each other and a command base. Under the most primitive conditions there would have been arrangements to call in, and another officer to remain on watch. But she was alone. Could she hope to approach the building, burst in, hold them all under the gun while she used their telephone to call the station for help? No way. She'd be crazy to try it. Then she remembered she didn't have a gun anyway. So what she had to do was get to the nearest phone and report. That meant the gas station two miles down. But report what? That she had seen people enter a building. While she was convinced of what was going on inside, she had to be able to say that she had actually observed it.

Norah picked herself up, made an attempt to brush off the dirt, and approached the building. As far as she could tell, there was no lookout. Nothing appeared any different than it had all the other nights except for a stack of packing cases beside the loading dock. Norah made a quick dash and then hunched down behind them. She waited a moment or two to be sure that she hadn't been detected before moving along the wall to the place where she had made a peephole on an earlier visit by slitting the wood of a rotting window frame. Even before looking, Norah could feel the vibration of the machines inside.

She closed one eye and put the other to the hole. The big shed was lit by lights directly over the rows of sewing machines and by well-shaded lamps hung low from the ceiling. Women worked feeding the dark blue fabric, turning and shaping, all in a steady rhythm, foot never easing off the treadle, never a break. It was, if anything, more expert. Certainly a more intense pace than she had observed during the day shift. As quickly as a garment was completed, it was placed in a hamper at each woman's side and a new one begun. There were no trips to the water cooler, no coffee breaks. Norah could not see faces, only bent heads, but they were all dark-haired. Two men patrolled the aisles; they were mere hazy forms to her, but she could make out that they were collecting the finished product and taking it to the rear. She deduced that an order was being readied, one on which LaBate could no longer hold up delivery.

She supposed that there were packers at the rear, but her range of vision was limited. As she watched, one of the men returned from dumping a load and turned frontally toward Norah. She had a clear view of a bulge of belly and the gun tucked in the belt.

Guards, of course! What else? But why not guards outside?

Now was not the time for analyzing. Keeping low,

Norah cleared the building and made her way through the fields before crossing over to the lane where she'd left her car. She got in and headed for town and the police station.

"Where is he? I have to talk to him." Norah spoke calmly and firmly, but her eyes were bright with anxiety.

"What about?"

"Is he at home? Please call him and tell him that Sergeant—"

"Mulcahaney. Yes, I know who you are, Sergeant." Max Fleischman looked through his steel-rimmed reading glasses at Norah, squinting to bring her face into focus. From the first he had sensed a quality, one he hadn't been able to classify in a rather limited set of categories. Now that he knew she was a policewoman, he should have been at ease, but he wasn't. For one thing, they were of the same rank, so he couldn't give her orders, but he wasn't prepared to take them, either.

"I'm sorry," Norah said. "I don't mean to tell you what to do."

"It's just that the chief doesn't like to be disturbed at home," Fleischman replied, a bit mollified.

"I'll take the responsibility."

"You don't work here, Sergeant Mulcahaney," Fleischman snapped.

"I'm sorry." She was handling this all wrong, Norah thought, letting haste and anxiety dictate. She took a deep breath, held it, and released it very, very slowly. "Look, Sergeant Fleischman . . . Frankly, what I've got here is too big for me." Her eyes fixed on his forced them out over the tops of the glasses to look at her in normal perspective. "I don't want to dump it on you. If our places were reversed, I wouldn't want you to put it in my lap."

Sergeants were supposed to be foremen in the management ranks of the police department. Foremen were supposed to stick to routine; they did not make decisions. When confronted by something outside routine, they were supposed to pass it upstairs. Fleischman got the message. He reached for the phone.

He dialed, then he waited. After a couple of rings he tilted the receiver toward Norah so she could hear. After six more rings, he hung up. "I'm sorry."

Norah scowled. "Don't you know where he went? He must have left a number? You must know where to reach him."

Fleischman shook his head.

"That's incredible!"

Fleischman clenched his teeth.

"All right, I'm sorry again, Sergeant. But we can't just sit on this thing. It's too big and tomorrow morning will be too late." She barely controlled her exasperation. "Who's the watch commander? Who's in charge? Somebody has to be in charge when the chief doesn't want to be disturbed." That had slipped out, and she didn't care.

"We're not country hicks, Sergeant Mulcahaney."

Oh, Lord, what's the matter with me? Norah thought. Why am I antagonizing this nice man, this competent officer who's only following regulations?

"I'm upset, Sergeant Fleischman. To be honest, I don't know what to do next. I need help."

"You could talk to Deputy Kimmel upstairs."

"Jess Kimmel?"

A nod was all Norah needed to dash for the elevator. It wasn't there. She couldn't wait, so she headed for the stairs. She paused just long enough to call over her shoulder, "Thanks, Sergeant Fleischman.

"Call me Max."

Max Fleischman was smiling when it occurred to him that he should warn Deputy Kimmel of what was heading his way.

Kimmel was still on the phone with the desk sergeant when Norah walked into his office. He waved her to a seat and she took it. She had just been reminded downstairs that no matter the urgency, respect for the position of the person one had to deal with was, in the end, the shortest route to action. So she sat and waited for Kimmel to hang up. Then she leaned across the desk to extend her hand.

"We've met before, Deputy Kimmel, at the LaBate house. I'm Norah Mulcahaney."

"Sure. What can I do for you, Sergeant?"

"It's about the LaBate plant. I've suspected for some time that Roger LaBate is running an extra shift and employing illegal aliens. I've told Chief Blegen, but there was no proof. I told him I was going to stake out the place. I've been on it a week, and tonight . . . I saw them." She didn't mention that the chief hadn't been pleased; on the other hand, he hadn't forbidden it, either. Blegen would be surprised! Norah gloated. "They're out there now, working. The plant is in full swing. You can catch them in the act—the illegals and a couple of armed guards."

Kimmel gaped at her.

"It's not a big job," she assured him. "It shouldn't take more than half a dozen men to surround the place and, say, another half-dozen to take the suspects into custody. I figure there are about sixty women and the two guards, plus maybe a couple more personnel I didn't see. You'll need two vans and the drivers."

Kimmel continued to stare. "You want me to mount a raid?"

"That's right. Believe me, you won't have a bit of trouble."

Kimmel was appalled. "I can't do that."

"Why not?"

"I don't have the authority."

"I thought you were in charge. Sergeant Fleischman said . . ."

"I'm in charge, but I don't have the authority." He was beginning to sound regretful.

"Then we have to get hold of Blegen. Where is he?" Norah demanded. The night was slipping away.

"I don't know, but even if he were here, he doesn't have the authority. They're not breaking any laws. And we don't know they're employing illegals. What you want is Immigration or the Department of Labor. They could mount a raid after conducting an investigation."

Norah groaned. She wiped her eyes with her open left hand in a gesture of frustration.

"I'm sorry." He was, for her and in part for himself. If LaBate was running an extra shift and employing illegal aliens, then he was taking jobs away from the local people who badly needed them. If Kimmel could prove that, it wouldn't hurt his reputation one bit and it wouldn't do Blegen's any good. "Look, Sergeant, it pays to be sure before making a move."

"I tell you I saw—"

"Yes, I understand. But you can't prove that the workers you saw are aliens. Now, I'm not saying that we should forget about it. They'll be working other nights, won't they?"

"Maybe. I don't know. I suppose so."

"So there's really not that much urgency, is there? We'll move when we're ready. And we'll get them."

What he said made sense. If LaBate wasn't interrupted in tonight's work, he'd gain confidence to do it again. On the other hand, they *knew* that the aliens were there tonight, now. Now was the time to move. She had an idea. She looked up, eyes bright, a slight smile. "You know that Jane Doe discovered in the ditch? That's officially a homicide now, right?"

"Sure. Shot in the back of the head with a twenty-two."

"And the book on her is still open?"

"Of course."

"So if you had reason to believe that she was one of

the aliens and that she had been working out there for LaBate, then you'd have every right to go there, round them up, and bring them in for questioning."

Kimmel didn't take long to make up his mind. Visions of solving the single mysterious murder during his entire five years as an officer and of breaking an illegal-alien operation at the same time was too tempting to resist. "I don't have enough men on duty, but I can round them up within the hour."

Norah nodded. An hour wouldn't matter. They'd be working out there till daybreak.

Once convinced, Jess Kimmel moved efficiently and with good speed. He organized four cars for his men and two vans to transport the suspects. Norah rode with him. The cars were to approach in pairs from opposite directions to cut off any getaway attempt should they be spotted before taking up position. But nothing like that happened. They entered the dirt-packed parking lot without incident. Stealthily they got out and surrounded the factory. When everyone was in place, spotlights were focused on front and side doors, and at the signal, turned on. Jess Kimmel made the announcement over the bullhorn.

"Attention! Attention, everybody inside. This is the police. The building is surrounded. Come out, hands over your heads."

No response. His amplified voice died in the night. He tried again.

"This is the police. We have you surrounded. Come out peaceably, hands over your heads."

Nothing.

Setting the amplifier aside, Kimmel reached for his gun. Raising his hand, he indicated for his men to draw the ring tighter, and approaching the side door, aimed his gun at the lock. Two shots followed by a kick and the door swung open. Into darkness. Reaching his free hand around the post, Kimmel felt for the main light switch and flipped it on. The metal-shaded ceiling lamps left the corners dark and sinister, but there was sufficient light to see that the place was empty.

Kimmel turned to Norah, who was at his shoulder. "Well?"

Every machine was neatly covered, every table swept clean of fabric scraps or threads, each hamper stood empty.

"They were here. I saw them."

Had they simply finished the night's work and left? Or had someone informed, tipped them off to the raid?

On the grim ride back to the station, Norah considered the two possibilities. She had plenty of time, because Kimmel wasn't saying a word. She couldn't see LaBate working the aliens only on a partial shift, so she dismissed that and concentrated on the second. Somebody had given the warning. But who?

She picked up her own car and started home. She had confided only in Kimmel and she had been with him the whole time until they drove up and he made his announcement over the bullhorn. Of course, he had made a series of phone calls to round up a raiding party and had been assisted by Fleischman. Though none had been told what the duty would be, any of the men they called, if involved with LaBate, could have guessed.

Norah drove slowly along the now familiar route back to the house. She was deeply disappointed and depressed because she had judged this community of York Crossing to be as decent a place to live, as free of crime and greed, as it was possible to find. It was hard to believe that involuntary servitude, for that was what hiding illegal aliens and keeping them under armed guard amounted to, could exist where people lived their religious beliefs. There couldn't be the excuse that nobody knew. How could Roger LaBate run an operation of that size without someone seeing something? Without word getting out? And in this town where, as she had been told over and over again, everybody knew everybody else's business, the knowledge apparently had extended to the police.

Tired, but mostly disheartened, Norah turned into her driveway. She got out to raise her garage door and became aware of a presence. Someone was sitting and rocking on her front porch.

"Hello?" she called out. The porch light wasn't on and her headlights were pointing in such a direction as to form a barrier through which she couldn't even make out a general outline. "Hello? Who's there?" she called again, instinctively reaching into her handbag for the gun she no longer carried. "What do you want?"

"It's only me, Sergeant," the man answered. "I'd like to talk to you. It'll only take a few minutes."

Norah marched up the front steps. "All right. Come inside."

Chapter II

THE HOUSE was hot, hot, hot!

Norah got up on the step stool to reach the thermostat and turned it down. She pulled the soft lamb's wool sweater off over her head and tossed it aside. She unbuttoned the blouse down to the cleft between her breasts and rolled up the sleeves. She lifted her long dark hair off the back of her neck, but there was no relief, no perspiration to evaporate and cool. Flopping down on the nearest chair, she bent over to unlace the heavy boots, took them off—and the thick wool socks too. The exertion brought high color to her face and she breathed as though she'd just run the marathon. Still she didn't sweat.

No wonder she was hot, Norah thought; the fire was blazing in the hearth! She didn't remember lighting it. She removed the fire screen, picked up the bucket of sand that stood to one side, and dumped it out on the leaping flames.

Unsteadily she padded out to the kitchen and got the pitcher of ice water out of the refrigerator. Instead of drinking it, she splashed it on her face, soaking the entire front of her blouse. Now she felt clammy. She tore the blouse off impatiently and let it fall. Better. Ah, that was finally better. She unzipped her slacks and stepped out of them, leaving them in a pile on the floor beside the wet blouse. Much better! In bra and panties, arms extended out from her sides at shoulder level and curved gracefully, Norah raised one leg, pointed her toes, and began a slow dance back to the living room. When she had been a little girl, Norah Mulcahaney had dreamt about becoming a ballet dancer. The childhood ambition remained in her subconscious. The rudimentary positions and combinations she had been taught all the years back were embedded too, and she now began awkwardly to execute them; the pliés, the glissades, the fouettés. She turned on the radio and, dark hair streaming, eyes bright but unfocused, Norah twirled and leaped and swayed to the music.

In the midst of a pirouette, she felt a touch on her leg, like a bug crawling. She looked down—a small figure, a small, stunted man was stroking her calf. "Ugh. Get away. Get away." She grimaced with disgust. She tried to shake him off. She kicked, but he wouldn't let go. She spotted another. And another. The room was full of them—midgets, slimy, creeping, obscene little people.

Norah screamed. They were climbing up, up her legs. They swarmed all over her; by their sheer weight they pulled her to the floor.

Richard Blegen heard music blaring even before he got out of his station wagon. It rolled out of the open window, a carpet of sound that swamped the senses. Scowling, he marched up the front walk and onto the porch. Every damn window was wide open! It was a nice morning, all right, sunny and warm and with a promise of spring, but not that warm. He rang the doorbell. Nothing happened. How could anybody inside hear it over that music? Going over to the nearest window, he bent down and stuck his head inside, intending to shout. What he saw made him gasp instead.

The room was a shambles. Furniture knocked over, smashed bric-a-brac on the floor, clothing strewn everywhere, and Norah Mulcahaney sprawled on the couch, arms and legs outflung, nearly naked.

Without a second's hesitation, Blegen threw one leg over the windowsill, folded his big frame under the sash, and climbed in.

He went right over to Norah and knelt beside her, placing his fingers at the neck just below her jaw to feel for the pulse of the carotid artery. He found it, steady. Thank God.

"Norah?" He shook her gently. Then he took her hand in his and slapped it a couple of times.

She stirred. Her color was high, her hair disheveled, her eyes, when she opened them, vague. "Chief?" she asked as though she weren't sure who he was.

"Are you all right? What happened?"

"Fine. I'm fine." She sat up and stretched her arms over her head, apparently unaware of her nakedness.

He stood and backed off. "It's freezing in here. You'd better get some clothes on."

She gave him a sweet, vapid smile before looking down at herself. "Oh." Then she looked around and the mists of whatever hallucination had held her in thrall cleared away. She blushed and searched for something with which to cover herself. Not able to find anything, she got up and ran out of the room.

Blegen closed the windows and turned up the thermostat to seventy. The furnace clicked on comfortingly. He didn't try to put anything right. He didn't touch a thing. He wanted Norah to be able to see it all as it was when she came back.

That didn't take long. Norah returned fully dressed in dark slacks and a shirt that buttoned right up to her throat. Her hair was neatly combed and severely tied back. She was confused and very embarrassed. More than that, she was frightened. As she examined the chaos of Gus Schmidt's living room, Norah shuddered. "What happened?"

"That's what I came to talk to you about," Blegen replied. "What happened last night."

"I don't know. I don't know what happened."

"I'm talking about the raid at LaBate's."

"Raid? There was a raid?"

"Come on, Sergeant . . ."

"I don't know about any raid. I swear."

He stared at her. "Are you putting me on?"

Her mouth was dry. She licked her lips. They were dry. She couldn't bring up any saliva. A terrible fear grew. "I don't remember anything about last night. Not anything."

"You talked Jess Kimmel into mounting a raid on LaBate's."

Norah shook her head.

"You stormed into the station claiming you'd seen people enter the factory, that they were illegal aliens working a pirate shift. You couldn't wait for the sergeant or Kimmel to locate me—I was only out for a few minutes. But you couldn't wait. You had to go ahead on your own. When the raiding party got to LaBate's, there was nobody there."

"Oh, God . . ." Norah was stricken. "I don't remember any of that. You know, I have been staking out the factory for the past week, but last night . . ." She began to tremble. "Last night, I don't remember going there at all."

Blegen fumbled in his pocket for the usual crumpled pack and lit up.

"What happened afterward? After the raid?" Norah asked.

He looked at her through the first cloud of blue smoke that hung in the still air of the closed room, gauging her sincerity. "You all left, naturally. Kimmel drove you back to town, where you picked up your car. The last he saw of you, you were driving off—presumably to come home."

"Alone?"

"Yes."

"I was all right to drive?"

"Apparently." Blegen took another slow drag on his cigarette. "Look, Sergeant . . . Norah . . . you meant well. You expected not only to round up a group of illegal aliens but to nail LaBate for murder, or at the least as an accessory. Right from the start, you had him picked for the killer."

"I did not *pick* him," Norah retorted indignantly. "Common sense points to him."

"Based on what? On his owning a vehicle similar to the one into which a woman, who may or may not be our Jane Doe, was forced on Sunday, but who wasn't killed till late Monday or maybe early Tuesday? On the supposition that he's running a night shift to manufacture illegal merchandise that he's authorized to produce in the daytime? You can't prove he's running the extra shift. You can't prove he's importing and keeping aliens to do it. You're assuming the victim was a member of a group that we don't even know exists."

Norah bowed her head. It sounded amateurish. Worse, vindictive.

"You convinced yourself that Roger LaBate is the perpetrator and you were going to show us all that you were right."

"No, it wasn't like that. . . ."

"You staked your New York reputation on it and it was a washout. Naturally, you were disappointed and depressed. You tied one on."

"I don't drink." The mention of drink made her aware that she was thirsty. Her mouth was very dry. Alcohol dehydrated.

Blegen waved his hand in a sweep around the

room, then at Norah herself. Though she was now fully dressed, she blushed fiercely.

"Do you have another explanation?"

"I'm trying to find one," she retorted with a flash of spirit.

"Fine, but meanwhile I've got a problem." Blegen ground out the cigarette and lit another. "LaBate got onto me first thing this morning. He reported that his place had been broken into; apparently Kimmel shot out the lock and the rest of you trampled the place down." He sighed. "I had to admit that we were responsible. I had no choice. So now he's claiming all kinds of damage to property, to reputation. He's talking police harassment and threatening to sue."

"I'm sorry." She had never apologized so many times in her life, and never without real reason.

"I've offered my apologies," Blegen went on, "and attempted to placate him."

She just couldn't say "sorry" once more.

"Oh, don't worry, he's not going to do anything. But . . ." Blegen hesitated. Basically he was a decent man and he had made compromises recently that were against his nature. He had bowed to expediency, reminding himself that there was a difference between ignoring blatant and proven criminal activity and turning your back on mere suspicion of fraud. "I had to tell him you were off the case."

Norah nodded. She had to take it. What else could she do? How could she argue?

"I also told him you were leaving. Going back to New York."

"No!"

"It's for the best."

"No! He's got no right to run me out of town!"

"Come on . . . Nobody's running you out of town." Blegen came close to smiling.

"I'm not going to let him do that." Her eyes were bright and clear. There was no doubt that whatever had been wrong with her before had passed. "I'm not going to let him, or you, do that to me." Her chin went up.

"I want to help you, Norah," Blegen replied quietly. "Believe me, that's my main purpose." He paused for just a moment. "I don't know what went on here last night. You say you don't either. All right. I do know that you've been under severe emotional strain. I think really what we have here is a delayed reaction to your husband's death and to the way he died. You came down here to run away from it and from your police responsibilities. In fact, it's all one package, isn't it?"

Norah didn't answer.

"Instead, you got involved in police work again. Because you saw that girl in trouble and didn't do anything right on the spot, you're holding yourself responsible for her death. You feel obliged to solve her murder. This temporary amnesia is an attempt by your psyche to protect itself."

"Are you a psychiatrist?"

"No, but maybe you ought to see one."

"I shouldn't have said that," Norah put in quickly. "I think you mean well."

"In fact, I do. I think you're too much alone here. I think you should go back to your family and your friends and your memories. You should learn to live with your memories. Learn to cherish them."

Norah's eyes fixed on Blegen's. He had offered an explanation for not taking part in last night's raid, though she hadn't asked for it. How could she ask a question about a series of events of which she had no recollection? From the beginning her insistence and unsolicited suggestions had been an irritation to the chief. Asking her to work with him had been almost forced on him as the lesser evil. She knew all that, yet she believed that he was not dealing sincerely with her.

"I'll think about what you said."

* * *

She did think about it. As Norah worked straightening the house and herself, she agonized over it.

As soon as Chief Blegen was gone, Norah almost ran to the bathroom, but nothing happened. Still the need to urinate continued. What was wrong with her? She looked into the mirror and examined herself closely as she had not had time to do in the hurry and embarrassment of getting dressed. The flush was gone; the glow, or call it the high, had faded. She was pale, drawn, and felt unutterably drained—down. Norah had never tried drugs, not even to experiment, to get the feel—as some citizens and even cops rationalized it. Anyhow, drug users didn't forget. To the contrary, they couldn't get rid of the memories. Often they were haunted by the horrible hallucinations long after they had stopped using.

Blackouts resulted from alcohol abuse. Yet Norah had told the truth when she said she didn't drink—not hard liquor beyond the odd cocktail, and even that not alone. To get so drunk that one had a blackout predicated either chronic alcoholism or an enormous consumption. If she'd gone on a drinking spree, she would remember the start of it. But she didn't. The period which the blackout covered was also puzzling in that it included a time during which, by Blegen's own admission based on what Kimmel had told him, she had behaved normally. She must have, because if there had been anything at all questionable about her, Kimmel would never have agreed to mount the raid.

Where did that leave her? With a breakdown. Blegen had called it emotional. But she hadn't had any kind of a breakdown! No way. Norah refused to doubt herself. There was an explanation. There had to be. She would find it.

So she set about to reconstruct the events of the previous night. The last thing she could clearly recollect was cooking dinner, eating it, and washing up afterward. Back in the parlor, Norah surveyed the scene carefully, hoping that something out of the disorder would stir her mind. Slowly Norah collected the scattered pillows, straightened the overturned tables and lamps, picked up the shards of broken china, coffee cups, and noted a coffee stain on Gus's good braided rug. Probably it wouldn't clean, she thought; she'd have to replace it. She stared at it. She'd eaten in the kitchen as usual, in the breakfast nook. Apparently she'd brought her coffee in here. Except that she didn't often take coffee after dinner; of course, if she'd expected to go on stakeout at the factory, she might have. She examined the pieces in her hands. She put them together and made two cups. So someone had dropped by. Quickly Norah returned to the kitchen for another look. Yes, everything had been washed up and put away. The visitor, therefore, had come by later and they'd had coffee together in the parlor. The percolator, half-full but unplugged, remained on the counter.

Could the visitor have put something in her cup? Who? Someone she knew well enough to have coffee with. Why? She hadn't the vaguest notion. All right, say that she had been drugged; that would account for her apparent wild behavior, maybe even for a partial loss of memory, but not for the loss of memory of events *before* the drugging took place. That was the troubling, distressing, terrifying thing.

As Norah cleaned out the fireplace, removing charred logs and sweeping up the sand someone had dumped to put the fire out, she felt a burning in her nose and throat from an acrid smell. It reminded her of the odor . . . at the LaBate house. There had been cold ashes in their livingroom fireplace, and according to her husband, Millicent LaBate had passed out from drinking the night before.

All at once, something clicked. She was reminded of a case, rather a series of cases. She hadn't worked on them but they had been so puzzling that the whole department had taken an interest. They were muggings in which the victims, usually tourists, were discovered out in the street or else they presented themselves at the precinct, but always in the same condition—ranting and raving, disheveled, their clothes torn or even without clothes, their money and valuables gone. In certain instances, the victim was not found till the seizure had passed, but his state was the same and *he couldn't remember how he had got that way!* Norah felt a tremendous surge of hope. In none of these cases did the victim have any recollection of what had happened, nor, most conveniently for the perpetrator, of whom he had been with or where. At first, the police had been merely intrigued, but the doctors had taken it more seriously. The instances which had been seen as oddities at the beginning escalated to the ordinary, rising from one or two a month to seven or eight each week.

Norah got up off her knees, left the bucket of sand and ashes and her cleaning cloth on the hearth. Pulses throbbing, she went to the kitchen telephone. She didn't need to look up the number; it was as familiar as that of her own home or office. She dialed direct.

"Asa? This is Norah Mulcahaney. I need some information."

Dr. Asa Osterman was the chief medical examiner of the city of New York and had been for as long as most cops, lawyers, and judges could remember. He was a small, dapper man of an age most often characterized as ageless, but nobody dreamed of his retiring. His reputation was nationwide. He was not only almost miraculous in his forensic skill, but a precise administrator. Strict protocol was observed between Osterman and the other branches of the criminal-justice system. Some complained he carried it to taciturnity. But he knew when to unbend.

He didn't ask Norah how she was, where she was, what it was about. All he said was, "Shoot."

She had expected no less; just the same, she was deeply grateful. "You remember a series of muggings and robberies in which the victims turned up with their clothes half-off, raving without any memory of how they'd got that way?"

"The anticholinergic poisonings, of course. After the job we had tracing the stuff, how could I forget? It had to be odorless and tasteless, and readily available."

"I think I may have run into another case of it. I wanted to check the symptoms."

"You described it: manic behavior, retrograde amnesia. Followed by shock and embarrassment when it's all over."

"Yes." Oh, God, Norah thought, yes!

"Also, typically there seems to be a hallucination of being attacked by little people—dwarfs or midgets in swarms. Of having to beat them off. You would have to observe this yourself, since the victim, once recovered, has, of course, no remembrance of it. He would, however, be aware of an arid condition of his body; mouth very dry, no saliva, no sweat under arms, no perspiration. Of course, no body odor."

"Yes, that's right."

"He would feel the need to urinate but not be able to."

Right, right, Norah repeated silently.

Osterman was curious but he didn't pry. "That rules out alcohol and is a strong indication that you're dealing with an anticholinergic. Probably what we had before—scopolamine in the form of eyedrops. Want to send me something for analysis?"

Of course he knew that she wasn't in New York. Of course he knew she wasn't on active duty, Norah thought, but that didn't stop Asa Osterman from helping a friend.

"There's only the dregs of some coffee in a broken cup."

"We'll do our best."

"Thanks, Asa. Thanks a lot."

"For what?"

Norah swallowed. "Asa? Could the scopolamine be fatal?"

"Depending on the dose. It is a poison."

"If the victim had high blood pressure?"

"Then the risk would be high on even a small dose."

"Thanks."

"Norah . . . the eyedrops are available only on prescription."

Norah carefully placed the broken coffee cups into a plastic bag and sealed it. She put that into a small corrugated cardboard box, cushioning it with plenty of crushed newspaper. Even if the lab should find traces of scopolamine-base eyedrops, she wouldn't know who had introduced the drug into her coffee, not unless he had obligingly left fingerprints. She added a postscript to her note to Osterman, but she didn't have much hope.

Now that she knew *what* had happened to her, the *why* followed logically. The intent had been not merely to wipe out the memory of certain events, but to discredit her, to make her appear unreliable, her word and her evidence tainted. All of last night's scenario had been planned. She had been allowed to see that night shift in operation on purpose. Then, while she went for help, the place had been emptied. After that, her lapse of memory and the psychotic condition in which Chief Blegen found her had finished the job. The *who* followed inevitably. Only one person stood to benefit. Roger LaBate. He had to get rid of her in order to continue his illegal operation.

Sometime after she'd returned home, Roger LaBate must have shown up. Maybe he'd been waiting for her. Probably he tried to justify his use of the aliens, pleaded with her to listen to some explanation or other . . . have a cup of coffee, talk. She would have gone along.

Scowling, Norah recalled what Doc Osterman had told her. No body odor. That applied to her symptoms and also to Millicent LaBate's. Though the underthings Norah had found in the bureau drawer had shown evidence of having been worn, they had been absolutely odor-free. If only Blegen had agreed to have those martini glasses analyzed . . . Of course, they wouldn't have known what to look for, back then. Still, Blegen's refusal had protected Roger La-Bate.

It was three-thirty when Norah parked in the La-Bate driveway. Neither the Mercedes nor the Bronco was in the garage, so she could reasonably assume that the master was not at home. She hoped and expected that Bridie Deely would be, as she preferred not to add a breaking and entering to illegal search. It was a very long time since Norah had even considered entering a place to search without a warrant. She'd actually done it only once, when she was a rookie cop. Joe had lectured her on it. She had thought he didn't like her. Later she learned he had been trying not to like her too much.

Tears stung her eyes, but she was smiling, for she was remembering not the mutilated face of his death but the young, darkly handsome sergeant, the ladies' man with the flashing grin and the teasing gleam in his eyes. There were good memories, she thought, so many. Blegen was right; she should learn to cherish them. The core of pain she carried was a little less sharp, a little less heavy. She got out of her car and marched up the front steps. Nobody was going to label her a drunk or emotionally unbalanced! Even Joe, if he were here, would go along with her on this one.

Norah rang the doorbell and to her relief Bridie
Deely answered. Surprisingly, she greeted Norah
with a smile.

"Hello, ma'am." She stood there beaming.

"Hello, Bridie, how are you? May I come in?"

"Oh, sure." Instantly the girl stepped back to admit Norah while regarding her with what could best
be described as awe.

"I'm here on an errand for Chief Blegen." It was a
lie but it didn't worry Norah because it would spare
Bridie from any possible blame later on.

"I know."

"You do?"

"Sure. You're a cop."

The word does get around, Norah thought. It made
it easier.

"Is it hard to be a cop?" Bridie wanted to know.

"To be a good one, yes."

"Could I be a cop?"

"I don't see why not."

"Gee . . ."

"I'd like to go up and take another look at Mrs. La-
Bate's bedroom."

"Why?"

That took Norah aback, but children were straightforward—they asked right out what adults would
speculate about. "I want to take a look at the clothes
she was wearing."

The girl's eyes widened; her chubby, freckled face
was grave. "You think he killed her? Roger? You
think he did it?"

Norah wasn't as much surprised by Bridie's jump-
ing to that conclusion as by her use of her employer's
first name. Probably she was showing off. She
wouldn't dare do it to his face. "What makes you
think so?"

Bridie shrugged. "Why else would you come
back?"

"I just want to check a couple of things."

"Why would you come when I was here but not him?"

She was shrewd. "All right, Bridie, I'll be straight with you. I do suspect Mr. LaBate, but I can't make a case unless I find certain evidence."

"Can I come up with you and watch?"

At norah's nod, Bridie Deely scampered up the stairs ahead of her and entered the bedroom.

Naturally, it had long since been cleaned and made up; even a lazy worker would have done that much, and Bridie was not lazy. After a cursory look around that offered nothing new, Norah went directly to the closet. It was still there, the outfit Millicent LaBate had worn on the afternoon Norah visited, exactly where she herself had replaced it. It hadn't been sent to the cleaner's, and for that Norah allowed herself one small sigh of relief and surge of hope. She took the knit overblouse from the hanger and folded it over one arm. Then she went into the bathroom and opened the medicine cabinet. She did recall the brightness of Mrs. LaBate's small blue eyes, and there on the bottom shelf was the bottle with its eyedropper cap. The label identified it and named patient, doctor, pharmacist. Norah made a note and replaced the bottle. Even if it had Roger's prints on it, he could say he had used it for his own eyes. She needed the blouse, however.

"I'm going to take this with me," she told Bridie, who was watching her every move. "I'm going to give you a receipt for it."

From her handbag, Norah brought out a small pad on which she wrote the item, a brief description, the place, and the date. "Now, don't lose it," she told the girl. "It's important that we be able to show when and from where I took this. Also, its condition. I've noted that there's a stain on the front. I want you to take a good look at it. You may be asked about it. All right?"

"Yes, ma'am. Is that going to prove he did it?"

"We'll see." Eager to get away before LaBate's return, Norah was about to pass over Bridie's insistence on her employer's guilt, attributing it to too much television. Still, the girl was eager to help, and she was sharp.

"Didn't Mr. and Mrs. LaBate get along? Did they fight?"

"Oh, no, ma'am. They was real lovey-dovey." She smirked.

"Well, then?"

"Well, he was a lot younger than her, and considering the kind of work he'd been doing before they was married . . . the place he'd been working . . ."

"You mean a nightclub?"

"A special kind of nightclub."

Norah raised her eyebrows.

"He worked in one of those places where the men take off their clothes and the women watch. The women give them money. They stuff the money into their . . . thing." The child pointed to her crotch.

Norah was shocked, not because Roger LaBate had been a male stripper, nor because he had lied about it. It wasn't something to brag about. Norah was shocked at hearing it from the child, from this child. Bridie Deely, along with all the children in this part of Pennsylvania, whether Amish or "English," as all the non-Amish were referred to, was sheltered from the outside world, protected from its evils. Yet somehow the prurient knowledge seeped through. "How do you know?"

"Roger told me."

Again the familiar use of his first name. This time, Norah couldn't overlook it.

"He was teasing you."

"Oh, no." Bridie's hazel eyes glittered. Her face flushed red as her hair, and beads of sweat formed along the golden down over her lip. "He did his act for me—one afternoon when the missus was out."

Norah was furious. All qualms about entering La-

Bate's house without a warrant and removing evidence were wiped out by this blatant corruption of the child. She drove home and quickly made up a new package containing the coffee cups and the blouse to send to Doc Osterman. Then she called the Meyers. She got Willie.

"Hi, this is Norah. I want to send a package express mail overnight. What post office has that service?"

"You have to go into York."

"Okay. Thanks."

"I'm going that way myself. I'll be glad to take care of it for you."

"I don't want to put you to trouble."

"No trouble."

Suddenly Norah didn't want anyone to know that she was sending a package to the medical examiner of New York City. "When are you leaving?"

"Right now."

"Oh. Well, the package isn't quite ready. Anyway, I feel like taking a ride." Quickly she hung up.

Chapter 12

NORAH DIDN'T sit around to wait for the results of the analysis from New York. The next time she approached Blegen, she wanted to be able to present a solid case against LaBate for the murder of his wife, and also to vindicate herself. Both required that she prove LaBate was employing illegal aliens. She certainly wasn't going to be permitted a second look at them working in the factory, so she had to find out where they were living. Wherever they were hidden, they had to be fed. Somebody had to go out and buy food for them and deliver it.

The job required a team. It could be done on her own but it would take a little longer. She got out her road map and drew a circle around York Crossing, using a twenty-mile radius to scale. Choosing to assume that the aliens were housed within that area, so must be the market from which their needs were supplied, she reasoned. Next, Norah made a list of the towns inside the circle. By consulting the Yellow Pages she noted the markets and grocery stores, feed and supply stores.

Assuming sixty people were employed, the same number as in the daytime, bulk purchases of dry comestibles—rice, beans, flour, bread—would be required. She doubted that the captives got much in the way of fresh meat and vegetables. Probably the marketing was done once a week, maybe only every ten days. She hoped it was done in the same place. The LaBates had been married two years, but according to what she'd been able to find out, the plant had started to show a profit only within the past eight or nine months. So she was looking for someone who had started buying in bulk no earlier than that.

By nature and by habit, Norah Mulcahaney was methodical. She set about this task intending to devote all her time and concentration to accomplishing it. Visiting the indivudal markets, large and small, chain or individually owned, she introduced herself as a New York detective. Along with gun, she had left her shield and official ID with Jim Felix. In its place she presented her PBA card, holding it up just long enough for a quick look, and it worked. It got answers. It also risked reports going back to Blegen about what she was doing, but that was a chance she decided she had to take. With every day that passed, Norah became more anxious that the chief would find out and order her to stop.

A week passed. It was Saturday, early evening. Norah was tired, but not discouraged. The job was tedious, typical of routine police work, but if done thoroughly, it would get results. She was accustomed to long hours and to the repetitiousness, and though she wasn't aware of it, she was deriving a certain solace from the very dullness and familiarity. It was only at night when she returned to Gus's empty house that reaction set in, that she had to face the void within herself. The widow's lament, she thought, the emptiness of the nights. How often had she heard it from grieving women, the bereaved of other cops. She began to think of Joe on these nights, reluctantly at first. Resisting, fearful of the memories, then eagerly, welcoming them, letting them wash over her—forgotten moments of private joys. Even the sorrows they had shared now brought a measure of consolation. For this she could thank Richard Blegen.

Sitting in the big wing chair by the fire that Saturday night, Norah stared into the flames and acknowledged that she was a different person from the one she had been before she met, loved, and married Joe. He had guided her in more than her professional life; he had released her emotional inhibitions. She had been shy, introverted. Through Joe's influence, the shell of her shyness had been crushed, her natural compassion released. She had gained confidence and vitality. Now she must not allow herself to lose ground and slip back. Joe's essence, even his humor, had become a part of Norah and must remain part of her always.

Would the rapport have had the same intensity if they'd been in another line of work? Yes, Norah thought. A shared belief, a shared dedication to a cause must strengthen the bonds between two people in love. For Norah and Joe it had been police work. Though he had insisted on treating the job as no more than a job, while Norah had a more intense attitude, both readily admitted that there was drama in it and even glamour sometimes. And both cared and had wanted to help the victims. My God! Norah thought, watching the flames change color and throw off sparks and smoke as they bit into wood that was still slightly green, Joe had given his life for an unknown woman screaming in a parking lot.

He had given his life, and she had walked out on what had been the core of their shared lives. She had run away. She had never denied that she was running away. Now she was ashamed.

The phone rang in the kitchen. Lazily, more at peace with herself than she had been in a very long time, Norah got up and went to answer.

"Norah? Karl Droste."

"Karl . . ." She felt a surge of pleasure, but she tried not to show it fully. "How are you?"

"I'm fine. How are you? We haven't seen you in such a long time. You haven't been around to ride. Dandy misses you."

"I miss him." She paused. How much should she say? How much could she say? "I understood he wasn't well."

"Who told you that?"

So Karl didn't know about her conversation with his wife; Kate hadn't told her husband of the ruse to keep Norah away. She was pleased, but she hesitated over what to answer.

"Who told you?" he insisted.

Norah took a deep breath and released it. "Kate."

"Oh. I see. Well, she tends to be overprotective of Dandy. Anyhow, he's fit again and eager to get out."

He was covering for her. Of course, what else could he do? For herself, Norah was anxious to accept the invitation, yet she didn't want to add to the troubles between the two. "Are you sure?"

"I wouldn't be calling otherwise. When are you coming?"

"Soon."

"How about tomorrow?"

Norah smiled. "I don't know. I have a lot on my hands right now."

"Take a break. I will. We can ride together tomorrow. After church, of course."

Tomorrow was Sunday. Only a few markets would be open. She hesitated. A day's respite out in the open air, the exhilaration of the exercise and companionship . . . It was tempting.

"Everything's greening up. The buds are swelling; there's a fine green fuzz over those muddy fields. You'll be surprised at how pretty our barren acres are becoming."

Driving around in the Honda, intent on her purpose, Norah hadn't noticed. "I shouldn't . . ."

"It will do you good."

Norah caught her breath. So he knew! Apparently everybody in town knew about her loss of memory and her erratic behavior. She blushed.

"No, thank you," Norah said firmly and finally.

"Why not?"

She would visit what markets were open, Norah decided. She felt a new urgency. She had left too many jobs unfinished lately. She would see this one through as quickly as possible. Then she would leave York Crossing.

"Why not, Norah? Have I done something wrong? Have I offended you?"

"I'm not well," she replied. Let him make what he wanted out of that! Let the word that she was incapable, unbalanced . . . whatever, spread.

"Oh. I'm very sorry. Can I come over? Can I bring you anything? Do anything for you?"

"No, thank you. I just need to rest." She hung up. And was instantly sorry. Karl had sounded sincerely concerned about her. He had meant only what he had said. She had to stop imagining that every remark was a veiled allusion. She had to stop being so sensitive. Should she call back and say she would join him tomorrow after all? Norah stared at the telephone. No. The friendship couldn't continue. It was as well to end it right now.

After mass, driving along Route 30, Norah found a farmer's cooperative set up at the side of the road that was not on her list. At first glance she nearly drove past, for it looked like a small country fair. Booths had been set up outside a one-story structure that might have once been a Howard Johnson's. They were gaily decorated—selling toys, gadgets, notions for the delight of squealing children, baked goods and preserves, tea cozies, pot holders, and quilts for beaming housewives. On second look, Norah saw that there were as many people inside as out. Counters, booths, and all restaurant decor had been ripped out and free-standing shelves and bins set up. Presto, a market! To locate the manager of such a place would be useless, she decided, for he would not be familiar with customers but rather with individual concessionaires, the men and women who stood beside their produce anxious to sell. This would be exactly the kind of place to which someone provisioning a large group, and not anxious to attract attention, would come.

She parked and went in, mixing with the crowd. She inspected the offered produce. There was little in the way of fresh vegetables and fruit, for this was local and it wasn't the right time of year. But there was what had been stored in root cellars over the winter, and plenty of dairy products and animal feed. There was also an area where sacks of grains for human consumption were piled on the floor.

The feed, Norah noted, moved the fastest. Next came things like cornmeal, dried peas, beans in varieties she had not known existed, lentils, rice, all available in bulk. The seller was a tall, rangy youth in faded jeans and a much-washed plaid flannel shirt. He looked about twenty except that he used his arms and legs awkwardly, as though he wasn't quite accustomed to them, like a young foal Norah had seen in the Droste stables. He was probably nearer sixteen, she thought. He had nice brown eyes that lit up in a friendly way as she approached. His lank brown hair fell over his eyes as he bent toward her—he was that much taller than she.

"Yes, ma'am, what can I do for you?"

Most boys his age, stuck indoors on such a day working at what she assumed was a family venture, would be sulking, Norah thought. This young man very evidently was exactly where he wanted to be, and eager to make a sale.

"Does this place operate only on Sunday?" she asked.

"Yes, ma'am, that's right."

"I thought most people around here didn't conduct business of any kind on Sunday."

"Some don't. Others do, if the price is right."

"Do you deliver?"

"No, ma'am, I'm sorry. But if it's a problem for you, then maybe if you could wait till we close, I might be able to . . ."

Good, another break, Norah thought. It meant whoever was buying had to come in person. "No, I'm not buying myself," she explained. He was certainly a go-getter, an entrepreneur in the making. "I'm a police officer." She flashed her PBA card.

"From New York!" His eyes widened.

'I'd like to keep this confidential, please." She looked around to be sure no one had heard his exclamation.

"Oh, yes, ma'am. Sure." His voice dropped to a conspiratorial whisper. "What can I do for you, Sergeant?"

"Mr. Hockheimer"—his name was pinned to his shirt pocket—"I'm looking for someone, probably a man, who's buying a lot of grain, not feed, and buying it in large quantities on a regular basis, say every week or two weeks."

"Gee, I don't know, Sergeant." He frowned thoughtfully. "Call me Ike."

"Thanks, Ike. I'm Norah. How long have you been here running this concession?"

He liked that. "About a year." He smiled shyly.

"Well, the person I'm looking for would have been coming for the last eight or nine months."

"He could be buying from one of the others. I could ask around if you want."

Norah licked her lips. "He's driving a brand-new dark brown Ford Bronco."

Now the bright eyes really shone. "Yeah! That's some beauty, that vehicle." He put the accent on the second syllable. "Some beauty."

Norah smiled along with him. "So you know who it is."

"Two of them. They come together; Ben and Will. Don't know their last names. Like you say, they come every week, just about."

"Have they come yet today?"

"No, ma'am . . . Norah."

"So I'll browse over there by the baked goods, and when they come, you give me the high sign. Okay?"

"You bet. Sure!" He was very excited.

It was a long wait, but Norah remained confident. They would show. She had a strong hunch that the case was going to break. Both cases. For she was convinced that the Jane Doe murder and Millicent La-Bate's death were linked. Time passed quickly. She had only one bad moment—when Chief Blegen appeared. She thought that he had heard what she was up to and had come looking for her. She primed herself to argue, but it wasn't necessary. The chief was with a plump little brunette, his wife probably. They were doing what everybody else was doing—shopping. Blegen moved around greeting neighbors, while Mrs. Blegen picked over the merchandise. Relieved though she was, Norah decided not to risk an encounter and slipped behind a display of the latest in Rototillers.

Now she was as anxious for her suspects not to turn up as she had been eager before. She chafed waiting for the Blegens to leave, watching with growing exasperation as they blandly browsed. The time dragged. Finally Mrs. Blegen had selected the largest eggs, the best of the cheeses, tapped the melons—the only nonlocal items—and they seemed ready to go. As the Blegens approached the doors marked "Exit," two tall, hefty young men pushed through the one marked "Enter" just alongside. They passed face to face, long enough to exchange greetings. Then the two proceeded directly to young

Hockheimer's stall and he gave her the sign they'd agreed on.

So Blegen knew them, Norah thought, as he must know just about everybody in York Crossing and for miles around. It was his job. All it meant was that the two were locals, a foregone conclusion because strangers would have stood out. Still, she didn't like it. While young Hockheimer was getting the order ready, Norah went out to the parking lot. Locating the Bronco, she positioned her own car so that she could tail it when they left.

A continuous stream of traffic in and out of the market made it easy at first. As it thinned along U.S. 30, Norah had to fall back, but there was still no problem, not till the vehicle turned onto an unmarked side road. She kept straight on at an even speed, rounded the next curve, then made a U-turn back. The suspect vehicle was not to be seen. Norah cut across the highway to follow. She went a good half-mile along the road they had taken, without any sight of habitation and without encountering another car. Should she continue or turn back? She could come another day, maybe on Dandy, to make it seem more casual. But she was here now, and the paved road suggested that it was used frequently enough so that she could travel it without attracting particular attention, less probably than if she were on horseback.

So she kept on. The terrain changed, becoming not hilly, but gently undulating. There were no plowed fields; the land was not under cultivation and that in itself was unusual in these parts, but nature protected it with its own ground cover of wild grasses, among which clusters of violets nestled. A mile farther on, behind a stand of ancient apple trees, where it would have been well hidden if the trees had been in leaf, Norah saw a big Dutch barn. It was in shambles, neglected, even its round hex symbol in need of paint. Off to one side, she noted a pair of smaller structures in similar condition. She didn't slow down, not even when she spotted the Bronco. She waited until she was well out of sight before pulling over. Then, map on the seat beside her, Norah marked the spot and studied the best way to get back to the highway and home.

INS, Immigration and Naturalization Service, didn't answer its phone on Sunday. Naturally, Norah thought, and hung up. She'd make a better case in person anyway. She had intended to go to Blegen with her discovery, but the greeting between the chief of police and the two suspects had shaken her more than she'd realized. Both Blegen and his deputy had kept insisting that they didn't have jurisdiction in the matter of aliens, so they could hardly complain if she applied to those who had. She drove into Harrisburg that night, stayed in a motel, and was on the INS doorstep when they opened on Monday morning.

Nor did she have to worry about the Immigration agents notifying Chief Blegen: the feds weren't interested in sharing credit for a roundup. In fact, they were not anxious even to have Norah along. Special Agent Bruce Creech mulled it over. Creech was in his middle thirties, medium height and build, undistinguished but for a mass of black hair that ran in long sideburns down to a heavy, squarecut beard. His light gray eyes focused piercingly on Norah from beneath overhanging brows. He looked fierce as a pirate or an NHL hocky player. Vocally, he was softspoken, forcing one to lean forward and listen very hard. It was a contrast carefully nurtured, Norah suspected, doing as she was meant to do—leaning forward to catch his decision.

"All right. But you're to stay in the car."

They both knew that a spot on the map wasn't enough: he needed her to show the way. Restricting her to the car was the special agent's way of defining his control.

"Whatever you say," Norah had to agree.

The operation was neither particularly elaborate nor cunning. Not that subtlety was required, Norah mused as she sat up front with the driver of the sleek black Oldsmobile. Bruce Creech rode alone in the back. The rest of the caravan consisted of Jeeps. They left the road as soon as she pointed out the objective, bouncing across the fields to form a battle ring that included the outlying buildings. Every blacked-out window and door, front and rear, was covered. There was no doubt that those inside must by now be aware of their presence, must have heard the roar of the motors, but what could they do? As soon as his people were in position, Bruce Creech emerged from the backseat, was handed an amplifier, and in unexpectedly stentorian tones made the official announcement.

By now the sun was high in the sky. A light breeze blew from the south; it ruffled the hair on the back of Norah's neck as she crouched in the lee of the sedan, but it was too gentle to stir the young leaves and its soft sigh merely intensified the waiting silence.

Creech raised the horn again and repeated the warning. "You are surrounded. Come out with your hands up."

Still no response from inside. No sound. No movement.

God help me! Norah thought with a sudden spasm of self-doubt. *Have I goofed again?* She had told Creech that she had not actually looked inside the building, but to remind him of that now would neither soothe him nor remove the stigma of the mistake from either one of them. For her it would be the second time around, and when word of it got out, she might as well leave and go back to New York—if Jim Felix would even take her back.

Agent Creech tried once more. "This is your final

warning. Come out with your hands up or we'll open fire."

Another wait, the side door opened to a crack, then wider. Two men emerged blinking in the noon sunshine, hands over their heads as ordered. They were the two Norah had seen in the farmer's cooperative, the ones she'd followed. She came out from behind the Olds.

"Where are the others?" Creech demanded in his loud voice.

The taller of the two, the blond with the skimpy sideburns and scraggly mustache, shrugged. "They don't understand English."

When the feds burst into the dark, cold building, the aliens were still hudled in their cots under drab army blankets. They lay silent and motionless for several moments, frighteningly so. Then there was a stirring. One or two sat up and looked at the raiders with eyes that spoke of hopeless resignation. Though there was no outcry, the alarm was communicated. It passed from one to the next, wakening those who somehow still slept, or pretended to, till all of the women and the handful of men in the barn had been alerted.

"Everybody up. This is a raid."

Perhaps they did not understand the words, but the intent was clear. The women, some young, some old, some pretty, others plain, got up and stood beside their cots. They were shivering with the cold and, despite the fact that each one wore some kind of enveloping garment, with embarrassment in the presence of strange men.

Creech eyed them in one comprehensive sweep, assessing only the number. INS agents were conducting raids all over the country, expending big manpower for minimal results. Recently, forty agents closing in on a suspect operation had bagged only ten illegals. On another dismal occasion, every Mexican arrested was proven to be in the U.S. legally, and was back at his job the next day. Creech had brought fifteen agents and had rounded up an estimated fifty or sixty aliens. Of that number, he was certain not one would prove to have valid documentation. His lips twitched with satisfaction.

In the excitement, he'd forgotten about Norah Mulcahaney. He saw that despite her promise to stay with the car, she'd followed inside. But how could he be angry?

Looking along the double row of cowering women, Norah spotted a cot beside which no one stood. It had not been used that night; it was neatly made up with its blanket tucked tightly from head to foot. Norah pointed.

"Whose is that? *Quien duerme aya?*"

And Creech, because the tip had panned out so well, felt he owed her. "Okay, you . . ." He pointed a finger at the bigger of the two guards. "What's your name?"

"Connick. Ben Connick."

"Okay, Connick. Where is she? Where's the missing woman?"

"I don't know anything about any missing woman. There's nobody missing. Everybody's here."

"How many are there supposed to be?"

Connick started to answer, then caught himself. "Fifty-nine."

"Is that right?" Creech asked the other prisoner. "Maybe your buddy can't count so good. How about you? You can make it a lot easier for yourself by cooperating."

Will Haney jerked his head toward Norah. "If you ask me, she's imagining things."

Instantly, Norah tensed. What did he mean? Was it a sly allusion to the other, abortive raid, the one she couldn't remember? She gave the two suspects a long, hard look, then resolutely turned her back on them to try her halting Spanish once more.

"Donde está la otra mujer? Ella que duerme aya."
Again she pointed to the empty cot.

Not one of the women would even raise her eyes to look at Norah.

Creech had to put an end to it. "Sorry, Sergeant, we've got to move."

"I thought they'd be eager to help." Norah was deeply disappointed.

"Why should they?"

"Well . . ."

"You don't think they're grateful to us for busting in here, do you? You don't think they're glad to see us? Hell, they've been avoiding us from the time they crossed the border. We're the enemy. We're going to deport them, send them back where they came from. They know that. Why should they tell us one damn thing?"

"The girl was one of them."

"Maybe. But she's gone and they're here. Look, ninety percent of the aliens we deport come back, not once, but over and over, time after time. They don't give up. Tough as the trip is, lousy as the conditions are once they make it, it's worse back home. And they have families there to support. As long as they're here and working, they can send money home, and that means everything to them.

"That's one thing the employer does," Creech continued. "Whoever he is, no matter how venal or how inhumanely he treats the workers, he sends a part of their wages, small as it is, back to the families. And he sees to it that they get the letter from home that tells them so. How else could he keep them and work them—like this?"

Norah sighed.

"So they're not going to tell you anything that would get their employer into trouble or antagonize him—they might be working for him the next time they cross over. Or if it should get out that they're troublemakers, they won't even find a coyote willing to take their money and guide them the next time."

Norah searched the faces of the women, haggard with overwork, lack of air, bad food; some of them looked sick. She knew what Bruce Creech had said was true. She examined the two guards, Connick and Haney. There was no mistaking they knew it too. They returned her look with a sneer. Norah seethed inwardly, but what could she do? What had started as a hunch, that these were the two she had seen abduct the girl, became conviction. She appealed to Creech. "The women are afraid, physically afraid of these two. If you could just take them outside . . ."

"I'm sorry, Sergeant. You'll get your chance to interrogate anybody you want later on at the detention center." He waved her aside. "Okay, listen up, everybody. Let's see your green cards. Anybody that's got a green card, I want to see it right now."

That didn't need translation. If any of the women had had one of the coveted green cards enabling the bearer to work legally in the U.S., she wouldn't be here.

In spite of himself, Creech sighed. The rationale behind the current series of raids was to take the aliens out of jobs and make them available to unemployed U.S. citizens. But there was a flaw: the average citizen didn't want this kind of job. It was too menial. Meantime, employers faced the danger of going out of business because they couldn't get help they could afford. Some European countries were recruiting workers from poorer lands on a "guestworker" basis. Foreign workers were not merely cheaper, they were eager, reliable, and enthusiastic. This country was built on immigrants. Hell, instead of deporting these people, we should be welcoming them, Creech thought. His scowl made him look more piratical than ever. Then he shrugged. If that ever happened, he'd be out of a job.

"Okay, let's line 'em up and move 'em out."

"You're going to let them get dressed, aren't you?" Norah asked, remininding him that they were still in their nightgowns.

Creech looked around to make sure the building was secure. "I guess so. You stay here and keep an eye on them, Sergeant."

Norah nodded.

"And hurry it up," Creech added as he signaled for his men to escort the two guards and the few male aliens outside.

As soon as the door was closed behind them, Norah addressed the women. "Does anyone here speak English?"

They ignored her. All glumly went about the business of putting their clothes on and collecting their few possessions.

Norah moved from one to the next, appealing on an individual basis. "Please, I know there was one more woman with you, a young woman. I can't believe you don't care about her. I can't believe you don't care what happened to her." She looked directly into the face of a woman who had been kneeling to get a zippered nylon bag from under the bed. The woman got up off her knees and turned away. But not before Norah had seen tears in her eyes.

Viorica Amara pulled a long black wool dress out of the bundle, a dress much like that of the girl in the lane, Norah thought, and saw that among the other things were pants and a shirt, small in size. A child's? There were no children here. She had a sudden insight, a hunch as to why they were so doggedly uncooperative. It was not for the reason Creech had cited.

"That girl, that young woman . . . she hasn't escaped. She's dead," Norah told them. She raised her voice for all to hear. "She was killed. Shot. Shot in the back of the head." Norah pantomimed. "She's dead. I saw her body."

The women stopped what they were doing. There was a low wail from Viorica Amara with the child's clothing clutched in both her hands.

"Ay, ay . . ." she keened softly. "Benita . . . *chica . . .*"

An older woman, much older, though probably not as old as she looked, came up to Norah. "You are sure that Benita is dead?"

"Yes."

They had believed that she had escaped. That was why they had been silent; they had been loath to put the feds on the hunt for her. They had thought that she had got away and lost herself within the population—that she had found the freedom they had all come here seeking. They had been protecting her. "I saw her," Norah repeated, sharing their sorrow. "She was young, perhaps twenty, with dark hair. She was beautiful." Then Norah added as specific identification, "She had a mole on the right side of her chin. I'm looking for the man or men who killed her."

A quick glance toward the closed door, then the woman, the one who could speak English, made up her mind. "We don't know nothing."

But Viorica Amara was not satisfied. *"Conteste, conteste,"* she moaned. "Tell her everything."

The older woman sighed. "Benita, she runs away. They catch her and they return her here."

"Who? Who brought her back?"

"Those two. *Las guardias.*" She indicated the door.

"Digale como, la suya condición. Como que la abusaron, batieron, violaron."

"They treat her very bad."

"She was raped. I know."

The woman looked down.

"Did she tell you who did it?"

"We wash her and we clean her and we try to cure her, but she is very bad. At night we go to work and leave her behind. When we come back, she is gone."

"Did she say who did it? Did she say who beat her and raped her?"

The woman pressed her emaciated lips together, clenched her teeth so hard that the pulses at her temples throbbed. She had gone this far, but she dared not make a direct accusation. Norah had one last card to play. From her handbag she took the newspaper with the artist's rendering of the dead girl.

"This was Benita?"

With an intake of breath that began as a sigh and ended in a gulping sob, the woman who had served as reluctant translator turned away. Viorica Amara snatched at the paper. *"Dios mío! Fueron ellos, ellos, las guardias! Benita Cruz me lo dijo."*

One by one the women filed by to examine the drawing. Then they slowly resumed dressing and gathering their belongings.

"Ask her if she's willing to testify in court," Norah appealed to the translator. "Tell her I'll try to help her with Immigration. I can't promise anything, but I'll do my best."

The woman whispered with Viorica for several moments. "She don't ask for no special treatment. Her son died on the trip, and Benita Cruz made sure he had a decent grave. She will do whatever you want."

Chapter 13

THE AGENTS had trampled through the aliens' living quarters handling, overturning, destroying any evidence that might have supported Viorica Amara's testimony, or at least rendering it unusable in court. Norah herself always made sure nothing was disturbed till the arrival of the forensic team, but Bruce Creech had all the evidence he needed in the persons of the aliens and their guards, so no care was needed and no experts would be called. Norah wasn't overly disturbed; she suspected that the clues to link Connick and Haney to the rape of Benita Cruz and perhaps her murder would be elsewhere, most probably in one of the nearby buildings.

There were three: one, small and dilapidated—an abandoned outhouse; another, a stable with six unoccupied stalls; the last, a larger, well-constructed building used apparently as living quarters for staff.

"Coverted chicken coop," Bruce Creech observed.

Norah's eyebrows went up. Her idea of a chicken coop was a wire-mesh cage about four feet square with maybe half a dozen chickens screeching and scratching the dirt floor. She knew that farming had become sophisticated, but she'd had no idea it had progressed to two-story residences for chickens.

"This whole complex was once part of the biggest farm in the county," Creech explained. "Five hundred acres. Belonged to the Rostal family. Everybody around here has had some bad years, but they had invested the most, modernized and so on. So they hurt the most. They had to start selling off parcels. I hear some city realtor bought up all of this and is planning to construct one of those recreation villages complete with manmade lake. Along with everything else, whoever's behind this is going to get hit with a trespassing charge."

He held the door for her and they went in.

The front room was a sitting room furnished with hand-me-downs, plain pieces made of good solid maple. The bedrooms upstairs were small, limited to the essentials. The larger of the two held a double bed with spindle headboard, a bureau, and one wooden chair. Men's clothes hung in the closet. A letter on the bureau was addressed to Ben Connick.

"They could have brought her here," Norah suggested.

Creech nodded.

Where else? Norah wondered. Why anywhere else? This was handy. This was private. They had brought Benita Cruz here for her punishment and their pleasure. The first time. The room was neat enough superficially, but there must surely be evidence of the girl's presence—blood, hair, fibers. She pulled down the faded quilt; the bed linen was clean, so was the mattress underneath. Tucking the sheets back under, she noticed a hair caught around one of the headboard spindles, a long dark hair. She pointed it out to Creech.

"Could be."

Norah knelt on the oval braided rug beside the bed to examine the floorboards. She couldn't find anything. The rug itself seemed very bright, almost new. Abruptly she got up and stepped off it. She turned it over. The other side was faded and badly stained. Some of the spots were fresher than others; they were spatters and they looked like rust.

Norah itched to take Connick and Haney in on an assault charge, but she had no jurisdiction. Anyway, she would have to turn them over to Blegen, and she was still reluctant to do that. It was academic anyway; Creech was not likely to let anyone else have them, not for a while. He had been considerate of her position and needs, even helpful where he could be. She didn't even suggest it.

The two guards were held by the INS on a charge of conspiracy to harbor aliens. Creech hoped that an investigation would reveal they were also guilty of conspiracy to smuggle and transport. Meantime, they were taken, along with their victims, to the detection center. There Creech got down to serious interrogation. What he wanted was the name of the employer, the person or persons behind the operation. He wanted to turn them.

But the two, together and separately, refused to name anybody. They refused to admit that the women found in the dormitory worked a night shift at any factory anywhere. They refused to say what the women were doing there or where they came from. They didn't utter a word.

They were arraigned and bail set at one thousand dollars.

Though he appeared calm, Creech seethed inwardly. His black beard bristled in his frustration. These two were no better than slavers! Fortunately, low as the bail was, neither one of them could make it. Whoever their employer was, he didn't care to reveal himself by coming forward or by sending someone to pay it. Now that he knew he'd have them till the case came to trial, Creech could afford to let them stew awhile. Not too long. He waited the rest of the week, then had them brought up again.

"I've got to tell you that the law is very loose on the matter of sentencing for this kind of offense," he informed them regretfully. This was no act. In Creech's opinion a stiff sentence should be mandatory. He went on. "You could get three months; you could get five years. My recommendation could make the difference."

No reaction.

"Or I could turn you over to the local police. They want you real bad on a charge of aggravated assault and rape. Now we're talking real time, up to twenty-five years."

Benjamin Connick, blond, macho, obviously the leader, and William Haney, younger and bigger, with a pudgy baby face and bad skin though he was twenty-four, exchanged one agonized glance. Creech caught it; that was when he picked up the phone. "Ask Sergeant Mulcahaney to step in here, please."

He noted their reaction to that too; apparently they didn't take the lady seriously. In the short time Bruce Creech had known her, he did and he was looking forward to watching them change their minds.

Norah tapped at the door but indicated to Creech that she wanted to speak to him privately. They stepped outside. After a brief conference, they returned.

"I'm going to release you," Creech told the prisoners.

Their eyes lit up.

"To Sergeant Mulcahaney," he added.

Connick smirked. Haney grinned unabashedly.

"An officer is on his way over from York Crossing with a warrant for your arrest on the charge of murder," Norah told them.

The smiles disappeared. They looked incredulous. "Murder!" Connick gasped. "What are you talking about?"

"The murder of Benita Cruz."

"Who's Benita Cruz? I don't know any Benita Cruz. Do you, Will?"

Haney joined in the act. "Not me. Never heard of her."

"She was in your room," Norah said to Connick. "Her blood, menstrual blood, was spattered on your rug and along your baseboard. One of her hairs was caught in the headboard of your bed. The soiled sheets were still in the laundry hamper when the forensic people searched. You didn't do a very good cleanup job. But I don't suppose that you expected anybody would go looking."

Connick's eyes glazed over. "I don't know what you're talking about."

"Maybe it was your buddy who raped her and beat her. Maybe your buddy did it in your room."

Before Haney could respond, Ben Connick jumped in. "Don't try that old ploy on us. You can't prove any of this stuff. You're a crazy lady; everybody knows that. Nobody's going to pay any attention to anything you say."

Creech threw her a questioning look, but she ignored it. In fact, she was glad that Connick had made the remark. For all her doubts about Chief Blegen, she didn't think he had advertised her condition after the raid; the most he might have done was discuss it with Dr. Gruenwald, and she certainly didn't think Gruenwald would gossip. The fact that Connick knew indicated he and Haney had been involved in setting her up. She would vindicate herself, she thought, but in her own way and in her own time.

"We have a witness," she said.

"What witness?"

"A witness who will swear that you assaulted Benita Cruz."

Haney looked scared. Streams of sweat ran down his fat face, but his blond partner laughed. "How the hell can you have a witness to a rape?"

"Your victim identified the two of you as her assailants. She pointed you out to her friend, and her friend is going to stand up in court and testify."

"So what?"

"She'll also testify, based on her own knowledge and observation, that you were part of the escort on her trip along with seven other women across country from California, that you acted as guards and stood over them with guns. She'll tell that Benita Cruz planned to escape and that she succeeded. She got away in the late morning while everyone else was still sleeping. The two of you were on duty. When you discovered that she was gone, you questioned the women, but no one knew anything about it. She remembers that you made a phone call and the night guard came to take over. Then you left, obviously to search for the girl.

"When it was time, the women went to work as usual. They worked all night and came back to find Benita Cruz lying on her cot. She was sick, bloody, and bruised. She told them that she had been kept prisoner all night, beaten, and violated, over and over again. She told them who did it."

Connick's eyes were hooded. He shrugged. "It's her word, a spic's word against—"

"Against that of a pair of fine upstanding citizens caught in the act of harboring illegal aliens," Creech put in. "Or are you going to claim that you didn't know the women were in the country illegally? Not that it matters; you were holding those women against their will and that's involuntary servitude, peonage, slavery."

"Shit!" Haney couldn't stifle a groan.

"Benita Cruz's blood on your rug and on your walls, her hair on your bed, and the soiled linen will back up the spic." Norah spoke quietly but her blue eyes were ominously dark.

"So what do you want from us?" Connick asked.

Looking for a deal, Norah thought. Okay. So was Creech. So was she, for once.

"I want to know whose van you were driving when you first went out looking for the girl on Sunday." She looked from one to the other. "Yours or his?"

"We borrowed it," Connick answered.

Norah didn't ask from whom; she would later. "How about the second time? On Tuesday morning when you showed up for work, she was missing again. You did go out looking?" Neither replied. "Did you still have the vehicle?"

"No," both blurted out at the same time.

"So you went out in your own car?"

"No." Again together.

"We didn't go after her," Connick explained. "I swear to God, we didn't go. Look, it was snowing. We had no way of knowing how much of a head start she'd had; she could have been gone all night, then how the hell could we track her? We called the boss. He said don't bother; he'd take care of it himself."

"How was he going to do that?"

Connick shrugged.

"Well, if it was that easy, he must have known where she went, right? So then why didn't he take care of it the first time? Why did he send the two of you after her then?"

Connick shrugged again.

"We'll have to ask him. His answer could be very important for both of you."

"Damn!" Connick exclaimed. "Don't you ever give up? We didn't tell him the first time. We figured we could get her back without anybody knowing she'd got away. I mean, it didn't look good for us that she'd escaped. So Will borrowed the Bronco and we went looking. We found her and we brought her back."

Norah waited. So did Creech.

"Okay, so we roughed her up. Okay, we raped her. It wasn't such a terrible thing. She didn't put up much of a fight." He paused. "She was no virgin."

Norah clenched her teeth and forced herself to be silent.

Connick realized instantly he'd made a big mistake. "Hell, we all had a little fun." He knew he was making it worse and gave up. "We didn't mean to hurt her. We did . . . what we did . . . then, but we don't know nothing about the second time. We knew that we didn't have a chance in a thousand of catching up with her, and we didn't even try. You got to believe that."

"That'll be up to the jury."

Will Haney looked to his buddy and then, for once in his life, made his own decision. "Ask Roy!" he cried. "Go ahead, ask Roy. He'll tell you he said not to bother."

"Roy?" Norah repeated.

"Roy Lee Bates. He's the one got us mixed up in this whole lousy thing. He's the one running it."

"You don't mean Roger LaBate?"

"Yeah, yeah. That's what he calls himself now."

Special Agent Creech wanted Roger LaBate for bringing in and transporting illegal aliens, for subjecting them to involuntary servitude. Sergeant Mulcahaney wanted LaBate for the murder of his wife and possibly that of Benita Cruz. Creech argued for immediate arrest; Norah thought they should wait for the lab report from New York.

Without her having spelled it out, Bruce Creech understood there was a possibility that somehow Chief Blegen might be injolved. No matter how remote, it couldn't be overlooked. They both reasoned that as long as LaBate believed no one knew, he would stay and tough it out. To run would be to give up the house and the plant he had inherited and shut down what had become a very profitable business. So Creech agreed to wait for a reasonable period. He didn't have to wait long. Norah got the call that night.

"We found what we were looking for in both samples you sent," Asa Osterman told her.

"Both?" She had hardly dared hope for that.

"That's what I said. The stain on the blouse yielded scopolamine in an eyedrop formulation. The sediment in the broken coffee cups was suggestive. The first piece tested negative. The second yielded a minuscule amount, but as that evidence seemed of particular importance . . ."

Had he guessed? Norah wondered. Or had word of her condition somehow got back to New York? Osterman would never tell and she would never ask. "Yes, it is, very important."

Osterman grunted. "We made an extra effort. The coffee in one of the cups was laced with the same ophthalmalogic formula."

She sighed with relief. "I can't thank you enough."

"Forget it. Where do you want the official report sent?"

So he did know, Norah thought. "To Chief Blegen in York Crossing."

"He'll have it by morning."

"Morning?"

"Be seeing you." Osterman hung up.

Norah hung up too, slowly. Though it was night, she felt as she leaned against the yellow kitchen wall that the sun was shining. The only way the lab report could reach Chief Blegen so quickly was if Asa had already sent it. He had done so because he had trusted her professional integrity. His parting words, "Be seeing you," underscored that confidence. He knew she would be back to face her responsibilities.

"Illegal search and seizure!" Blegen protested, slapping the New York report he had received in the morning mail. "The evidence isn't admissible. You ought to know that, Sergeant."

Norah sat quietly while the chief ranted. Special Agent Creech, who had met her at the York Crossing police station by arrangement, also remained quiet, appreciating that the chief was in a difficult and embarrassing situation. Creech, however, was not quite as sympathetic as Norah. In his opinion, the man had brought it on himself.

Blegen's eyes were bloodshot, his jowls hung loose. He was sweating. "You had no right to enter and search the LaBate house . . ." he muttered, beginning to run down.

"I had Bridie Deely's permission," Norah pointed out in a conciliatory way. "I gave her a receipt for the blouse."

"The hired girl!"

"She was the only one there. Anyway, there's nothing illegal about the other piece of evidence. The coffee cup came from my kitchen."

"That would be great if you could remember who drank the coffee with you." Blegen was bitingly sarcastic.

"You think there's more than one person running around doctoring drinks with scopolamine?" Bruce Creech asked.

Roger LaBate was not at home when they arrived. Norah's first thought was that they had misjudged him, she and Creech, and that he had run out after all. She dared not look at the immigration agent.

They proceeded to the plant. It was in full operation. The machines hummed; women bent over them working with even more intensity than on Norah's first visit. There was also a sense of distraction. They looked up at the entrance of the three law officers and never quite got back full concentration. These were townswomen, legally employed, members of the union, earning good wages with all benefits, yet their shoulders slumped and they were . . . dispirited. Just as the aliens had known instantly that they were being rounded up, so these women knew that their jobs were suddenly in jeopardy. Along with Creech and Blegen, Norah climbed the stairs to the mezzanine office. LaBate was on the telephone. She shot a glance at Creech and they shared a brief grin of relief.

"I can't get the order out by the twelfth!" LaBate was both angry and anxious. "We're working as fast as we can, but . . ." He caught sight of the visitors and his tone moderated. "I'm sorry, we're just not going to be able to ship the order on that date. You'll have to be patient. . . . Fine! If you feel you can do better somewhere else . . . all right. *All right!*" he snapped, his attitude veering sharply yet again. *"Go ahead and cancel!"* He slammed the receiver down. "No patience," he commented with a thin attempt at a smile. "Everybody wants his—yesterday."

"You should put on more people," Creech suggested.

"I can't afford it," LaBate replied.

"You miss your night shift."

"I never ran a night shift. Who are you?"

Creech continued. "Two of your employees, Benjamin Connick and William Haney, say you did. They have testified that you employed illegal aliens."

"What's he talking about?" LaBate demanded at large. Then he turned on Blegen. "Is he with you?"

"Special Agent Creech, Immigration and Naturalization Service," Creech answered for himself, and showed his credentials.

LaBate's florid complexion turned to ashes but he was far from giving up. He kept on Blegen. "What's he doing here?"

"I'm sorry, LaBate."

"Sorry? Sorry doesn't make it, man!"

Blegen flushed, but he kept his eyes level and held onto his official demeanor. "Connick and Haney say they were working for you. They have signed statements swearing that you employed illegal aliens in a night shift in this factory, and that you transported and harbored them."

The ex-disco dancer, stripper, male prostitute, swelled his broad chest in a show of indignation. His blond brows drew together and he seemed ready to explode. Then he changed his mind. "Damn!" he muttered. "I don't suppose arguing will do any good." He glared at the chief, but he addressed Creech. "Okay, what's it going to cost me?"

"That'll be up to the judge."

"You're going to put me out of business; you realize that. You realize what that means? That means all those people down there are going to lose their jobs." He pointed dramatically with extended arm to the women on the floor, who were by now doing very little besides casting anxious glances up to the office. "Most of those women are the sole support of their families; farmers' wives whose salaries are paying off bank loans and staving off foreclosure. You're sentencing them. You're putting them on unemployment, and when the benefits run out, what the hell are they going to do? This town needs this plant."

From Creech he looked to Blegen and then finally, reluctantly, he included Norah. "What's so terrible about employing aliens? If I could have afforded to hire another sixty locals, believe me, I would have. But I can't pay the inflated salaries and benefits. My God, the benefits! So I hired people that were willing to work for less. Because of the low costs, I'm able to sell at a more attractive price and beat the competition. That's business. That's the American way. Because of the aliens, I could keep those local citizens down there employed." He paused. "That's right, isn't it, Chief?"

Blegen sighed.

"The chief is a realist. It's too damn bad that the government isn't." LaBate reached for the phone.

Blegen watched as though in a trance.

Norah jumped forward. "Hold it."

"I get to call my lawyer, don't I?"

"Not yet. There's more."

"Listen, you busted in here the other night, damaged my property, started rumors—libelous rumors that smeared my reputation . . ."

Norah marveled at his continued arrogance, but she had her own counteraccusation to make. "And you poisoned me."

"What?"

"Over a period of fourteen hours I lost all memory. Was put into a psychotic state, rendered irresponsible for my actions."

"That much is true, all right, but I can't claim credit."

"The seizure was caused by scopolamine which I ingested with my coffee."

"Do either of you know what she's talking about?" LaBate appealed to the two men, then back to Norah. "I think you've lost your marbles for good, Sergeant Mulcahaney."

"I have here a copy of the lab report which states the coffee I drank was mixed with scopolamine contained in a prescription-eyedrop formula."

"So?"

"So the stain on the blouse which your wife wore on the afternoon she died was also analyzed. It was from a martini laced with the same eyedrop formula. That formula was specifically prescribed for her by her ophthalmologist."

For once LaBate had no quick response.

"You poisoned me, and the poison wore off; you poisoned your wife, and it killed her."

He shook his head incredulously. "The woman is out to nail me. God, it should be obvious that she's trying to explain her craziness."

"You've admitted mixing your wife's martini," Norah reminded him. "Are you asking us to believe that she poisoned her own drink?"

Abruptly LaBate sat down. He wiped his face with

his open palm. "It was an accident," he said. "I didn't mean for her to die."

There was a hush in the small glass-walled office. The whirring of the sewing machines below was distant. Up here, for a heartbeat, it had stopped.

"I only wanted Millie to forget," LaBate explained. "To forget what you'd put into her head," he accused Norah. "*You* made her suspicious. You showed up asking questions, making insinuations. Millie was shrewd; she was also old-fashioned, scared to death to do anything a little out of line. You put it into her head that we were running an extra shift. When her first husband was alive, she used to be the bookkeeper. So as soon as you were gone, she went up to the attic and got out the old accounts. She compared them with the current figures, and of course, even allowing for expansion and higher prices, they didn't jibe. She asked for an explanation. I managed to put her off, but I knew that wasn't going to be the end of it. She'd worry at it till she got the whole story. And she wouldn't have gone along. No way. Not Millie. She would have shut us down. All I wanted was to wipe out that particular set of memories. That's all. That's all."

Norah sighed. "You'd used the eyedrops before."

He looked down.

Norah thought of Bridie Deely. "To cover up flings with other women."

"Yes. All right, yes. She was old, an old woman. I'm still young."

Bridie was young, Norah thought. Thirteen years young, Bridie was. "You fed your wife the poison over and over."

"I didn't mean for her to die!" he shouted. "It was an accident."

Blegen stepped forward with the handcuffs.

"I want my lawyer." LaBate pulled back.

"Not yet," Norah said.

Now LaBate was thoroughly frightened. From Norah he looked to the chief, still hoping for help. "What the hell is she trying to do to me?"

"I've got to read him his rights," Blegen said to Norah.

"Go ahead."

She stood beside Bruce Creech while the chief took out the little-used plastic card he carried in his wallet and mumbled through the printed warning. When he was finished, he put it back in its compartment. "Do you understand these rights as I have explained them to you?"

"Sure. It means I can call my lawyer and I don't have to say another word till he gets here."

"Right, Mr. LaBate," Norah replied for the chief. "Not unless you want to."

He just stared, lips pressed together.

"According to your employees Connick and Haney, one of your captive aliens attempted to escape. Her name was Benita Cruz. She was found by them and brought back. They used your new, shiny Bronco to go after her. That was the first time. She tried again, but the second time they couldn't go after her because they'd returned the Bronco to you and didn't have another suitable vehicle. So they called you to tell you she was gone. You said not to worry, that you'd take care of it."

Norah paused, but LaBate waited her out.

"The next day, Benita Cruz's body was found in an irrigation ditch five miles from the place where the aliens were housed. She'd been shot in the back of the head with a twenty-two. But you know all that; it's been in all the papers. The only major murder case in York Crossing in . . . how many years, Chief?"

"Is she accusing me of being involved in that girl's murder?" LaBate was incredulous.

"I'm giving you a chance to explain," Norah said.

"You're something else! Okay. I'm telling you that I don't know anything about that girl. I don't even know that she worked for me; maybe she did, maybe she didn't. I never said I'd take care of finding her because I didn't know she was gone, not the first time, not the second. *Nobody* ever called me."

"How about the Bronco? They claim they returned it to you on Monday morning."

"Sure, with the gears stripped. It went right to the garage."

"I saw it in your driveway two days later."

"Right, that's when I got it back, on Wednesday. Cost me seven hundred bucks. Check it out, lady."

"You still had the Mercedes."

"Which I used to take Millie to Philadelphia to a big dinner and fashion show. It started to snow early that night, so we stayed over. We didn't get home till nearly noon on Tuesday."

"That, they both knew, was well after Benita Cruz's body had been found.

Gloating, Roger LaBate was ready to rub in his triumph. "You can ask . . ." he began, and then stopped.

"Millie?" Norah finished for him.

Chapter 14

THE CHARGES and countercharges almost wiped each other out.

Both LaBate's home and the factory were searched for the gun that had been used to kill Benita Cruz. It didn't turn up. The quarters of the two guards didn't yield it either. Lacking it, there was no positive proof of murder against either employer or employees so each would be tried on the lesser charges: Connick and Haney for assault and rape, LaBate for manslaughter.

Then a witness came forward, Emmanuel Wien, a farmer. Mr. Wien stated that Ben Connick called him at approximately eleven-thirty on Monday night, the night of Benita Cruz's second escape attempt—he kept his watch half an hour fast as was the custom of a great many Dutchmen who valued punctuality to the point of obsession—making it actually eleven P.M. Anyhow, Connick wanted to borrow Wien's pickup truck for a couple of hours. Wien said all right, but he would need it in the morning and Connick promised to have it back no later than five A.M., English time, and kept his word.

Confronted with Wien's testimony, both guards now admitted that they had not called Roy Lee, as

222

they continued to refer to him. As on the first occasion, they had been afraid of getting fired for having let the girl escape. They went out in Farmer Wien's pickup truck to look for her. At first light, they gave up. The storm had intensified. They rationalized that since she was in the country illegally she wouldn't go to the police, that they didn't need to be afraid she would turn them in because that would mean revealing herself as an illegal and betraying her friends as well. It would get them all deported. It was the last thing in the world the girl wanted, they assured themselves, and went back to the barn dormitory to stand their daylight shift.

Nobody bought the story. They had a strong motive for wanting to get rid of Benita Cruz once and for all. Now that it was known they'd had transportation, the county district attorney decided to up the charge to murder. Though the case was circumstantial, Norah believed he would get a conviction.

It was time to go home.

But there was still one unresolved problem: what to do about Richard Blegen. Strict justice demanded that she speak out, yet she was reluctant. As she put out the suitcases and started to pack her country clothes and select what she would wear for the trip back to the city, the doorbell downstairs rang. Probably the Meyers come to say good-bye, she thought and, glad of an interruption, ran down to answer.

"Chief!" She was both surprised and a little embarrassed.

The big man was pale, his sagging face oiled with sweat, his eyes almost swollen shut. It could have been an allergy, except that Norah smelled liquor as rank as though he'd doused himself with it. Nevertheless, Blegen held himself remarkably straight. Only a tremor of the hand in which he held a burning cigarette betrayed that he had been drinking heavily.

"May I come in? I'll only take a few minutes of

your time." His voice, low and hoarse, was under control.

"Of course. Come in."

Norah led the way into the parlor and indicated the wing chair, which Blegen did not take. Instead, he located an ashtray and put out the burning cigarette only half-consumed and lit another. In the process, the shaking of his hands became more pronounced. The fresh cigarette lit, he inhaled the smoke desperately. His presence filled the small room, his unease communicated to Norah.

"May I get you some coffee? A drink?" Sometimes the hair of the dog really did help.

It cost him an effort to turn it down. "Nothing, thank you. This isn't a social call. Well, it is and it isn't. I came to say good-bye, to thank you, and to wish you well."

She wished he hadn't come. All of a sudden she had reached a decision, and his having come here made it that much harder.

"I also came to tell you that I'm resigning."

"Oh?"

"You're surprised?"

Norah sat down. "No, actually, I don't think so. I am glad."

"I never took money, you know."

So. She had wondered at LaBate's silence. She had been surprised that he hadn't tried to drag Blegen down with him.

"I knew what was going on," Blegen continued. "A lot of people did. How could we help it? We kept quiet, all of us, in the best interest of the community—we thought. The town is dying. The loss of sixty jobs would have been, will be, a severe blow. It's not the jobs themselves, of course, but the chain reaction."

Norah sighed. That had been LaBate's justification.

The police chief paused. He was not calmed by his

admission. It brought no relief; to the contrary, sweat broke out again on his flabby face, settling into the creases. He took a couple more drags, then ground out his smoke. "The truth of it is, I didn't want to lose my job. I was . . . encouraged to retire from my previous positions—first from the force because I turned in men who were on the pad. I gave evidence to Internal Affairs. Nobody wanted any part of me after that. I got a good security job in private industry. I was eased out when I discovered a couple of the top executives were running a scam, stealing hundreds of thousands from their own company. So when I found out what was going on here, I was afraid to call INS; I was afraid I'd get booted out another time."

Norah waited.

"I realized that those women were being held in virtual slavery," he admitted.

It wasn't enough.

"I let it slip to LaBate that you were staking out his plant. I'm sorry for what happened . . . for what he did to you. I'm sorry."

Still Norah waited.

"I'm responsible for two deaths," he said at last.

She sighed, very softly.

"If I had reported what I knew was going on at La-Bate's, both women—the girl, Benita Cruz, and Millie LaBate—might still . . ." He shook his head and took a deep breath. "If I had reported what I knew was going on, both women would, in all probability, still be alive."

Then he crumpled. He reached a hand to the chair Norah had offered and fell into it. He fumbled for his pack but did not light another cigarette. Instead, he tossed the pack aside and the hands folded in his lap were finally still. Norah pitied him but could offer no consolation. Evidently he wanted something from her; he kept looking at her and waiting.

"I don't intend to seek another job in law enforcement," he told her. "Is there anything to be gained by making it public that I knew?"

He was basically a decent man, a good cop whose honesty had been tested too many times, Norah thought. He had learned his lesson. A harsher discipline demanded formal charges and public disgrace. Would it be any worse than the punishment he had chosen himself? True, there would be no prison sentence, but neither would there be an end to the self-imposed penalty, no probation, no parole.

"No," she told him. "Nothing."

Norah finished packing and went to bed early. Tomorrow would be a long day. She was already thinking past the drive back to the actual arrival. To being home again. It would be good to be in her place, among her own things, the familiar things she and Joe had accumulated, reminders of their life together. She wanted to think of Joe easily, in a warm but ordinary, everyday context. She could handle that now. And the family; she could handle that too. How about the job?

She had run away from crime and violence only to learn it was inescapable. Jim Felix had warned her. He'd been right. On the other hand, she hadn't been completely wrong. There was more respect for the law outside the cities. She had not felt overwhelmed with apathy and indifference. She'd been able to work with concentration and had solved her case.

But had she?

Lying awake in the now familiar and comforting country silence, Norah wished that the case against Connick and Haney were stronger. She reviewed it and was stuck, as she had been at the very beginning, on the abandonment of the body in the open ditch. That was the flaw. Why had they left the body where it could be so quickly and easily discovered? They could have transported it. But where? They could have buried it. But how? First they would have had to clear the snow to find a likely spot, but could they break the frozen ground? They would have had to come prepared with pickaxes as well as shovels. They might have dug a grave under the floor of the unused stables, but that was too close to home. Norah had gone over and over the problem. The only logical explanation had to be that the two killers intended to bury the girl, maybe just by piling snow on her in the very ditch where she had been found. Perhaps they'd been interrupted in the process and forced to flee.

Now, on the eve of her departure, Norah simply was not satisfied, and, as so often happened after she'd worried a problem from every possible angle, when she'd given up and was ready to go on to other things, her subconscious mind, unbidden, presented a solution. As always, once she had it, it seemed obvious. Undoubtedly the prosecutor had already thought of it. Just in case, Norah promised herself she would check with his office before leaving in the morning.

Trying to get the information the next morning, Norah was reminded yet again how difficult it was to work from the outside. Okay, she thought, if they didn't want to answer a simple question, she could find out for herself. It would mean putting off going home. For just one day. Norah realized suddenly how very much she wanted to go home; how very eager she was to pick up her life again. But first, she had to finish up here. Joe would have agreed, she thought. And he would have been pleased.

"I didn't expect to see you again."

Norah couldn't tell whether Bruce Creech was pleased or not. She decided to react positively and smiled. "I couldn't go without saying good-bye."

"Really? You made the trip all the way over here just to say good-bye to me!" He leered, black beard bristling, light gray eyes twinkling as he searched her face. "I'm flattered."

Norah's smile broadened into a grin. "You made a big impression," she teased, but she meant it. "I also wanted to talk to the women."

"Ha! I knew it! What's up?"

"It's about Benita Cruz. Has the M.E. fixed the time of death?"

"He couldn't because of the cold. You know that. The body was as good as refrigerated."

Suddenly Norah had a clutch of anxiety. "She hasn't been buried yet, has she?"

Creech shook his head. "We've notified the family in Palmas al Lago and we're waiting to hear how they want it handled."

Thank God, Norah thought, more than ever convinced that her idea would work. "We can determine the time of death through how far digestion had progressed."

Creech frowned; not only was that simplistic, but it had been the first thing the M.E. had considered. "We don't know when she had her last meal."

"It doesn't matter." Norah was charged up. "We know that when the women got back from work on Monday morning and found Benita beaten, nearly comatose, they revived her, washed her, tried to make her comfortable. Presumably, they also fed her. If we know what they gave her and when, it doesn't matter what else she may or may not have had later on. All that's necessary is to trace the digestion of those particular foods."

"You've got it," he said.

"So?" Norah waited expectantly, then caught her breath as another possible impediment suggested itself. "They're not gone? The women? They haven't been shipped back?"

"It's quite evident that you're not familiar with the workings of federal agencies, Sergeant Mulcahaney," Creech replied sternly. "We move with all deliberate speed."

"What does that mean?"

"That means, my dear Norah, that they won't be out of here for another month at least. Let's go."

On the day of her second and final escape attempt, Benita Cruz had shared the women's regular afternoon meal consisting of dark pumpernickel bread and thick lentil soup. The stomach contents indicated she'd had a light snack consisting of a ham sandwich on white and milk. That remained in her stomach, indicating it had been ingested between two and four hours prior to death—give or take. The dark bread and soup had passed into the duodenum, then the jejunum. Taking into account the weakened physical condition of the victim, the amount of food, the strength of the gastric juices, the pathologist cautiously estimated that she had died sometime after five A.M. of the Tuesday—give or take.

By five that morning Connick and Haney had returned the borrowed pickup truck to Farmer Wien and were back in the dormitory. The women confirmed it. Having found Benita missing again, they had waited anxiously for the two guards, fearing that they would be dragging her with them, expecting that they would have to care for her as before. Some of them even wondered what they should do. There had been talk of refusing to work unless a doctor was called. When the guards returned without the fugitive, there had been a silent, but common, sense of relief. Benita was free. They would not be called on to do anything. Nevertheless, it had been hard for them to settle down. They had slept through the daytime hours only fitfully. They were able to affirm, reluctantly, that the guards had not left their post.

Ben Connick and Will Haney had an alibi supported by fifty-nine witnesses.

* * *

Norah went back to the house and unpacked. It all depended on why the body had been left in the ditch.

Could the shooting have been an accident, committed by a stranger who walked away secure in the knowledge that there was no connection between him and his victim? A hunting accident? But who would have been out hunting in the middle of a snowstorm? Who went hunting with a twenty-two revolver?

On the day of the storm, Bridie Deely had gone to work early, school having been canceled, and she had testified that Mr. and Mrs. LaBate hadn't returned from Philadelphia till well after noon. So, though his wife wasn't alive to support it, Roger's alibi stood. Just the same, Norah continued to dwell on his part in the events that led to Benita Cruz's death far from home in the open fields of the Pennsylvania farm country. It was Millicent LaBate who had the business background, yet Roger had set up a sophisticated and duplicitous operation without her knowledge. She had provided the premises for the work, but how had he, a stranger in these parts, discovered the old deserted barn in which to house and hide the aliens? The spot was not only lonely but also fortuitously located on land recently sold but not yet put to use. He had to have had advice, guidance from someone local. Norah phoned Bruce Creech.

"The land on which the dormitory was located—who owned it originally?"

"I told you, don't you remember? The Rostal family."

"Yes, but I can't locate any Rostals in the county."

"The only one left is the daughter. She's Kate Droste now."

Karl Droste had married the daughter of a neighboring farmer, joining the two largest tracts in the county; Willie Meyer had told her that! He'd also told her Karl had been selling off parcels of his land because he owed the banks, that he was down to the central core of his holdings and still hurting.

"What have you got?" Creech asked, but she had already hung up.

Norah remembered Karl Droste's surliness when she had first approached him for the hire of a horse. She had put it down to the ingrained local resistance to strangers, but perhaps he had already known about her police connection and simply hadn't wanted her around? Then, being the man he was, he'd decided to face the danger, to challenge his destiny, and so he'd invited her to come and ride, to look, to find—if she could. At the same time, he'd kept her under observation, gained her confidence. If she should suspect anything, she'd go straight to him. And she had. Oh, yes! Norah thought bitterly, on the day she had witnessed Benita being forced into the Bronco, she had gone directly to Karl Droste. She had allowed him to still her fears and allay her suspicions. She had accepted him as a friend, and he had used her.

She had sympathized with the aridity of his marriage. She had believed that he was reaching out from his loneliness to hers. She had believed that they were helping each other. The long rides together, the discussions, had been both consoling and stimulating. She had grown to depend on them, had built her days around them so that later on solitude was bearable and became healing. How could she have been so gullible? Such a willing dupe? Even now Norah found it hard to visualize Droste as partner with Roger LaBate, but necessity, much more than politics, made strange alliances.

Assuming Karl had been informed that the girl was missing a second time, how had he managed to track her in the middle of a raging storm? And then back to the original question: having found her and shot her, why did he leave her in the ditch?

Norah paced the parlor. She sat down; she stood

up; she made coffee and let it grow cold. When she finally remembered to drink it, it was fit only to be poured down the sink.

Suppose that instead of his finding her, Benita Cruz had found him?

Norah's heart beat faster: the answer was within reach. Put yourself in the girl's place, she thought. Think as *she* thought; reconstruct what she must have done. Start after the rape. Benita is returned to the dormitory. The women nurse and comfort her. Then they have to go to work and they leave her. She is considered too sick to go with them, too sick to do anything. So nobody guards her. She knows that this will not happen again. If she is to get away ever, this is her chance. Okay. She leaves as soon as she is physically able, knowing that a good head start is important but not enough. To succeed, she needs help. So where does she go? What direction does she take? Except for the first attempt the day before, she has never even seen the surroundings by day. She has no more idea now where the town lies or even where there are any houses than she did then. Correction: she knows where there is one house.

It was almost five when Norah got into the Honda and drove to the Droste place, late for Karl to be at the stables, but she looked there first anyway.

He wasn't around. Bert Hadley, the hired hand, was, and unaccustomedly busy, in his element in fact, directing two boys in threadbare breeches and scuffed boots, rosy-cheeked and eager. The stable that had been nearly empty was now completely full. Every stall occupied. Yet Karl had told her that he was going out of "the horse business."

"Hi, Bert," she called. "I see you've got a full house."

"Hi, Miz Capretto. Yes, ma'am, we sure have. Beauties, ain't they?"

Exceptional, Norah thought. Fine strong animals

of noble aspect, far superior to what Droste usually traded in. "They look like thoroughbreds."

"Yes, ma'am, they are." Bert Hadley swelled with pride. The cracks in his rawhide skin were gleaming with the sweat of exertion and his faded eyes were bright with enthusiasm. "And they belong to us. We're gonna race them ourselves. Us."

Quite a turn, Norah thought. "Congratulations," she said. "And good luck."

"Thanks, Miz Capretto," he replied, but his attention was quickly distracted. "Hey, you—Josh! You call that mucking out?" He grabbed the shovel from the boy. "This is the way."

Thoughtfully, Norah walked down the aisle to Dandy's stall at the rear near the double doors. She found him looking forlorn amid the attention being given the newcomers. She had no sugar or carrot for him but she stroked him quietly for several minutes, murmured to him, savoring with particular poignancy the contact between them, the smell of horseflesh, of good leather, of hay and manure, knowing it was for the last time. She was saying good-bye to a friend. Finally, with a deep sigh of regret at parting and even deeper regret for what lay ahead, Norah left through the back and headed around to the house.

As usual, Ilse Raisbeck answered the door.

"I'd like to see Mr. Droste, please."

"Not home."

"Do you know where he is?"

"Beresford Farms."

That was in Maryland. It suggested he was still buying. "Please ask Mrs. Droste if she can see me."

"She's busy."

"Please go up and tell her I'm here. Tell her it's important."

Before the housekeeper could make another excuse, voices—a man's and a woman's—could be heard. Ilse tried to shut the door, but Norah brushed past her just as Kate Droste started down the stairs. She was dressed in simple, beautifully cut black satin pants and an artist-style white crepe shirt with graceful full sleeves cuffed at the wrists. She walked unassisted, neither leaning on Roger LaBate, who was beside her, nor using the handrail. She walked with confidence, even energy. Till she saw Norah. Then she stopped. Everyone froze. LaBate took the offensive.

"I thought you were supposed to be in New York," he accused.

"I thought you were in jail," Norah countered. "How good to see you up and around, Mrs. Droste . . . Kate."

The lady was not at all discomfited. "I have my good days." As though to prove it, she continued down the rest of the way with ease.

"I'm out on bail," LaBate explained.

Norah nodded but said no more.

"What can I do for you, Norah?" Kate Droste asked in her sweet, high voice.

"I came to talk to Karl, but maybe I should talk to you instead."

"I'll do my best."

"It's about Benita Cruz."

"Benita . . . ? Oh, yes." She cast a quick look at LaBate, an angry look that was at the same time intimate. "What could Karl possibly be able to tell you about her?"

"Benita Cruz made two attempts to escape from . . . her captivity." LaBate flushed, but Kate Droste remained unperturbed. "The first time, she managed to get within sight of this house, almost to the gate at the end of the lane, when she was caught and carried away. I wonder whether she made it the second time?"

"God! Don't you ever give up?" LaBate snarled.

Kate Droste put out a hand for his support. "I'd like to sit down, please," she murmured, and Roger instantly jumped to help her over to an upholstered bench against the wall.

Norah was not impressed. "Think back to March 8, Kate, a Monday. Was that a good day or a bad day for you?"

"I don't remember. How can I possibly remember? I don't have any point of reference." Delicately she raised a hand to her forehead as though she had a headache. But she was only shielding her eyes.

"You don't have to answer," LaBate told her. "This woman has no rights here." He turned on Norah. "You'd better leave before we call the real police. We can charge you with harassment, invasion of privacy, trespassing."

Norah ignored him, watching the woman on the bench, who was now genuinely pale and wan. "Was Karl at home on the night of the eighth and the morning of the ninth?"

"I don't remember."

"Ilse?"

The housekeeper's thin lips barely parted. "I don't remember."

Norah shrugged. "I can ask Karl when he gets back. I'm sure he keeps a calendar and he'll be able to tell me whether the girl found her way back here on that night or not."

"No, he won't, because he wasn't here," Kate Droste snapped. "I remember now. It was the night of the storm. Karl was away. This . . . Benita. Nobody was out that night. Nothing moved. Does that answer your question, Sergeant?"

Yes, Norah thought, it certainly does. It clears Karl. Not till this moment, when it was lifted from her, did she realize how heavily his betrayal had weighed.

"I have another question: does Karl own a twenty-two revolver? I know that he has a gun collection; does it include a twenty-two?"

"I haven't the slightest idea."

"You don't mind if I take a look." Without waiting, Norah started down the corridor toward the study.

"Yes! I do mind," Kate called, voice firm, commanding.

Norah stopped. She had to. "All right. I have no search warrant. By the time I'm able to get one and come back with the local police, you can quite easily get rid of the gun. Of course, Karl will know that it's missing. The next question, the crucial one: will he lie for you?"

Kate Droste had already dropped the pretense of friendliness; now her cautious reserve gave way to silent but open dislike.

"That will depend, I think, on whether or not he knows about your affair with Roger," Norah continued. "Unless you've been putting scopolamine in his drinks. Do you use prescription eyedrops, Kate?"

"Prescription eyedrops?"

"So that's a secret Roger didn't share. There are others: that he had women besides you—his hired girl for one."

"Don't believe her!" Roger snapped. "She's trying to make trouble between us. She's fishing."

"Has he performed his strip act for you? He did for Bridie Deely."

In a flash, Roger had raised his hand and struck Norah across the face. Her cheek flamed scarlet.

"You just got your bail revoked, Mr. LaBate," Norah told him as her eyes filled with the sting of pain. "Maybe that kind of violence arouses some women. It turns me off."

"You provoked me. You did it on purpose to provoke me."

"Shut up, Roger. It's me she wants to provoke," Kate Droste told him.

"I saw some fine new horses in the stable, Kate," Norah said. "And I hear you're going into racing. That takes a lot of money. Where did Karl get it?"

Kate didn't answer.

"You gave it to him, didn't you? What did you tell him? How did you explain suddenly coming into that much ready cash?"

Still no answer.

"Does he even suspect that the money for those fine animals and the others he intends to buy from Beresford Farms, for hiring grooms, a trainer, feeding, transportation to the tracks, all the expenses of the new venture, is the profit from slave labor?"

"I sold off some family jewelry."

"And of course you have the receipt."

The sham invalid cast off her fragility. "Those people were eager to work for what we paid!"

Though she was careful not to show it, Norah was relieved by the admission. She had the picture now, almost complete. Filling in the missing pieces was largely intuitive. "You and Roger were in business together. The affair—did that come before, or was it business insurance? Did you make love in order to tie Roger to the deal? Did he accommodate you for the same reason?" What would all this do to Karl when he found out? Norah wondered, and pitied what he faced. Of one thing she was sure: "When Karl finds out, I don't think he'll be inclined to lie for you—not about the gun, not about anything else."

While Kate Droste was formulating a defense, while Roger LaBate was backing off toward the door, the housekeeper spoke.

"I did it. I did it. I killed the girl," she announced flatly. "I took the gun out of the cabinet in Mr. Droste's study and I shot her."

Ilse Raisbeck's face was haggard, her eyes protruding and turned up so that the white was dominant. Spittle formed at the corner of her wrinkled lips and trickled down to her chin.

"No, no, Ilse . . . Don't say any more," Kate Droste pleaded. "Don't speak."

"I did it. I killed her."

"No!" Kate Droste appealed to Norah. "She's an old woman; she doesn't know what she's saying."

"Why? Why did you kill her, Ilse?" Norah asked.

The question appeared to confuse the housekeeper. She glared; then her eyes rolled down to a normal focus and narrowed craftily. "She came in the night." She paused as though she had explained everything; then she added condescendingly, "We were alone, Mrs. Droste and me. Mr. Droste was away. I heard a noise, somebody prowling around the house. I was in bed and nearly asleep when I heard the noise. I got up and looked out. It was snowing. I couldn't tell who it was, man or woman. All I could see was a figure going from window to window."

"But all the windows were locked securely and all the doors?"

"The bolt on the kitchen door was broken. I remembered that. She . . . the person . . . whoever it was . . . could get in that way. I went down and got the gun. Then I went and waited, and when she broke in . . . I shot her."

"Without asking what she was doing, what she wanted?"

"She . . . the person . . . had broken in. Why else could it be, but to rob and murder us."

"So without a single word . . . you just fired?"

"Yes."

"As she walked in the kitchen door?"

"Yes."

"Benita Cruz was shot in the back of the head."

The woman was confused, her determination shaken. She shivered, then pulled herself together. "I suppose when she saw the gun she turned around and tried to get away."

"You suppose?"

"It was dark. Naturally, I didn't turn on the light."

"Then how could she see the gun?"

Ilse Raisbeck smirked with satisfaction. "She didn't have to see it. She heard me. She knew she had been discovered, so she turned and tried to run."

"Then why did you shoot her? Never mind. She turned, and you shot her in the back of the head. Then what happened?"

"Then I had to get rid of her."

"How did you know she was dead?"

Pause.

"I knew. She didn't move or groan or anything."

"Why did you have to get rid of her? She was an intruder. You shot in self-defense. Why didn't you just call the police and tell them?"

For the first time since her confession, the housekeeper sent a glance, quick and beseeching, toward her employer. Norah waited, giving both women a chance—the one to change her story, the other to give some help. Neither availed herself.

"I didn't think of it," Ilse Raisbeck replied. "I was afraid they might not believe me. I don't know . . ."

"So you decided to dispose of the body. Tell me exactly what you did."

"Well, I went to get the car."

"Which car?"

"The van. And I put her into it."

"Just a minute. I want you to show me." Norah started for the kitchen. Though she had never been in that part of the house, it was easy to find, a matter of passing through the open arch to the formal dining room and then through a swinging pantry door. The three followed, too dazed to protest anymore. At the back door, Norah examined the bolt, which was in working order and showed no signs of having been either repaired or replaced, but she made no comment. She merely opened the door, letting in the cool spring breeze. Only Kate Droste shivered.

"All right, the intruder stood here." Norah took the position just inside the threshold. "Sensing that she'd been discovered, she turned." Norah did so.

"You fired, hitting her in the back of the head, and she fell."

Norah got down on her knees. "Show me the position of the body."

"I . . . I'm not sure."

"Did she fall forward or backward?"

"Forward."

"Like this?" She lay down, head outside the door, feet inside. "Then what did you do?"

"I went to get the car."

"You just left her lying across the open doorway? Suppose Mrs. Droste had wakened and come down to find her?"

"I pulled her outside."

"All right, do it."

Despite her age—she was well into her sixties— Ilse Raisbeck had always carried herself erect. She was thin, her flesh hanging in raddled folds, but her frame was rigid. Since childhood, by training and as a reflection of her ethic, she had never allowed herself to slump in weariness, either of body or of spirit. At this moment, drawing herself up and calling on every bit of her will, she seemed to fill out and to grow in strength. She seized Norah under the armpits and heaved.

She couldn't budge her.

Color suffused Ilse Raisbeck's gray face. She straightened, took a couple of deep breaths, bent lower, and tried again. Though she strained every sinew of muscle and every effort of will, she couldn't drag Norah's inert and unresisting body a foot.

"You're much heavier." She was gasping. Her face was flushed with the exertion—and the failure.

Norah got up. "No one realizes how difficult it is to handle a deadweight unless he's tried. You had help."

"No. I did it alone."

"In moments of stress, a person can summon superhuman strength," LaBate asserted.

Norah paid no attention. "Did you help her, Kate?"

The answer was a long time coming. "No," she said, and for a while Norah thought that would be all. Then Kate Droste sighed. "No," she repeated. "That isn't the way it happened."

"Nein, Katerina! Nein, liebchen . . ."

Kate Droste, beautiful and scented, took the woman, haggard and shivering, rank with despair, and clasped her into her arms and kissed her raddled cheek. "My mother died when I was five years old," she told Norah. "Ilse came to take care of me and she's been taking care of me ever since."

The housekeeper began to cry, helplessly and hopelessly.

The pale, delicate face of her mistress quivered. Compassion was in her green eyes; the first and only time Norah had seen it. It was quickly gone. Kate separated herself from her old nurse.

"The girl arrived at about midnight on Monday," she began with her usual cool composure. "She came to the back door, rang, and Ilse let her in. The girl explained that she had run away and she asked Ilse for help. Ilse, of course, informed me, and I came down.

"The girl wanted help to get to New York, where she said she had friends. She said she would pay me back for her bus fare and whatever other cost was involved. Well, on the face of it it sounded all right, and I was inclined to do it. Then I thought: suppose she gets picked up later on? In New York or wherever else she might go? There's a big push on to round up aliens and deport them. Once they got her, they'd squeeze everything out of her: how she entered the country, who arranged it, who had first employed her. Immigration would shut us down." She paused. "Karl would find out.

"I couldn't take the risk. There was no use returning her to her . . . keepers; she'd just go on trying to escape till she succeeded. The only sensible solution was to send her back home to Mexico.

"I had Ilse prepare a light snack for her and then put her in one of the spare rooms for the night. I figured Roger would have no trouble getting her out of here by the next afternoon, when Karl was due back. But when I called Roger, there was no answer. Then I remembered that he and Millie had gone to Philadelphia for the fashion show and I reached him at his hotel. He said they were staying over because of the storm and that all the airports in the northeast were shut down so I'd have to keep her for another day anyway. I didn't like it, but there was nothing more I could do. I went back to bed. But I couldn't sleep. I tossed and turned for hours. Finally, around five, the storm seemed to have let up and I decided I should take her to an airport myself. I got up and went in to tell her to get ready. She was gone.

"I suppose she'd been up looking for something, the bathroom probably, and she'd overheard my talking with Roger. She'd understood just enough."

Norah nodded. "She ran away—for the last time."

"I took the van and went after her. The snow had stopped temporarily, so her tracks were still discernible and I had no trouble following and catching up. I reasoned with her, but she wouldn't listen. I told her it was best for her to go home. I told her she would never be able to get a decent job in this country; she would never be allowed to stay legally. I offered money. I reached out and grabbed her arm and tried to pull her up into the van. Instead, she pulled me down into the snow. We struggled. We rolled in the drifts. We tore each other's clothes and hair. We were at the edge of the irrigation ditch. She had managed to push me off. As I made one last lunge for her, I slipped on a patch of ice and fell." She lifted up the bottom of the left pants leg to show a bandage. "I sprained my ankle.

"The pain was severe. The girl saw that I was

hurt. She could have gone then; there was no way I could have stopped her. Instead, she picked up a rock and stood over me. Her eyes were wild. She meant to finish me. I knew it. I took the gun out of my pocket and I fired. I had no choice."

"She found a rock under eight or ten inches of snow?" Norah was openly skeptical.

"I know it doesn't sound likely, but it happened."

"All right. She stood over you with the rock. How did you come to shoot her in the back of the head?"

"I don't know. It was a wild night. It's very difficult to recreate exactly what happened. I suppose that when she saw the gun, she instinctively turned away."

"Then she was no longer threatening you," Norah pointed out.

"She still had the rock. She didn't drop it. She could have whirled back and hit me anytime."

"So you shot her and she fell into the ditch," Norah summed up. "You couldn't have hoped to move her under any conditions, certainly not with your injured ankle. She was far enough away from your house; there was no known link between you. So why not just leave her? It must have seemed an easy way out."

"I didn't intend to kill her. She tried to kill me." The composure broke. The control was slipping.

Indignation, anger, that was what Kate Droste portrayed, but underneath, Norah glimpsed fear. "I would like to believe you, Kate, but if you didn't mean to kill Benita Cruz, why did you take the gun? You were in a hurry to go after her, yet you took the time to go to your husband's study, unlock the gun cabinet, and take a weapon."

"I only meant to threaten her with it, to make her get into the van and come with me."

"And were you going to hold the gun on her to force her to get on the plane?"

"No, no, I meant to take her back to the house for Roger to deal with."

"But you didn't want her in the house. You didn't want her around when Karl returned."

Kate scowled. The contradictions were piling up. "He was delayed by the storm too, like everybody else. He called to say so. Didn't I mention it?"

"That's one more thing I'll have to ask him about," Norah said.

Kate Droste bit her lip and a bubble of blood appeared at the right corner. Her green eyes locked with Norah's. Then she began to shake. It was over, Norah thought. Kate knew that her husband would not back her up. Without his support, her story was fabrication. She could fall back into her invalid pose, but Norah didn't think that Karl would be gulled by it any longer. Maybe Kate didn't think so either. Maybe after all the years of holding him through pity, she knew that she couldn't now expect him to respond with love, Norah thought as the suspect's eyes dropped in acknowledgement of defeat. But even as Norah looked around for a phone from which to make her call, Kate Droste stopped shaking. She literally jumped from the kitchen door over the steps and fled across the backyard.

"Kate!"

There was no indication of a weak ankle; she was running fast and headed straight for the stables.

"Kate!" Norah called again, and lunged forward, only to be brought down in Ilse Raisbeck's steely embrace. What LaBate had said about the strength of desperation surely applied. As she struggled to break free, the housekeeper used her arms like tentacles—as Norah pried one loose and went to work on the other, the first tightened again. And she hung on Norah, inert, like the deadweight Norah had demonstrated as being close to an insurmountable impediment. While they struggled, both were watching out the open door and both saw Kate

Droste, mounted on Dandy, ride out of the stable. She almost paraded across the yard; then, setting her heels to his flanks, she kicked him into a gallop.

"What in the world . . . ? Ilse, for God's sake, let me go!" Norah was more annoyed than desperate. "Will you please get her off me," she appealed to LaBate. But LaBate wasn't around. He had taken his opportunity and fled. Then, all at once, Ilse Raisbeck let go. Surprised, Norah looked out and saw why— Kate astride Dandy had just jumped the fence and was headed across open country.

Norah only stared after them. There was no point in chasing them. By the time she saddled and mounted, it would be too late; besides, she lacked confidence for a chase on a strange horse. Not that it mattered, Norah thought; Kate couldn't get far. She must realize that. If she didn't, she would soon. The flight had been an instictive reaction. Still, why hadn't she taken the car? Wouldn't that have been logical? Suddenly, with a sinking feeling, Norah had the answer. She knew why Kate Droste had chosen to escape on Dandy and exactly where they were headed. She ran to the Honda.

The sun was setting fast, slashing the western sky with vermilion, but Norah headed east toward the dark. The narrow paved road seemed to be leading away from the direction taken by horse and rider, but it would actually curve up ahead and double back to a point where Norah could get out and intercept them on foot. The macadam was badly cracked by the cold of winter, heaving in spots, sinking in others, but she drove as though it were a perfect surface. At last, as she was rounding the curve, she could see Kate and Dandy nearing the top of the well-remembered hill. Dandy was at full gallop, Kate bent low over his neck. How she could ride! Norah was now driving along a parallel line. She kept on till she got well ahead. Then, stopping the car, she got out and started up the slope on foot, intending to step directly into the horse's path and somehow make him stop.

But Kate saw her and anticipated. She jerked Dandy to one side, at the same time urging him to greater speed. They flew past Norah. They passed so close that she looked directly up into Kate's contorted visage and smelled Dandy's sweat and terror. He left behind a cloud of his hard breathing in the cold air. There was nothing more she could do but stand and watch as they approached the lip of the quarry. Kate Droste was bent forward so low she could whisper almost into Dandy's ear. She slapped him with her open palm, for she carried no riding crop, then she rose in her stirrups for the jump.

Dandy did not jump. At the last instant he refused. Forelegs trembling with strain, head high and thrown back, he stopped as he had once before when Norah had been riding him—at the very edge. But Norah had been leaning back, resisting, and they hadn't been going nearly as fast. Now Kate Droste, up and out of the saddle, was urging the horse on, leaning as far ahead as she could. She went soaring over Dandy's head. Norah didn't hear the splatter as the body hit the rocks below; her heart was pounding too loud. She heard the scream. So did the horse. He began to shake convulsively and to whimper.

Norah ran to him, took his bridle, talked to him quietly. She stroked him and soothed him. The sun set. It was night when he had calmed enough so that Norah could lead him at a slow walk back to the stable.

At last Norah was home. Really home. She entered the closed, musty apartment and, looking around at the covered furniture, the dusty tables, shrouded lamps, felt a letdown. She had steeled herself for an onrush of memories and was confronted instead with an impersonal, empty set of rooms. She didn't know whether to be disappointed or relieved.

Meantime, she carried her suitcases into the bedroom and began doggedly to unpack. In the midst of it, the downstairs bell rang.

She hadn't advised anyone she was coming. She went to the vestibule and spoke into the intercom.

"Yes?"

"Jim Felix, Norah. May I come up for a few minutes?"

"Of course." She buzzed him in.

Norah hadn't even informed Gus Schmidt that she was closing his house and coming back. Probably the Meyers had told him and he had passed it on. Well, she'd been planning to visit Felix in the morning; his visit merely advanced the timetable. She whipped off a couple of the sheets so that they'd have somewhere to sit. At the sight of the familiar pieces, she suddenly felt a stirring of that ache, part happiness, part sorrow, that she had hoped for and dreaded. Quickly she yanked off the rest of the sheets and dumped them in a pile in a corner. Then she went to the desk that she and Joe had both used and opened the bottom drawer. His picture taken on the occasion of his promotion to captain was lying facedown. She turned it over. The silver frame was tarnished; there was dust on the glass, but when she rubbed off the grime with her fingertips, his eyes looked up clear and happy. Norah set the picture where it belonged —on top of the desk. She would not hide it away again.

The doorbell rang.

Jim Felix could hardly miss noticing the tears in her eyes. "It's good to see you," was all he said as he leaned over and kissed her cheek.

"It's good to be back."

Felix also noted the sheets hastily piled on the side and the dust on surfaces that had not been protected. "We expected you back several days ago."

"Something came up."

"I know." He ensconced himself on the sofa. "I've been hearing a lot about you."

Norah took a chair opposite. "I'll bet." She grimaced. "I didn't exactly make a hit down there."

"On the contrary. Only this afternoon I had a call from the mayor. He wanted to know all about you. He's considering offering you the job of chief of police."

"Me? You're kidding!"

"He wanted to know if I thought you could handle it."

"I don't believe it."

"I also had a call from INS. Special Agent . . . uh . . ."

"Creech? Bruce Creech?"

"Right, Creech. He was very upset. Seems you left without giving Special Agent Creech your New York address. He says there's a job for you in the Harrisburg office anytime you want it. He'll be getting in touch."

Norah shook her head in disbelief.

"So I came prepared with an offer of my own," Felix concluded, eyes bright and fixed on hers.

"No, please, Inspector . . . Jim. I've already—"

"Norah, for once, just once in your life, shut up and listen to the whole thing before you start objecting."

'I'm trying to tell you that I'm not—"

"Be quiet. As a personal favor—shush! Thank you."

Felix opened the zippered briefcase he had set beside him on the sofa. From it he removed a sheaf of papers in various folders which Norah knew were from police files. "You remember Sister Therese of Our Lady of Perpetual Help?"

"Of course."

"The case is still open." Felix separated one section of the folder, placing it on the coffee table in front of Norah. "These are the reports of the detectives who worked on it."

The stack was impressive.

"These others"—he indicated the pile he held in his lap and which was much larger—"are reports of similar attacks on the religious all over the city, from every precinct and borough. Nuns, priests, rabbis, ministers, have become prime targets. They haven't the physical strength or the spiritual inclination to meet violence with violence—in other words, to defend themselves. The assaults have to be stopped."

Norah folded her hands in her lap, clenching them tightly.

"The P.C. has decided to make up a task force to deal with crimes against the religious of every faith."

"I thought he didn't want a special team," Norah retorted. "I thought he'd decided that since the crimes were haphazard and widespread, it would be useless. The whole department, every cop on foot patrol, traffic detail, special and detective assignment, Italian, Irish, Polish, Jewish, of every faith and ethnic background, would constitute the task force."

"It's not working."

"So?"

"So he wants the best team we can put together. It's to have citywide jurisdiction. You're to set it up and head it."

Norah's hands were clasped so tightly the nails of one dug into the palm of the other, but she felt nothing.

"Well? I'm through. Now you can talk," Felix said.

"Yes."

"Yes what?"

"Yes, I want it. Yes, I want the job. Thank you, Jim. Thank you, Inspector."

"My pleasure, Sergeant." Smiling, Felix got up and began to stuff the papers back into his case.

Norah put her hands over his. "You might as well leave those. I'll start going over them tonight."

"Are you sure? I don't want to rush you. Tomorrow . . ."

"You wouldn't have brought them unless you expected to be leaving them. Right, Inspector?"

"Right," Felix admitted, and grinned.

"And if you hadn't offered me the assignment, I would have asked for it." She grinned back.

ABOUT THE AUTHOR

Lillian O'Donnell, who also writes the Mici Anhalt thrillers, lives in New York City.

CLASSIC
JAMES
MICHENER